HALLOWED PROMISES

ALSO BY W.J. CHERF

The Manuscripts of the Richards' Trust

Bow Tie

Recovery

Children of Ptah

Imhotep

Maat-ka-ra. Memoirs of a Time Traveler

Iron from the Sky

The Adventures of J.J. Stone

The First Soul

The Lictor of Magic

I Am the Storm

Adventures in Paranormal Archaeology

The Magician's Tomb

Netherworld's Gate

Dhampirica

Hallowed Promises

Adventures in Paranormal Archaeology IV

By

W.J. Cherf

FBP

Foxbat Publishing

Foxbat Publishing
ISBN: 978-1-7329779-5-2

Cover and frontis image. Plowing scene in the afterlife. Note
the tall wheat and fruit ladened date palms. 19th Dynasty
tomb of Sennedjem and his family. Deir el-Medina, Theban
Tomb 1. Discovered in 1886 by the workers at Qurna.

DEDICATION

The process of storytelling is not an easy one. Yes, there must be a proper tale to tell. But frankly, it is also a test of stubborn discipline as well. Still, I enjoy the process and that's what counts, for me, the storyteller.

To my editor, Cassidy, thank you always and forever for your careful attention and helpful suggestions. You have transformed a sow's ear into a silk purse.

To my Sweet Sue, you who faithfully slog through the pages and ferret out my blunders. As I have said so many times in the past, receiving your stamp of approval is all that really matters.

PREFACE

A most remarkable book, *The Knot of Eternity*, is oftentimes considered inscrutable by the dimwitted and cabalistically challenged. The work, organized into a series of lessons, explains the Cosmic Order and the beings that govern and inhabit it. By all accounts, it seems to have been an ancient sourcebook for those of a priestly status.

Fortunately, an English translation of the anonymous text is available, itself based upon a Sanskrit text dated to the fourth century BC, if not earlier. As for the work itself, its place of origin has been assumed to be the Indian subcontinent. The translator also noted a reference that this work, written on an animal skin, was first discovered illicitly hidden aboard a trading ship. Ptolemaic Greek law at the time stipulated that all such works had to be sent to the Alexandrian Library for their translation into Greek and inclusion into that institution's vast collection. At that point, a wise and knowledgeable adept commissioned a private copy of the scroll. Ever since then, many copies have been made, as the old papyrus or parchment versions deteriorated over the many centuries. The main library of The International Integrated Interface Society currently holds a Byzantine Greek version that dates back to the sixth century of our era.

From a historical perspective, *The Knot of Eternity* and its message have not been well received. In fact, the Christian Church declared the treatise heretical at the First Council of Nicaea in AD 325, and subsequently ordered all copies of it to be burned. Why? Because the organized religions of the West and East, mortal institutions all, have placed themselves as the only rightful intermediaries between the mortal and divine. They chose to explain the unexplainable or ambiguous with autocratic religious tenets to be accepted on faith, and faith alone—tenets which were nothing more than self-serving and aggrandizing guesses. In short, *The Knot of Eternity* represented a dangerous voice, a heretical alternative to organized religion, the contents of which threatened, if not refuted, the established tenets and authority of Judaism, Christianity, and Islam.

It is to be lamented that the age-old coven, the *Consilium magorum et sagarum*, or Council of Magicians and Witches, chose to turn its back upon the wisdom of this text. Due to this conscious decision, that society of exceptionally gifted adepts have followed a disastrous path blinded by their own arrogance and ignorance. To attribute one's place in the vast universe to the vagaries of chance is folly. But to ignore the experience of generations of adepts, confirmed by this text, reveals their fatal flaw. That being, that every soul is responsible for its own development or damnation. Bluntly, a choice must be made between good or evil. The *Consilium* never recognized, for to do so would require the establishment and enforcement of ethics and law, this foundational basis for the accountability for one's actions.

Cosmology, or "the study of the universe," is one filled with marvel and the extraordinary—all things far beyond the rules and regulations of organized religion. Only *The Knot of Eternity* told its story and offered guidance. Nowhere else is explained the interactions between, much less existence of, the Dark, Light, and

Mortal realms, the entities that rule them, the relationship of the soul to its carrier, much less the function of The First and Second Souls. Why is that? Because organized religion was primarily concerned with the material sphere, and only possessed a vague notion of the supernatural—a realm that was far beyond their earthly, materialistic control. In truth the rabbis, priests, and imams lacked a fundamental understanding of the true nature and landscape of the supernatural. As a consequence, they could not provide their brethren with a framework of its workings and interactions. Only *The Knot of Eternity* did deliver on this hallowed promise.

--Gregory L. Love, translator of *The Knot of Eternity* and author of its first commentary.

PROLOGOS

W hat may seem to us as irreconcilable, the old ones took as complementary, and thus as confirmation of the manifold powers of the gods. Although ancient logic is not ours, it has its own consistency and integrity. Consequently, one must leave behind the world of rational and scientific causality in order to gain entrance to the world of magic.

The Knot of Eternity. A Commentary. G. L. Love. 2nd. edition with T. Good. (Old Oaks Academy Press, 1960), vol. I.1, 1.

THE FIRST LESSON

From somewhere deep within the vast void of the earliest Universe, the Creator smiled as the grand plan went into motion. For out of that abysmal darkness, it created light and matter. From those constituent parts the realms of existence came into being along with their various guardians and overseers. Then, with great care and deliberation the Creator caused its greatest creation: the First and Second Souls.

The First Soul, a construct fashioned with free will, was tasked with the overriding desire to preserve and protect that which the Creator created. The First Soul, afforded with many protections, evolved through incarnation, but was not allowed to attain perfection and ultimate transcendence. For to do so would remove it from its primary task—the preservation and protection of the Cosmic Order.

Knot of Eternity.[2] Love, Good, vol. I.1, 13.

THE SECOND LESSON

C oincident in time with the creation of the dark, light, and mortal realms, the Creator caused energies to coalesce into several immortal entities. One came to be named by the ancients the Ledger Keeper. This self-aware, neutral overseer of the three realms, records the presence of every soul and tracks their every mortal passing and incarnation, to ensure that balance is maintained within the Cosmic Order.

The Creator also fashioned a terrible entity out of dark energies, one subservient to the Ledger Keeper. This entity came to be named by the ancients the Devourer of Souls. This self-aware incorporeal construct was tasked to destroy the demented and berserk of its dark realm. However, weak and susceptible mortals, enfeebled by hate or ignorance, could be influenced to do its bidding.

Knot of Eternity.[2] Love, Good, vol. I.1, 14.

THE THIRD LESSON

The Creator fashioned the dark, light, and mortal realms as distinct and separate. At a mortal's passing, its soul first arrived in the dark realm. There the soul chose whether to rise toward the light and pass into it, or to remain unperfected, and sink ever deeper into the endless darkness.

Souls that failed to rise toward the light did so because they were bereft of hope and love. They chose misery, became demented, and vengeful. Souls, so doomed, as their depravity mounted, continued to descend until they met their utter destruction. This journey was called damnation.

Those souls that chose to rise up through the dark and enter the light did so based upon their innate sense of contrition, hope, and capacity for love. From the light realm a soul continued its progress through a portal, provided for the purpose, to the mortal world. This journey was called incarnation.

Knot of Eternity.[2] Love, Good, vol. I.1, 15.

CHAPTER 1

"Magic. What is it? Well, for one, it's made up of a lot of things, and for another, if just one of those things is out-of-sync, then your spell is not going to work. At best, your first attempt will fizzle like the damp wick of a cheap firecracker. Magic must be embraced like a hallowed promise."

The Egyptian witch, Dr. Melaina Makris, senior lecturer of spell casting and ancient magical documents, paused to allow her statement sink in. She scanned the auras of her clutch and was not impressed. *Although, there were a few ... but does that young man over there near the wall even belong here?* She corrected herself. *The first lecture for a freshman rarely went well. For them sheer survival with a barely passing grade was considered a victory. There will be no 'participation' grades given out by me. How sad these times have become.*

"I can see that you're not listening. So I'll try again. To successfully cast a spell, you must do many things ... right."

Her pause was accompanied by a drumming of long and spider-like fingers on the wooden surface of the antique lectern. Remarkably, no one had yet to take a note.

"I see that you're still not listening. Fine. You'll flunk out ... and ... I don't give one wit about the failure rate in my classes. Grading curves and retention ratios do not count in my world. You see, I'm a freebooter. I do this class for fun, and the dean and president of our society know it. In short, if you do not apply yourself, then ... well ... you're screwed."

This time she paused to rearrange her lecture notes cursively written in black ink upon aged and perfumed papyrus. Much to her pleasure, the witch noted a mounting unease within Old Main's venerable lecture hall. She actually saw several furtively glance toward the exit, in confirmation that an actual escape route existed. Makris gripped the sides of her lectern and waited as a bit of odd and unfamiliar dizziness passed.

Now what was that? She soldiered on nonetheless.

"Be advised that the first step in becoming an adept is the firm belief that magic exists. There is absolutely no sense in pursuing something that you don't believe in. You must have certainty. The second step logically follows from the first—you must commit to magic. Making a commitment to something is far more tangible than some loosey-goosey feeling that something *might* exist. A commitment is a conscious forward step, a physical action, even a goal. Again, something tangible, something that your six senses can latch on to."

She now sipped from the chilled glass of water, around which a conjured wisp of hoarfrost slowly circled. When she had lifted it to her lips, many jaws dropped at the wonder. Again she leaned into her podium, this time because of an upset stomach. *What the hell is going on?* She thought as a slight sheen of moisture formed on her forehead and upper lip.

"Once you get your collective heads wrapped around the difference between belief and an outright commitment, then we arrive at everyone's favorite—memorization. You can't cast a spell if the words aren't right. Your next hamburger order, without the right words, in the right order, and with the appropriate options mentioned, will not be a hamburger. Instead, it will be a zucchini salad, but only if you are lucky."

She paused again, this time to stretch the growing tension out of her aching lower back. *Must be some kind of flu.* The lectern's blond oaken edges were worn smooth by the callused grip of generations, who had stood before their charges over the centuries. Old Oaks Academy, established in 1813, had been after all the heartfelt gift of a grateful United States president. Many within the society had sacrificed much to defend the young nation in its most dire time of need.

"Doubly important is the language of the spell. Facile translations, like botched pizza recipes, don't work much less taste good. So master a foreign language. Better, several. And ... get the accent and pronunciation spot on. When properly delivered in its native tongue, a spell takes on a luster and power like no other. And most important, your opponent's counter spell *must* also be expressed in that language, and that's what I call a distinct advantage."

She adjusted her half-reading glasses. A low grumble began to sound, the subtle shuffling of feet yearning to march. *They have yet to realize the perfect acoustics of this old wooden lecture hall... better ... chamber.*

"Perhaps the most difficult part of spell casting is the sheer ability of the individual to do so. While everyone has some modicum of innate psychic ability, not many possess it in sufficient measure. Yes, yes, I well-realize that one's psychic ability can be bolstered through training—much like prepping for those useless and faulty university entrance exams. But that tactic is only a temporary fix. Fortunately, for all of you here present, your entrance tests *say* that you possess the needed acumen. But what most of you do not possess is a disciplined mind capable of maintaining focus under stress. You see, that's where the great divide occurs. And, this is why you are here—to ... be ... challenged ... and stressed under contest-level conditions. Why? Because in the real world there are no do-over's. Because the real world is a frightfully brutal place, where only the prepared earn the right to live another day. When charged by a werewolf or vampire, your ability to cast defensive magic will be painfully apparent."

Another sip of water. She saw her words had her students shifting uncomfortably in their seats. *Good...*

"Finally, the proper casting of a spell requires will—not to be confused with emotion. Will provides the conduit through which an adept's energy triggers the spell. You cannot start an automobile without its electrical system. You cannot cast a spell without your will to power it. Will has endurance. Will does not easily tire. Will provides focus."

Makris paused for effect and saw that *some* were taking notes.

"Your will possesses an endurance that emotion never will. In a life and death contest, your will can provide sufficient defense against the most furious of emotionally-driven magical attacks. Our most bitter enemy, CMES, teaches its students to use raw emotion to power their spells. They deal in raw fear, rage, hatred, you name it, instead of mastering the will. As you all well know, the expenditure of emotion is exhausting. As a result, in any contest they tire quickly. This is why your mastery of the will, when used responsibly with restraint and logic, rules the day."

Again Makris paused, but this time she saw that a young man had raised his hand.

"Yes, Mr. Grissom." She encouraged after gently peeking into his mind to find his name.

"Ah, Dr. Makris. Is there some kind of handbook on all of this?"

"An excellent question. On your thumb drives, which you all received on the first day of classes, is a copy of *The Knot of Eternity,* provided in your native language. Our society believes that knowledge is power. *The Knot of Eternity* is our guide to that knowledge. I suggest that all of you familiarize yourselves with it."

Makris glanced at the time displayed on her personal device that rested next to her right wrist. "Consider what I have said. I fully expect that fifty percent of you will immediately drop this introductory course in spell casting. If unsure, drop and come back when you are more fully prepared to embrace it. Kindly don't waste either my time or yours."

* * *

Four weeks later and six time zones away, the same Dr. Melaina Makris put her opening lecture into practice as she sang with arms outstretched a melodious song in her family's ancient Egyptian Demotic tongue. The effort added considerably to the effectiveness of the spell's casting. She delivered this spell at the behest of her society in retaliation for a brutal vampiric attack upon the Vatican. The target of the chanting was a lavish Roman villa that she stood before. This structure contained the international headquarters of a much-hated and scurrilous coven, who had sent the vampire on its bloody rampage against a treaty ally.

To foil Makris' detection, the witch wore an Urban Combat Suit—just as did her heavily armed husband who stood next to her, which among other things, rendered the witch and her guardian invisible, because of a technological leap in light-bending materials.

Life, life, life is to be again granted to this place.

For too long it has been denied its place.

Wenet and *Wenenu*, the favorites of green Osiris,

Wenet and *Wenenu*, the fecund and abundant,

Goodly *Unnefer*,

He of 'Beautiful and Bountiful Renewal,'

Breathe life into this place that has been denied for
so long.

The witch repeated this chant thrice without blemish. Finished, she bent down and removed a beautiful and frisky male rabbit, perfect in every way, from one chamber of her also invisible shoulder bag. It was the very Egyptian image of *Wenenu*—aggressive fertility. Then, she lifted out of the bag a female, *Wenet*—the very personificaton of Egyptian procreation. Around their necks the witch had tied a white ribbon inscribed with the chanted spell of renewal.

Makris gently placed *Wenet*'s and *Wenenu*'s magical *Doppelgängern* down upon the sun-scorched, noon-time soil. With a whispered spell of encouragement and a gentle push, the rabbits began hopping forward. As their sensitive paws heated up, they quickened toward the villa and its cool shade. As the rabbits progressed, wherever their paws touched the barren soil, a marvel of nature occurred. Long dormant life germinated. Spotty at first, each point where the rabbits touched sprang to life, greened, and spread out like water dripped upon a paper napkin.

Smiling down upon this glorious miracle, Makris turned to leave, but could not help herself as she stopped, and turned around to see the rudimentary beginnings of a lawn forming, filled in here and there with colorful wild flowers.

The rabbits, those venerable images of fertility, now safely within the villa's shadow, nuzzled one another. Overcome with nature's own zeal, the rabbits began doing what rabbits do—the male vigorously coupled with the female, while she encouraged him ever on. With every thrust and every contraction, magical procreative vibrations, oscillations, and outright tremors were sent throughout the villa's isolated hillock.

The initial reaction of the life-giving renewal spell affected the villa's immediate grounds. Its secondary effects would take more time soak in, for deep beneath the hillock existed a vast labyrinth of inhabitable spaces, tunnels, chambers, and yes, even catacombs.

Within many of these places long-interred organic remains began rustle. Those high dignitaries buried intact stirred in their places. For those not so fortunate, the plaster that imprisoned them began to crack and give way. Their bones often supported tunnel walls. Their skulls sometimes formed archways and convenient places for torches or electrical lighting. These less-fortunate, uncountable numbers included the tortured, the half-devoured, those buried alive, institutional dissidents, and the merely hated—not to mention troublesome witches, wizards, werewolves, wraiths, vampires, and ghouls by the score. These wretches represented centuries, lo' millennia, of safe storage for the great unwashed and unwanted. They were consigned to the black inkiness of a forgotten pit with no name, by their masters who believed themselves better.

These pitiless forms, both the venerated and not, now tasted something rare and special—hope. They had been granted the gift of life once again—a hallowed promise, which also endued within each and every one of them a natural allegiance to something other than their former coven masters and oppressors. For most of them, sweet revenge was on their minds.

CHAPTER 2

The priest in the black cassock strode briskly into the museum library's main atrium. For a brief time he stopped under its arched ceiling, which was supported by stone-fluted   Corinthian columns with gilded capitals. Taking in the majestic expanse, his chest swelled as he took in a deep breath. The broad-shouldered clergyman noted the air was thick with the aroma of books, which caused an appreciative, fleeting smile. Nowhere reeked the pestilential stench of the unholy, something this cleric could easily detect.

Within that cavernous chamber's pre-dawn darkness, he chose a place at a long reading table before a lamp that cast an inviting, golden glow. Under his arm he cradled a thick personnel file. Its cover was stamped "Confidential," while the affixed white sticker said, "ERIK GERHARD REISSEN." He laid down the dossier, pulled out a chair, and sat down. The echoes of that act on the smooth limestone flooring were heard by no one but the priest at that early hour.

Alone in the pristine silence of this Renaissance temple devoted to the preservation of knowledge, Father Richardo opened the file and immediately encountered a large B&W glossy photograph. His arthritic hands fingered its white borders as a smiling face with strong features and dark hair looked back at him, as if in greeting. After studying the image for several seconds, the priest placed his right hand across the bottom-half of the photograph in order to better concentrate upon the man's eyes and what they revealed.

"'Eyes are windows to the soul.' Shakespeare could not have been more correct." He murmured. After several moments of examination he saw it. "The right is the soft one—the kind and generous one, while the left is … calculating, severe, and commanding. Hmm, a fascinating combination."

Father Richardo reached up and removed his round wire-rimmed glasses and carefully placed them above the open file, for what he was about to do didn't require them. As he did so, a crease left its mark along the temples of his neatly trimmed white hair.

In preparation for his next test, he rubbed the bridge of his nose and shaven face with manicured hands. Both were smoothed and moisturized by a fragrant and woody-smelling papyrus-based oil. Now ready, the cleric placed his fingertips along the edge of the man's image, closed his eyes, and concentrated.

"Ah, yes, there you are." He whispered over the photograph that he now viewed with his inner eye. "Your aura betrays you my friend. You're a powerful empath."

The priest's brow furrowed with greater focus. "You also have second sight. How very interesting and useful for someone in your profession."

Unconsciously, the priest's fingertips pressed

harder upon the photograph. "And, you're something else as well ... a telepath ... no, a student of that craft. Through sheer will you developed that talent. Impressive."

"Now, what else are you?" the priest whispered to the image full in the knowledge that the typical norm was a trio of paranormal traits, but something lingered in the background, teasing him, a basal trait that spurred on the cleric's intense curiosity.

A light perspiration formed on his wrinkled forehead. Then, "Ah, there you are. You possess claircognizance—an extraordinary ability for finding things." *So far, I would judge you as either a Fifth or Sixth Level Adept ... possibly even an unclassified. How very intriguing.*

Upon opening his eyes, the priest noted the nearing of dawn from the many stained glass windows overhead. Their leaking rose and pastel colors foretold the coming flood of the chamber with brilliant sunlight. Removing his fingers from the image, he cracked them to loosen up the strained joints, and sat back into his wooden chair with a squeak.

It's simply remarkable what a photograph can reveal about a person. Now for his dossier. I will no doubt find several useful tidbits that will flesh out my initial impressions.

Replacing his glasses upon his nose, Father Richardo carefully turned over the photograph, smoothing out several sharply defined creases left behind by his fingertips. He scanned and occasionally read the file's many documents, for there were many.

An hour later, the chief personnel officer of the Brotherhood of St. Paul finished with a tired sigh. *He's the fine choice for the operation's director of Pro Deo. My good friend Cardinal Alberti chose well. Long may his fine soul be venerated. While we had our differences, we also shared much in our common fight against evil in all its guises. Still, this Reissen walks a precarious path between our organizations with one foot treading within each. Perhaps the cardinal was right about him—that he represents that* rara avis—*a hybrid of research talent and tactical ability. Most certainly his recent exploits proved just that ...*

*   *   *

Sweat dripped down the sides of his lean face and deeply stained his tee shirt as the jogger completed a positively grueling morning run through the streets of Rome. Coming to a halt before his flat, he bent over and leaned on his knees to catch a breath before scaling the stairs to his third floor apartment. Once there, he showered, shaved, and dressed in his adopted tan cotton uniform of the Vatican's security force.

Finished, the man left his flat and made his way to his office within the Vatican's Gregorian Museum. En route Erik Reissen stopped for a pastry and an espresso-to-go. It was the best the Austrian-born archaeologist could manage, having been hopelessly spoiled on Viennese sweets.

* * *

Reissen could tell First Sergeant Lucius Agave had beaten him yet again to his office suite, because its wooden door was wide open and light flooded out. Ever since Reissen had selected him to be his assistant from the Vatican's security force, it had become a game of who could arrive the earliest. Yes, the Austrian admitted, there was much to do and manage, but he had arrived at half-past-six, which the Reissen thought sufficiently early.

"Good morning, Lucius!" the middle-aged Reissen bubbled at the short-cropped, black-haired youngster. "How early did you arrive this time?"

Sheepishly, "Oh-six-hundred," His assistant admitted, who sat behind his gray steel desk and open laptop. A steaming Starbuck's cup, a notepad, and pencil were the only items in view.

Others, of a more defensive nature, Reissen knew lurked within the soldier's easy reach. Ever since the ancient vampire Sigmund's attack on the suite, the Austrian thought it wise to "be prepared." Both of their automatic weapons were loaded with silver-lead alloy ammunition. The newly installed overhead lighting also reflected this grim reality, since they radiated a high-level of UV, guaranteeing that neither man would ever require any vitamin D supplements. Even the suite's fire bottles held a special surprise—pressurized Holy Water.

"I see. Well, I give up. From now on, I will be here at half-past-six. Make a note for future scheduling purposes."

His assistant nodded and made a quick jot on his notepad.

"And," Reissen pointed at the paper cup, "that swill will kill you, if not rot your brain."

The newly-promoted sergeant just shrugged off the comment with a congenial smile. Reissen pointed to his non-Starbucks' cup.

"This, sergeant, is authentic Italian espresso. Never forget that."

At that admonition, Reissen entered his office space through a fractured twelve-inch thick brick wall where a heavy door frame once filled. During a recent visit, the vampire Sigmund had destroyed that office's entrance and the archaeologist preserved the architectural carnage as a reminder of just what could happen. Hence their defensive upgrades.

Seated behind his industrial gray steel desk and laptop, Reissen signed-in, discovered a full e-mail box, sighed, and sipped at his espresso. Next, he checked his day's schedule, and to his delight, discovered that he had only one appointment, at ten, with a Father Richardo. Reissen called out—taking full advantage of his open door policy, "Lucius, who is Father Ricardo?"

"Head of personnel for the Brothers of St. Paul," Agave answered.

"Thank you." *Interesting ...*

That question settled, the archaeologist went back to excavating his way through his morning e-mail.

* * *

Just as his device indicated the top of the hour, the Austrian sensed the arrival of his ten-o'clock appointment. Reissen likened it to a change in air pressure or the sensation of a passing wave. Whoever this Father Richardo was, the Austrian felt the presence of a powerful psychic, something good to know.

Next, the archaeologist heard a soft, but firm command voice as he politely announced himself to his office assistant Sergeant Agave. Then the priest half-filled the open doorway to reveal a chiseled man with white hair, broad shoulders, about five-foot-four.

Rising from his chair, Reissen smiled and greeted with an extended hand. "Welcome Father to my humble office. I am Reissen."

Taking the proffered hand, the priest smiled back and returned a firm grip. Upon contact, Reissen received the warming psychic buzz of much, much more.

I was right. This priest is a high-adept—powerful and commanding.

"Please sit, Father."

"Dr. Reissen, it is indeed a pleasure to finally meet you. But no," turning toward the open doorway, "I think it best that we go somewhere more secure."

Without batting an eye, the archaeologist said. "As you wish, Father, lead on."

The pair made its way silently along the red terrazzo flooring of the museum's administrative level. Both men wore soft rubber soled boots—highly prized by the Vatican's normal and *paranormal* tactical units. The pair drifted soundlessly down a flight of marble steps, passed through the museum's main atrium, and out into the brilliant summer sunshine. A slight breeze tousled their hair with the scent of flowers and heady pine.

Striding alongside Father Richardo, Reissen commented. "I really do prefer to be outside on days like this."

Richardo smiled in agreement.

The priest led them over to a modest circular fountain with one central column and five noisily gushing spigots. As they approached, the breeze feathered away a portion of the fountain's plume creating a cooling rainbow. Beneath this light mist, the priest sat, indicating with a pat of his hand where the archaeologist should join him. Moving in closer, the priest dipped his hand into the fountain's waters, blessed himself and touched Reissen's forehead in benediction with the sign of the cross.

At the Austrian's look of surprise, the priest

shared. "Dr. Reissen, you just never know."

"Good point, Father."

"The waters of this fountain, Dr. Reissen, are blessed each morning by His Holiness. This comfortable setting, within its mists, provides us a very secure place to freely discuss what we all to often deal with on a daily basis. The white noise of the flowing water confuses most intruding listening devices. And most certainly, no demon, fiend, or vampire would dare approach us here, much less in the broad daylight." Father Richardo stated with a casual, but rock-like certainty that surprised the archaeologist. The priest then sighed, halted, and continued. "We have a grave crisis before us, Dr. Reissen. Even before recent events, CMES was in free-fall, but now it is outright crumbling before our eyes. We must decide what to do—if anything."

After a few moments of surprised consideration of what the priest had said, *CMES is crumbling?* "Father Richardo, Nature abhors a vacuum. CMES, as blasphemous as it is, serves a purpose. It firmly rules over its diverse and unruly membership in ways we never could or would. To witness to its fragmentation, while full knowing that we could have done something to preserve it, and yet do nothing..." Now shaking his head, "That is a course I would not support. I say, let us throw them a lifeline."

Father Richardo listened carefully to his colleague's words with warmth and approval. "I see that you are a practical man who practices *Realpolitik*, Dr. Reissen. You fully appreciate the gray areas of our world." The man smiled while reaching over to pat the archaeologist's tan and leathered hand. "So, how shall we assist our woefully errant colleagues?"

CHAPTER 3

Senior security guard Giuseppe Condé burped loudly into his hand as he made his rounds through the catacomb's Fourth Level. The sound of that bodily report echoed in the tight and winding corridors, but the security guard didn't care. *After all, who would hear me anyways?* He thought as he patted his plump and still-bloated gut filled with a large salami sandwich of olive oil, onions, garlic, and green peppers. Smacking his lips with relish from the lunch's aftertaste and licking his salt and pepper moustache for any missed morsels, the veteran security guard knew his way around this maze quite well. Almost to the point of being able to pad about blindfolded—well, upon consideration, perhaps not. After all, he had his nearing pension to consider so why take any unnecessary chances.

Scanning his helmet's light and hand flashlight back and forth cast gruesome shadows in those dark and gloomy spaces. In his left hand, Condé carried a dust whisk on a long stick. Ever since his first thirty or so days on his rounds, not one wisp of cob webbing could be found. Open burial niches, low horizontal slots hewn in the bedrock, stacked four and sometimes five high to the ceiling overhead, held the mummified remains of past dignitaries. These he dusted as well, considering it a hallowed promise, for Condé easily recognized his betters by the glitter of their gold. His only wish was that he knew who they were, what their lives had been like, what made them such objects of veneration.

But as for the rest, the countless skeletons plastered directly into the walls, they told a far grimmer tale, as did the row upon row of skulls and long bones artfully incorporated into the catacomb's walls and archways. Frankly, if the Italian had been superstitious, he would have gone stark raving mad years ago. But, the senior security guard dusted them too, as he felt an odd kindred with them.

So why did Condé stick with the job? Bluntly, it was a reliable, high-paying, day-job in a cool and dry environment—and the benefits were outstanding. On top of that, the surrounding clientele, as he thought of them, caused him few headaches and made even fewer complaints. Only during the occasional earthquake, did the security guard ever pause in worry as tendrils of dust and grit descended from the passage's ceilings.

*   *   *

It first began with the noisy and echoing collapse of ancient plaster. From the dust cloud created, came the eerie sounds of scratching, scrabbling. Then, other heavily plastered over wall sections of the deep catacombs joined in. Seemingly in concert, these once silent chambers filled with the sounds of movement— of newly resurrected life.

Amid this chaos, filthy and struggling for purchase, with limbs and fingers stiff with age, a resurrected entity slowly crawled its way out of its niche and unto the floor amid the fallen debris. A royal scion of the thirteenth century BC, Sethi, a *Consilium*'s former first voice, the *sem*-priest, and magician of Set, was seething with anger and for damn good reason.

Sethi, a son of Ramses the Great, who had enjoyed his afterlife, now had been rudely ripped from it.

This once long-lived magician and supremely powerful priest of Set, snarled out from long dried lungs in the language of the pharaohs. "Priestess-witch!" The effort cracked his face's parchment-like skin. "You have summoned me from my most-blessed eternal place, taken me from my wife's *ka*, denied me my children's, grand-children's, and great-grand-children's many attentions, and have cruelly returned me to this dried out husk. Such unthinkable abuse I do not tolerate. I will find another ... form ... and then I will find you witch, and fully leverage my vengeance upon you!"

This man's ire came with authority. After two hundred and sixty-three years of existence this priest-magician had led the *Consilium* for forty-three years as its first voice, its absolute leader, while centered in most-sacred Memphis. When the *Consilium* moved to Rome, Sethi, along with twelve other notables from the coven's past, made the journey as well, but as talismans to be interred in the hillock's catacombs.

*   *   *

As Sethi struggled forward amid the plaster debris of Level Four, others of his kind stirred as well. Then a poor beam of illumination scanned around through the dust-filled and choking atmosphere.

Then the ancient Egyptian dignitary heard the voice of a security guard curse into the gloom. "*Madre di Dio*, what a mess!"

The ancient priest and magician sensed the approach of hesitant, shuffling steps in the gloom. Instinctively, the Egyptian froze in place and waited like a horned-viper prepared to strike.

The security guard Condé slowly made his way forward because the floor was covered with plaster, rock, bones, and even mummified remains. Sethi waited and watched the guard who again noisily commented, "Now how did you get all the way here from your crypt?"

As the guard commiserated with himself, Sethi paused to realize that he wasn't quite close enough. The priest-magician knew that he had only one chance. Now was hardly the time to blunder. *Patience Sethi ...*

*   *   *

To Condé's credit, he moved about with extreme care so as to not step on his many misplaced clients. While doing so, the security guard imagined himself as an archaeologist, like that famous Hollywood fellow Indiana Jones, as he corkscrewed his steps this way and that in an ergonomically torturous manner.

*　　*　　*

As for Sethi, he didn't give a damn about the state of his current corpse, but did grudgingly appreciate the care the man was making. "Respect for the dead," that was what the Egyptian saw, and his heart softened—but only fractionally.

CHAPTER 4

In the dusty haze, the light from his helmet's lamp and flashlight was rendered practically useless by all the airborne particulate. Senior Security Guard Condé had to cautiously moved about to avoid tripping over the fallen plaster and rock debris, which included in it stray bones and more than one displaced mummified form. "Now how did you get all the way here from your crypt?"

He couldn't place why all the mess. He hadn't felt an earthquake. But the place looked like a storm hit it.

Suddenly, Condé's foot got suck. The guard tried to shake it free, but then one of Sethi's stiff fingers savagely punctured the meat of his lower leg, making a painful wound in his lower calf muscle. Instead of screaming in pain, the security guard became strangely disorientated, dizzy, and almost staggered as Sethi poured his resurrected *ka* into the man like a massive injection.

Nonetheless, the resurrected priest-magician quickly took command and stiffly righted the portly man. Awkwardly standing, and taking several tentative steps, Sethi put out his hands and steadied himself against a wall. Searching Condé's subconscious, he then made his escape from the villa in search of the witch who resurrected him. Along the way, he viciously kicked out of his path several sets of grasping mummies, former colleagues, but not of his lofty station.

"Find your own host!" Sethi snarled down at them.

During those early moments of the mass resurrection, Sethi remarkably encountered few full humans, and those that he did were quite preoccupied as they attempted to deal with the situation. In fact, three of them were in the fight of their lives as a small horde of the recently revived attacked them. Cagily slipping around this melee, moments later he passé through the level's steel crash doors and locked them behind him.

Why the Egyptian did so, he could not say. Perhaps it was Condé's idea to lock down the lowest level. Ascending another two sets of stairs, he secured Level Three's crash doors as well. After going up the remaining stairs to ground level, Sethi passed through the employee entrance, and out into the fresh air and bright sunshine of a summer's day. The experience warmed Sethi's angry heart and brought tears to his eyes.

"Divine Re, you are more beautiful than I remembered!"

Wiping them dry, the body of the senior security guard out of unconscious habit walked off the property in the general direction of the local train stop. But halfway to it, Sethi had to sit down and gather himself. It was difficult enough traversing this new and strange environment filled with unfamiliar sights and sounds. It was something else again internally, as the owner of the body that he had forcibly taken possession of was fighting back—hard. The pure effort of just walking, putting one step before another was taxing. Then there was this incessant internal whining, yammering, and complaining. A truce was needed.

Images of the two men met in Condé's subconscious, the place where Sethi's *ka* had boxed in his personality. The security guard was fit-to-be-tied, angry, and more than scared. He was desperate. Standing with his meaty fists up, the Italian wanted to fight.

Facing him was a short and muscular Egyptian, dressed in a starched white kilt, with two golden pectorals draped across his chest and a leopard skin over one shoulder. Narrow of face and with a shaved head, two painted eyes gazed back at the guard, regarding him.

"Who are you!" raged Condé. "What have you done?"

With a head held high, "I am Sethi, high priest of Set, and master magician."

"What's going on? What did you do to me?"

"I have temporarily possessed your body with my *ka*."

"What's a *ka*? Some sort of a disease?"

"No, it is my soul."

"This is nuts! I have to be dreaming." The Italian vented with his hands flung up into the air.

"No. It is true. A witch resurrected me and many others back at the crypts. Think back at the destruction and chaos. For this abomination, I will exact my revenge upon her."

"Why me? Why did you take me?" The Italian said while pointing to his chest.

"You were convenient."

"CONVENIENT!" The security guard screamed with a beet-red face.

"Yes, Condé. You were convenient. And the only reason I did not destroy your soul is because of the respect that you have shown me and my brethren over the years."

At that explanation, the security guard's jaw sagged open in understanding. "You can read my mind."

"Why yes, of course I can. And all things considered, you are a good man, and a hen-pecked husband. But for the next ten days I need to ... borrow ... your body."

"You need *ten* days to deal with this witch?"

"Precisely. And no longer. My *ka* cannot survive separated from my mummy beyond that period."

"Just what did she to you?"

"She had the audacity to resurrect me from my eternal place in the most-select of gardens!"

"Gardens?"

"Yes, gardens, and separated me from my wife, children, and grandchildren! Condé, I was happy,

fulfilled, and joyful in the afterlife." The priest
practically broke down.

"So heaven's real?"

"Yes, in so many words."

"Huh. And what then?"

"My *ka* leaves your body and returns to my
mummy."

"Will you go back to your family and gardens?"

"That is my fervent desire."

"And when we separate your *ka* from me, will I be
screwed up in any way during this … this offloading of
your *ka*?"

"No. That is my hallowed promise. And no longer
than ten days—maybe even sooner."

"Huh." Now the security guard squinted at the
Egyptian standing before him. "I can read your
thoughts too! You're a really famous CMES big-wig! A
priest-magician, a first voice too!"

"Yes."

"Can you do lots of magic?"

"If necessary."

"Can you make me rich?"

"You wish me to pay for the use of your body?"

"Yeah, sure. Why not? Let's just call it a rental
fee."

"I believe I can make that arrangement."

"Great! *Signore* Sethi, I think that we can work
together. Let's go find this witch of yours.

*   *   *

The initial chaos the security forces managed to contain with a minimal loss of life, but the chairman of the oldest paranormal organization on Earth knew that it was just a matter of time. As a stop-gap measure, the two upper-most levels of the regal villa, located in a northern suburb of Rome, had already been evacuated to a temporary site.

The international headquarters of CMES—the *Consilium magorum et sagarum* or "Council of Magicians and Witches," incredulously found itself under siege by its own ancestors. The coven's security force had battled the resurrected dead in the lower two levels. These catacombs included the remains of the enclave's noteworthy twelve, those impressed slave laborers, and the damned. No one truly knew how many had been so entombed since the coven's relocation from Egyptian Memphis following Rome's conquest of the province in 31 BC. Yes, there were detailed records, but in such times of extremis, who had the time to make that reckoning?

*   *   *

CMES's chairman, William DeSalvo, held few illusions as he managed the situation from his cube on the First Level. He estimated the newly resurrected in the thousands, and from all appearances, they were not at all happy. The problem for his security force was how to deal with the throng's incessant beating on the hardened steel doors, attempting to gain their freedom.

After all, how does one stop an animated skeleton or mummified corpse, when physical violence just creates smaller bits which slowly reorganize themselves back into the original? To resort to a magical remedy implied that the conjurer knew what the original spell was, in order to counter it. And therein lay the crux of the problem. Not only was the spell unknown, but so also was its intrinsic source of power. As a consequence, someone in security had selflessly sealed off the access points from the lower two levels. While a primitive solution, for now that would have to do.

DeSalvo worried, "What happens when they decide to dig themselves out? What then?"

His chief of security, a man named Paul Kiel, shook his head. "We need some serious magic, *Signore Presidente*. The sooner the better."

DeSalvo grunted in agreement as he gazed upon the hasty mess left behind by the main administration level's evacuation.

What has happen to us? He frowned. *First the tragic loss of* The Gathering *building in downtown Manhattan. Then, the embarrassment of the Contest in the Desert, followed by the massacre of the Barcelona coven ... and others. We have become a rudderless ship caught in high seas.*

DeSalvo then admitted to himself the full reality.

No, William, we are in full decline. And here I sit as our coven's chairman, powerless to do anything about it. My decisions are responsible for this.

*   *   *

President Betsy Silver Moon sat on her veranda in the late morning Santa Fe sun. Her favorite indigo blue coffee cup, made by her niece, still appeared two-thirds full. Yes, it was already getting hot, but Silver Moon's Navajo ancestry tolerated it well—no, craved it.

This was the president's quiet time, for the management of the Earth's second largest paranormal organization, TIIIS, seemed to literally suck the life-energy from her. The International Integrated Interface Society was the current name of this global enclave, which had undergone many evolutions since its founding in second century BC Rome. Originally founded as a conservative Roman faction to stamp out the practice of human sacrifice within the walls of the Eternal City, the group fell on bad times during the late second century, and especially early one during the reign of the Emperor Caracalla. TIIIS' greatest misfortune was when it became the much-smeared target of CMES, which orchestrated its persecution by both the Imperial Roman administration and later by the Early Christian Church. Long relegated to the shadows, only during the Age of Enlightenment did the members of TIIIS dare reemerge. And only during the early twenty-first century had TIIIS finally gained a parity of sorts with its age-old tormentor.

Laptop open before her, an e-mail chimed its arrival. Glancing at the screen, she read the address's suffix, ".it," and saw it was from Italy.

> Greetings from Rome!
>
> Erik Reissen here.
>
> We need to talk via an encrypted line, or even better, face-to-face and for a whole host of reasons. Unfortunately, I dare not leave my post here in Rome. Might I request that you make a visit?
>
> This Austrian is not one to cry "wolf," but your direct input would be most helpful.
>
> Best regards,
>
> --EGR

CHAPTER 5

Twenty hours later, a much jet-lagged President Silver Moon landed at Leonardo da Vinci International Airport. Despite the fact she made the journey in the TIIIS corporate jet, Reissen's polite request had troubled her to the core, denying her sleep. As she studied several pictures of the man, a nagging little voice wondered whether her organization was at fault for this current crisis. And then there was something haunting about Reissen's e-mail that screamed "Help!" in a way not often heard. Pulling a single wheelie, the short, middle aged woman from Santa Fe breezed through customs and entered the terminal thirsty, hungry, and bleary-eyed.

Bottom line: Silver Moon absolutely hated to fly, much less non-stop all the way to Rome. But all of that immediately was dispelled when she caught sight of Dr. Erik Reissen who was patiently standing behind the barriers. *Damn, he looks like shit. His aura is all blurred from stress. But I recognize that look. Management will do that to you, just as will knowing too much, bottling all of that up. Then, too, there are all the consequences to consider ... the Vatican once persecuted us, hunted us like animals. But now, we enjoy an informal treaty with the Holy See. Came to their aid regarding the vampire Sigmund, and even provided them with an answer to that monster's calculated carnage upon their clergy.*

Then and there the president decided, *Suck it up, buttercup! TIIIS to the rescue!*

She put on her best smile. "Well, at long last, Dr. Reissen!" she greeted while extending her hand.

"And to you as well, Madam President," the Austrian replied with a short bow of his head. "Was your flight uneventful?"

"Indeed it was, but I couldn't sleep a wink. That e-mail of yours worried me greatly. What is the local time?"

Glancing at his wristwatch, "Just after seven in the evening."

"Wonderful!" Silver Moon said as she tried to ignore the onset of a headache. "Let's grab an early dinner. I'm famished."

"Splendid. I know just the place."

*   *   *

"So, what seems to be the problem?" Silver Moon asked, hands folded, now all business after devouring a magnificent cold plate of sliced cheeses and salamis accompanied by a glass of crisp, dry white wine. Reissen, she noted, had chosen both well. It was now mid-course, and she was beginning to feel human again. Besides, her second glass of wine had done a good job of lubricating her tongue.

*   *   *

The directness of the American's question caused the Austrian to pause, psychically reach out, and take stock of his guest. *She's not blocking her mind one bit. She's exhausted. No, check that, completely shot. Yet, here she sits ready and willing to talk shop. Remarkable...*

Before Reissen could form a word, Silver Moon broke in. "Erik. That was perhaps the smoothest, gentlest mental intrusion I have ever experienced. Who was your teacher?"

The archaeologist blinked, then answered. "The late Sister Mary Gabriella."

Silver Moon heard the raw anguish in his voice. "I'm sorry for your loss, Erik. I didn't realize. The vampire Sigmund got to her, didn't he?"

A single nod.

"Shit."

Both paused to sip their wines in a silent toast to the dead.

Reissen finally answered Silver Moon's question. "Betsy, Dr. Makris' spell worked too well."

"Oh? How so?"

"Our distinguished competitors have evacuated their residence. It seems that their lower levels have come alive and threaten to escape. I do not know about you, Madam President, but I think it would be extremely bad form to have a hoard of revived corpses wandering about Rome. Don't you?"

"Oh my."

"Indeed. A veritable zombie apocalypse. Is there some way to reverse Dr. Makris' spell?"

"I am sure there is. One moment." Silver Moon fished out her device and furiously began working it with both thumbs. Reissen, perhaps for the first time in the past twenty-four hours, felt a modicum of relief flow through his body. Moments later, he received his confirmation.

"Dr. Makris will arrive within the next twenty-three hours. She indeed has a solution. I will send back the jet immediately to fetch her. In the meantime, I will remain to make sure that everything is tidied up in a nice bow."

The waiter arrived with a steaming bowl of pasta. The aroma of onions, garlic, and Italian spices flooded the air. Silver Moon raised her glass in benediction and smiled. "To rabbits, Erik. They make the world go round."

*   *   *

Reissen, experiencing *déjà vu*, returned to the airport the next evening, but this time accompanied by Silver Moon. When Dr. Melaina Makris appeared at the customs exit, her president caught her attention and waved her over. As the lean, graceful, and ageless Egyptian made her way through the throng, many cast appreciative looks her way. Exotic, if not stunning in appearance, Makris' honeyed visage possessed a narrow nose, high cheekbones, and full lips. Her shiny, jet-black hair framed a set of deep-brown, almond-shaped eyes.

Before long the threesome made their way back to the family-owned restaurant he had treated Silver Moon to the night before.

Their waiter from the previous evening noticed with a smile that the good-looking man now entertained two attractive women. He hoped his tip would reflect that fact.

"A bottle of Santa Margherita Pinot Grigio Valdadige, and three glasses, please," Reissen smoothly ordered in Italian.

"Si, signore."

"The same as last evening?" Silver Moon inquired.

"Indeed."

"Melaina, you're in for a real treat." Silver Moon said conspiratorially.

With the Egyptian witch sitting opposite him, the Austrian began. "So, Dr. Makris, what in the way of preparatory steps will be necessary?"

Makris' brown eyes stole a glance at Silver Moon before she answered. A deep sigh. "First off, I wish to apologize for any inconvenience that has occurred. That was not our intent. I had no idea as to what was contained *beneath* that hill. As for 'preparatory steps,' I need the villa and its grounds to be completely evacuated of all … mortal living personnel … for a period of twenty-seven hours. Thereafter, they will be safe to return."

Reissen took a moment to chew on that answer. Then, "Betsy, how well do you know Chairman DeSalvo?"

"Well enough to have his private cell number."

"Then may I suggest that you use it and outline to him Dr. Makris' 'preparatory steps'?"

"That would be difficult, Erik, as he still doesn't know that we cast the spell in the first place. Diplomatic relations between our organizations are at a very delicate stage. For the first time in centuries— millennia—we are cordial. I do not want to cause a setback, even if we are responsible. So I would suggest that someone connected with the Vatican give him a call, as a friendly suggestion, an overture."

The waiter returned with the mildly chilled wine, pulled the cork, filled Reissen's glass, the others, and departed. All during this ceremony, the Austrian felt the intense heat of a spotlight upon him. He had to make a decision. Should he call his colleague Father Richardo? No. That would be a mistake. Too much would have to be explained. *Verdammt!*

After taking a long sip, the Austrian said, "Betsy, give me the man's number."

"Certainly, Erik. Here it is." She passed him her business card. On the back she had already written DeSalvo's number.

Then the archaeologist shifted gears. "Dr. Makris,

is there a particular time of day that you wish to … begin?"

"Thank you for asking. Eleven-thirty in the evening. If I begin at that time, all should be in place to trigger at midnight. And one other thing, I need a young goat—the living variety—along with a heavy hammer, a wooden stake, and a length of rope."

"Glad I asked."

*   *   *

Reissen sat in his darkened office, illuminated only by his laptop's screen. He dialed the number and waited.

"*Caio*, DeSalvo," said a weary voice.

"*Signore Presidente* DeSalvo. We have never met. I am Dr. Erik Reissen, the operations director for the Pro Deo department of the Vatican. I have come across some information that I wish to share. I believe that it is vital to your organization. Do you have a moment?"

"I have all night, Dr. Reissen," said the suddenly alert voice. "Speak."

"It has come to my attention that a third party wishes to solve your organization's current dilemma. To do so, however, you and your *living mortal* staff must completely evacuate your headquarters by eleven o'clock tomorrow evening. Further, you should not attempt to reoccupy the villa until twenty-seven hours have passed. In other words, do not step foot on the property until three in the morning the following day. Do you wish me to repeat this information?"

Reissen clearly heard typing in the background.

"I have it. Out by eleven this coming evening. Return no sooner than three in the morning the following day. Now, Dr. Reissen, a question. Why are you telling me this?"

"Professional courtesy, *Signore Presidente* DeSalvo. We are both in the same business, but see things from opposite sides of the street. What is happening to your business is most unfortunate. It could happen sometime to mine."

The archaeologist heard a grunt from the other end of the line. "So what are you proposing, Dr. Reissen? An understanding of some kind between my organization and yours?"

"That is acceptable."

"Done. And, Dr. Reissen, if this all works out, I propose that we meet to discuss the future of our respective businesses."

"*Signore Presidente*, that would be most acceptable."

As Reissen thumbed off his device, he wondered. *Did I just begin the process of brokering a diplomatic* rapprochement *between the Vatican and CMES?*

*   *   *

As the hour approached for Makris to reverse the

resurrection spell from the CMES property, Silver Moon held an ace in reserve. When she disembarked from the TIIIS executive jet two days ago, she was not alone. Her society's Lictor of Magic had secretly accompanied her. J.J. Stone, who carried the First Soul of Creation, was once a highly decorated US Marine. Currently he held the post of instructor of demonology at Old Oaks Academy. This Fifth-Class Adept and husband of Makris had insisted—made a hallowed promise—on covering her back during this diplomatic junket. It was only providential that his wife now joined him, so he could guard over her as he had done on the original resurrection casting made less than a week before.

At the appointed time, about eleven-thirty in the evening, a plain panel van pulled into the general neighborhood of the stricken CMES villa. Its rear doors opened, its rear suspension noticeably lightened, and then the doors closed of their own accord. Oddly, only a young goat could be seen, which never touched the ground, seemingly carried by an unseen entity.

Once rounding the corner, they reached the villa. Makris and her husband stood on the pavement with the young goat hemmed in between them. Both wore Urban Combat Suits.

"Mel, do your thing while I mind the goat," Stone's voice crackled through the tactical communications rig in their suits.

"Enjoy," his wife said as she removed a pair of

wooden soles from her invisible satchel. These she attached to the bottom of her assault boots and then plodded off snowshoe-like across the lush lawn. Makris would recite the first spell repeatedly in Egyptian Demotic, as she circled the perimeter, or religious *pomerium*, of the villa's border. The ancient tongue only strengthened its effectiveness. The purpose of this magical delimitation was to contain the awful effects of the death spell that would follow. The witch had clearly learned her lesson on the delimitation of a casted spell.

Mark this *pomerium*.

Bless this *pomerium*.

Allow nothing cast or conjured to pass.

Contain within it, like a sealed vessel, all castings and conjurings.

This I adjure you, oh Anubis, master of the *necropolis*.

Makris quietly chanted as she slowly stepped around the hillock's limits, often brushing along neighbors' privacy walls. When finished with each chanting, the witch took one step back and repeated herself. In so doing, she overlapped each magical segment, ensuring that it would be one continuous magical barrier. Each recitation covered about thirty feet of ground.

While this entire spell casting took place, the Lictor

of Magic, invisible in his UCS, watched, listened, and stood by at the ready to draw his Bone Sword if needed. Meanwhile, the apparently prescient goat fussed, which caused the six-foot-two enforcer of good and destroyer of evil to bend down and hold it in his arms, soothing it.

Twenty-five minutes later, the Egyptian witch had completed her circuit. While she had been busy establishing the magical *pomerium*, Stone temporarily tied up the goat in order to set a wooden stake firmly into the lush and grassy slope of the property. Raised on a working ranch in North Texas, Stone adeptly carried the goat to the stake, roped its legs, and made sure that goat and stake were secure. Only then did he step back and return to the relative safety of the stone pavement.

"Are you ready?" Stone asked.

"Yes." His wife said as she left the pavement to stand next to the tethered animal. Then she removed from a flapped pouch-pocket an ancient obsidian knife. Its curved blackness shone in the moonlight. With a tight grip around its bone handle, Makris pulled the goat's head back and said to the air around her,

All-powerful Set, witness this innocent's sacrifice.

May this innocent's blood satisfy Thy lust for death.

As this innocent's blood is shed,

Allow this innocent's blood to spread within the *pomerium*.

Allow this innocent's blood to bring a swift death to all living and animated *things* within this *pomerium.*

This, mighty Set, master of the dark Underworld, make effective immediately, and to last only one day's time from this moment.

Finished with casting the death spell, the Egyptian witch cleanly sliced through the goat's neck. With blood fountaining upon the lush lawn, Makris held the squirming goat's head steady until it expired. Now standing in a pool of wasted life, she slowly and carefully backed out from her handiwork. As she did so, even in the bright moonlight, the vegetation nearest the sacrificial victim began to sag and wither.

Makris dragged her feet on the remaining lawn to cleanse her wooden soles of any trace of blood. When she reached the roadway's curbing, she carefully stepped off onto the pavement, where she removed the wooden soles.

Now holding them up to examine them, Makris said, "J.J., when we get back, remind me to dispose of these." And with that, the pair silently walked back several blocks to the concealed van and left the affluent northern suburb of Rome.

The local time was seven minutes past midnight.

"You're pretty good with a knife. Who taught you?" Stone inquired of his wife.

"My mother, when I was a child. I learned on

pigeons and doves."

"And again, what's with the wooden clogs?"

"Insulation. Wood is the traditional material to protect one from the power of a ley line or of a magical casting."

"Better than rubber?"

"Infinitely."

"Well, you two, anything else to report?" Silver Moon asked from the van's passenger seat, while Reissen drove.

"Yeah, we were definitely being watched," Stone answered.

"I didn't notice anything," Makris countered.

"Honey, you wouldn't have. You were busy chanting and keeping step. I was there to watch and listen. That was my job, and I picked up plenty."

"Such as?" Silver Moon probed.

"Twice I heard muffled tactical radio chatter. It came from behind one of the neighbor's walls. If they had been on my team back in Iraq, I would have busted them down two ranks for that. So, folks, we have to assume they had night-vision and infrared deployed on video cameras. That would be exactly what I'd do."

*   *   *

As the goat's blood pooled, spread, and was absorbed by the soil, death relentlessly followed. Once covered with verdant grass and wild flowers, now a swath of browning grasses stood, amid dying insects and wilting flowers. Birds and bats who had taken roost on the property fell to the earth with gentle thumps. Two feral cats and several rabbits died immediately. As the spread continued, it reached the villa's *pomerium*, stopped, collected, and moved on like a flood of mercury, looking for any rent in the barrier to exploit. Soon, the entire hillock was once again a dead and barren wasteland. As minutes passed, its spread traveled downward, affecting all those resurrected in the Third and Fourth Levels of the catacombs, returning to them a peace of sorts, and restoring the subterranean passages to the silent crypts they had once been.

*   *   *

"What do you have?" DeSalvo asked his head of security, Kiel, as he reviewed several videos.

"Not very much, but sufficient to identify the intruders as the TIIIS Lictor of Magic and one other."

"Your evidence?"

"Two sets of footprints, one a standard NATO boot pattern, and from the other, an indefinite, smooth pattern."

"Like a wooden sole?"

"Precisely like that."

A grunt. "Anything else?"

"*Si*, over the infrared we could see one individual, about 180 to 185 centimeters in height, who at different times either held or carried the animal. Mind you, we didn't actually see the heat-signature of that individual. We could only detect his shadow against the heat-signature of the goat. As for the other individual, we have only the footage of the actual sacrifice itself, when they lifted the goat's head and slit its throat."

"Any audio?"

"We believe we recorded the spell casting that took place during the sacrifice."

"You 'believe'?"

"*Si, Signore Presidente*. We believe only, because the 'chant' appears to have been delivered in a language that we did not recognize. The tape is currently being analyzed."

Another grunt. "Anything else?"

"*No, Signore Presidente.*"

"So how can you so confidently identify the intruders as TIIIS?"

"We know that only TIIIS possesses a tactical suit that renders its wearer invisible. One of the suits could reasonably have the NATO-style boot pattern. I think that they were Stone's. Secondly, we were in close proximity to the TIIIS Lictor of Magic when he killed the vampire Sigmund. His height matches what we have on the video. As for the other individual, they, too, wore an invisible tactical suit. Therefore, in my mind, both are TIIIS agents."

"I could not agree more, *Signore* Kiel. Good job."

*   *   *

On the appointed day, DeSalvo, showered, shaved, and dressed in one of his finest silk suits, and stood at the curbing of his coven's villa at three in the morning. Even dressed as he was, the chill in the air made him shiver. An introspective man, the chairman knew the hour after which he could proceed, but he couldn't move his feet at that moment to step upon the withered lawn. In this supreme moment of indecision, he was not alone. His security staff was there as well, standing in silent readiness, dressed head to toe in their heavily armored riot gear. He had told the rest of his staff that the property was off limits until after four that morning—just in case. But still, someone had to be the first to test the waters.

Even in the dusky pre-dawn light, the evidence that something significant had occurred on the hillock was everywhere in evidence.

"Death himself has been here," the chairman whispered with a shudder of horror.

Glancing once more at his gold Patek Philippe wristwatch, he stepped onto the dead lawn and strode purposefully toward the villa's arched entranceway. Successfully reaching the double doorway, he turned and waved forward his security force. "All clear."

As his security force flooded into the villa, DeSalvo began his own inspection, level by level. He had a rancid taste in his mouth. He still didn't positively know who had cast the resurrection spell in the first place, but he held strong suspicions.

"*Signore Presidente*. I just heard." Kiel jogged up to his chairman's side. "Levels Three and Four are all clear."

"*Gracie, Signore* Kiel. Finally some good news. I authorize the clean-up crews to begin. When the administrative personnel arrive at four, begin the move in."

"Si, Signore Presidente."

DeSalvo returned to his musings, head down and hands behind his back, as he strolled through the villa's corridors buzzing with his coven's revival. *How can I continue this recovery?* He challenged himself. *We have suffered greatly at the hands of TIIIS, the spectacular loss of* The Gathering *building in New York City, the embarrassment of the Contest in the Desert, and now the recent failure of the vampire Sigmund. We are in decline, William, and it is occurring during your watch. And now this latest situation, not solved by our own, but by an unknown third-party. Have we totally lost our compass? More importantly, how can I turn this fated ship around?*

*   *   *

It had been a hectic day. At its end, DeSalvo sat down with Kiel, for the post-move-in brief.

"What is our status?"

Kiel checked his notes and began. "Levels One and Two are, for the most part up, and functioning."

"'For the most part'—what do you mean?"

"Several key people quit. They had enough."

"I see. Continue."

"The IT and Communications Department reports that it's up and running. The repair of the plaster in Levels Three and Four has begun, which includes the reincorporation of any loose skeletal material. All of our former dignitaries have been placed back in their assigned niches." The security man then paused before he continued. "The bad news is that we lost four good men. Three were found ripped to pieces, and the fourth is missing entirely."

"Who is missing?"

"Senior security guard Giuseppe Condé. His responsibilities were the Third and Fourth Levels."

Again the security man paused.

"What's troubling you, *Signore* Kiel?"

The head security man sighed. "Two things, *Signore Presidente*. Condé's wife hasn't seen her husband over the past several days and is worried sick about him. And second, on one of our dignitary's mummies, we found blood."

"Oh…"

"After laboratory analysis, the blood turned out to be Condé's."

"How much did you find?" DeSalvo frowned with concern.

"The amount was not significant. We found it on the hand of a Memphite dignitary from the Fourth Level called Sethi."

"Sethi. That name rings a bell, but I am not sure why." DeSalvo said.

"I checked the archive. He was the twenty-fourth Memphite first-voice, and a priest-magician of the Egyptian god Set. He was known to be extremely long-lived, firm, and ruthless if necessary."

"I like him already." DeSalvo quipped with a wry smile.

* * *

Several days later, and true to his word, William DeSalvo invited Erik Reissen to lunch.

Once the greeting and introductions were made, a certain awkwardness settled over the two men. The coolness of hyper-European politeness threatened to take over until DeSalvo put a stop to it. He did not wish to spar with the stiff Austrian academic. He wanted to get to know the man.

"Dr. Reissen ... Erik ... my first name is William. Please feel free to use it."

A nod of acknowledgment.

"Erik, my headquarters is only now getting back on its feet. We lost three security guards before it was all over. Another is altogether missing. Regardless, I am compelled to thank you for your assistance. Your third party did a fine job of settling things out. Please let them know of our deep gratitude."

"Thank you … William. I surely will."

Now leaning forward against the restaurant's linen table cloth, "I also wish to tell you that we know who that third party is."

"Oh?"

"Yes, it was two TIIIS agents, and one of them their Lictor of Magic."

"How do you know this?" Reissen asked with genuine interest.

"We have worked closely with their Lictor of Magic in the past. We know his signature. But as for the other one, well, they did a marvelous job."

The waiter arrived with a bottle of white wine. DeSalvo approved it. Glasses were filled, and an appetizer was ordered.

"William, did you say that one of your security guards turned up missing?" The Austrian asked as he nursed his glass of wine.

"Yes. It is unfortunate. He was an experienced man. But something quite odd was connected with his disappearance." The chairman sipped at his wine as if deciding whether or not to share something.

Reissen, for his part, listened carefully to the man's mind and noted that it was fully shielded.

"Erik, I do not know how to share this. One of our former dignitaries, one that our coven brought from Egypt during those hectic last days of evacuation, a mummy, was found with the man's blood on its fingers. I suspect something dark occurred."

"Who, might I ask, was this former dignitary?"

"His name was Sethi—a son of Ramses II, a warrior, priest, and powerful magician."

Reissen's eyes widened in recognition at hearing Sethi's name. DeSalvo saw it.

"You know of this man?"

"No, no I do not, at least not directly." The Austrian backpedalled. "It's just that a Turkish scholar is studying a papyrus at the Vatican Library that purports to be a biography about a Sethi."

Now DeSalvo's eyes widened. "You are kidding." The man said as his fingers tightened around his glass.

"No, I am not. From all accounts, this Sethi was a formidable man."

"Yes," the CMES chairman said into his glass.

"So, William, why are you telling me this?"

"Because we have a grave suspicion."

"And that is?"

"That the resurrected *ka* of the priest-magician was infused into our missing security guard. A man named Giuseppe Condé."

Reissen took a sip from his wine, both to steady his nerves and disguise his shock.

"What is your concern, William?"

"That Sethi has taken over Condé's body. Why? We have no idea as to motive. There could be any number of possibilities."

"Interesting. Are you willing to share this security guard's image?"

"Absolutely."

"And if I happen to see this security guard on the street, what am I supposed to do?"

"That is a good question. Follow him for sure, and let us know of his whereabouts. We will do the same. But beware, as we do not know what this Sethi wants, or is capable of."

"I am still curious why this ancient Egyptian would want to possess a modern." The archaeologist said.

DeSalvo shrugged and shook his head. "At this time, we have absolutely no idea."

Reissen studied his glass of wine for a moment. "Actually, if I put on my Egyptology hat, this fellow Sethi just might be extremely angry."

"Why?" The chairman asked as he leaned in, genuinely curious.

"Presumably because his sudden and unexpected resurrection took him from his eternal Egyptian place of nirvana. Imagine, William, you're all comfortably settled down for eternity, surrounded by your family and close friends. To be ripped from that existence would be quite a shock."

"You are actually willing to entertain such a scenario?" DeSalvo said with more than a bit of dismissive mockery in his voice.

"Why not? All you have to do is carefully read *The Knot of Eternity*. It's our shared handbook. Just such a scenario is totally compatible with its guidelines for existence."

DeSalvo stared out into space and then looked Reissen in the eyes. "I have never read it."

"It is required reading within Pro Deo. I know for a fact that TIIIS requires it as well. Why is it not required within your society?"

A wan smile appeared on the chairman's face. "Perhaps because its content is not favored by our membership."

"How could that be?" Reissen leaned in. "It explains so much."

"Erik, I am surprised by your reaction. It explains so very much. Be advised that the religious organization for whom you work abhors human sacrifice, yet makes a mystical human sacrifice the centerpiece of its worship. This that hypocrisy?" The man theatrically shrugged. "Keep in mind also, that many of my brethren *prey* on human flesh." He said as he stabbed his finger into the table for emphasis. "Even *depend* upon it for their survival. So much for *The Knot*."

CHAPTER 6

After his luncheon with the CMES chairman, Reissen sent an e-mail to his colleague Father Richardo, the personnel director of the Vatican's paranormal tactical department, the Brothers of St. Paul. To the Austrian's delight, he received a reply that simply said, "Let us meet at the fountain in ten minutes."

The Roman afternoon's sunshine was steady and hot. Sitting under the fountain's misting spray was a refreshing reprieve.

Reissen found the priest waiting for him. As before, he patted the limestone surface next to him in greeting, followed again with a blessing of Holy Water.

"Welcome to my office *al-fresco*, Dr. Reissen." Father Richardo said with a smile.

"Hello again, Father. I have some good news to share with you."

"Wonderful. Please do."

"Our colleagues from Pennsylvania successfully assisted our errant local colleagues."

"Yes, so have I heard."

The Austrian cocked his head quizzically. "But did you know about their missing security guard?"

A shake of the head and the priest's face became one of concern.

"They think that one of their former dignitaries possessed a security guard." Reissen whispered.

"A *suspected* possession?" Father Richardo repeated with some disbelief. His eyes slitted.

"Yes."

"How did you come by this information?" The priest asked now crossing his arms and leaning in.

"From William DeSalvo himself."

"DeSalvo ..." now leaning back, "now that is most interesting. Do you know who this unfortunate is?"

"Yes. DeSalvo shared an image."

Again leaning in, "And what if we run into this poor wretch? What does DeSalvo want us to do?"

"He suggested that we follow and inform him immediately. The inference being that they will take care of their own."

"Anything else? Such as *what* might have possessed him?" The priest clinically inquired.

"Yes, the entity that is *suspected* of possessing the security guard is a master magician and member of the priesthood of Set."

At the mention of Set, Father Richardo's face darkened. He hissed through his teeth. "Are you sure of that?"

"Yes. And, perhaps coincidentally, a visiting Turkish scholar is right now translating a papyrus in our own library that seems to be a biography of the man."

"My God ... that surely sounds far more than mere coincidence to me, more like divine providence, if not an outright sign." The priest stated with firmness.

"But Dr. Reissen, did the CMES chairman assign any motivation for this *suspected* possession?"

"No, he did not. But possession, even *suspected* possession, is serious business in my book. That means this Sethi must have had a very good reason."

"How long has this security guard's body been missing?"

"Five days." Reissen answered.

"Is he married?"

"Yes, he is, but his wife has not seen him since the resurrection spell."

"So where can this poor unfortunate be?"

"That's the question, Father, but even more than that, what is Sethi up to?"

*　　*　　*

While Father Richardo and Reissen were discussing Sethi, Makris and her husband were busy being tourists. They wandered about everywhere shopping, sightseeing, and eating gelato from every street corner vendor.

At the same time, Sethi was on the street hunting, trying to find the witch responsible for his unexpected predicament. What Sethi used to track were the witch's subtle characteristics he had sensed during the resurrection spell. Every time an adept used magic, the spell's casting required the adept to pour out their will to empower it. Just like a hound scented an animal, so also can certain adepts—called spell whisperers—differentiate the scent of one's will. Magic always left behind the unique signature of its practitioner.

So how do you know that this witch is still in Rome? Condé wanted to know of his paranormal partner-in-crime.

"She is here. Moving about. What is shopping?"

The Italian shrugged. *Buying stuff like food, clothing, shoes, you name it.*

"Ah, now I understand. She is shopping. Where does one do this? Is there a central marketplace?"

That question caught the Italian short. *Uh, not anymore. Instead, places to shop can be found nearly everywhere throughout the city.*

"That answer is not helpful. What is gelato?"

It's a cold dessert, a sweet. It comes in many flavors.

"She is eating this now. Where can it be found?"

Almost anywhere.

"Again, that is not helpful." Sethi sourly said.

It's just that everyone loves gelato.

* * *

Meanwhile, both CMES and the Brothers of St. Paul had distributed Giuseppe Condé's photo among their members and operatives in hopes of spotting the security guard somewhere on the streets of Rome. They had not approached the Roman constabulary, as the security guard had not committed a crime. Besides, the explanation for "why" they wished to find the man would have been an interesting discussion that the Vatican was not interesting in having.

Rome normally had a population of nearly three million. In the summer, however, that figure swelled, because Rome was the third-most-visited city in the European Union. Among those hordes of tourists, the security guard, who, being a native of the city, blended in perfectly.

CHAPTER 7

New Tomb Discovered: Unknown Son of Ramses the Great

(Cairo, Egypt). Egypt's Ministry of Antiquities has announced today the discovery of a large and well-decorated tomb of an unknown prince of Ramses the Great at Sakkara, Egypt. Six later intrusive burials were also reported.

The Nineteenth-Dynasty tomb was found south of the Step Pyramid of Djoser and is comprised of six beautifully carved and painted chambers. The wall murals and inscriptions depict the tomb owner's military exploits and his lineage as a son of the Pharaoh Ramses II and his queen Nefertari. Following his military career, the prince became a *sem*-priest of the Egyptian god Set, and subsequently the chairman of a priestly council—a body heretofore never before reported.

The tomb's later intrusive burials are believed to date to the Ptolemaic period. The archaeologists made this estimation based upon ceramic evidence and papyrus found at the site.

During a ceremony that announced the tomb's discovery this past Saturday, Dr. Ahmed Salam, the secretary-general of the Supreme Council of Antiquities said, "We have yet to find an intact example of the prince's name written in hieroglyphics. All that we have are erasures, which is very mysterious."

According to the Ministry of Antiquities, who made the discovery in collaboration with the

Department of Archaeological Studies at the University of Milano, the intrusive burials are likely to be a familial grave of the "middle class."

The archaeological team began its work in February 2018, when it discovered a corridor cut into the bedrock. That corridor eventually led the six-roomed burial chamber.

"So, Erik, what do you make of this archaeological discovery?" asked Sister Josephina Busby, Ph.D. in Egyptology, specialist in ancient Egyptian magic, and Pro Deo counterpart.

"I find the erasures of the prince's name disquieting. You know as well as I the implications of such a defacement."

"Yes, to erase a name is to deny that person's memory, damn them from the afterlife, and destroy a portion of their soul. That trifecta is tough to beat," the fiery redhead concluded. "This unknown prince must have either done something egregious during his life, or more probable, fallen into disfavor after his burial."

"Interesting take. I wonder if anyone has examined those erasures. Sometimes the hints of several glyphs can be resurrected with the use of a directed light source."

Sister Josephina's eyes danced. "Do you think that this is Sethi's tomb? The same guy who is now running around Rome in somebody else's body?"

"Sight unseen, no. But the fact that this tomb is in the neighborhood of Imhotep's and Djedi's tombs, both who were serious magicians in their own right, means there is a strong possibility. Are you willing to do some reconnaissance work for me?"

"I thought you would never ask."

Reissen smiled. "Then it is settled. I will see to your travel arrangements. You leave tomorrow. When you visit the tomb, take Inspector Hassan with you. Remember: think like a sneaky magician. Look for anything that looks suspicious. And get some reads on those erasures. In the meantime, I will e-mail Inspector Hassan to let him know about your visit and need for an archaeological site pass. At least I think Ali still holds that post. Regardless, be sure to look him up."

"Will do. See you soon," the sister said before she turned to go, black robes trailing.

*   *   *

Sister Busby's flight from Rome to Cairo barely reached cruising altitude before its descent began. Traveling only with a light backpack and dressed in a comfortable outfit of light cottons, the nun breezed through customs and hailed a cabbie for Sakkara. Overjoyed at the distance to be covered and the fare to be collected, the man bubbled when Busby engaged him in his own Egyptian dialect.

"Tell me about the tourism. Has it returned back to Mubarak levels?"

The cabbie, a man named Mustafa from his name

plate, at first didn't know what to make of the potentially sensitive question, given the present regime. "It is difficult to say."

"Mustafa, do you have a family?"

"A wife and two daughters." The taxi driver smiled and answered proudly into his rearview mirror.

"How old are your daughters?"

"Seven and nine years."

"Are they in primary school?"

"Oh, yes! They are doing very well in their studies."

"Is their school an ordinary or religious school?"

At this point, Mustafa began to realize that his passenger knew quite a bit about Egyptian life. "Ordinary."

"How nice," the nun replied as she gazed out of the passenger's window.

About an hour later, as the traffic had been light, Mustafa asked, "Where at Sakkara do you wish to go?"

"Let's make a quick stop first in Memphis at the archaeological offices there. I need to pick up my site pass."

"No problem. Do you wish for me to wait?" Mustafa asked hopefully.

"Yes! Please."

"Arriving minutes later, Sister Busby hopped out of the taxi and disappeared into the two-storey brick building. She reemerged moments later with a grin on her face.

"Okay, Mustafa. Next stop, the south side of Sakkara. Drop me off in the bus parking lot next to the Step Pyramid."

After paying the cabbie his fare plus a good tip, Sister Busby slipped into her backpack and began walking. Soon she was crossing King Unis' causeway and passed between that king's adjacent boat pits and the tomb of Neferhorptah. From there she walked south in the direction of the tombs of Maya and Horemheb. About halfway there, she stopped and flashed her archaeological pass at the security guard, who stood before the newly discovered tomb.

Instead of allowing Sister Busby to pass, the man with the bushy moustache blocked her passage. "No, no entry." He said in broken English. "Forbidden."

"Yes, yes entry," the nun corrected in Egyptian Arabic. "This pass was given to me by Inspector Ali Hassan's office. Do you wish to keep your job?"

Surprised by the sharp retort, but seeking a bribe of *baksheesh* nonetheless, he still blocked her entry to the long, descending corridor cut into the limestone bedrock.

Realizing his none-too-subtle game, Sister Busby pulled out her device and called the inspector directly. The guard's smile froze.

"Hello, Inspector Hassan. This is Sister Busby. I am sorry to bother you, but I am at the entrance to the newly discovered tomb south of Djoser's pyramid. When might I expect you to arrive?"

"Ah ha, in about ten minutes." The nun repeated in Egyptian. "Wonderful inspector. May I ask of you a favor?"

"Yes. Yes, would you please tell your antiquities guard to allow me into the tomb?"

After a brief pause, Sister Josephine said, "Yes, yes one moment."

Then the nun handed the device to the petrified guard. Twenty seconds later, the lock on the steel-grated door was open.

"Thank you." She said to the ashen face.

Now standing before the descending corridor, the nun noted its ten-foot ceiling, low and sloped steps, and the ramp cut down its center. *All better to drag a sarcophagus...interesting.*

Continuing slowly toward the tomb's entrance, Sister Busby noted that two layers of limestone had been cut through to allow the passage. As for the tomb entrance itself, it was a simple rectangular cutting without decoration. *Probably blocked up and plastered over to hide its existence.*

Once inside the tomb, all was darkness, even though banks of lighting rested along the bases of the corridor.

Turning around, the nun saw the guard resting in the entrance's shade smoking a cigarette. She called out, "Excuse me, but can you turn on the lights?"

The guard just shrugged and raised his open hands in reply, but his smile suggested pure insolence.

"Damn asshole," Sister Busby murmured as she dug into a side pocket of her backpack. She withdrew a powerful LED flashlight. While the tomb's entrance was plain by design, once Sister Busby flicked the ON switch, the tomb's central corridor illuminated with a sun-like intensity.

What she beheld was a veritable treat for the eyes. The bright freshness and perfect condition of the wall paintings looked as if they had been completed the day before. The wall carvings seemed almost to breathe in their placement and form. Without question, this was no nobleman's tomb, but a version fit for royal blood.

The tomb's layout was based upon a central aisle, from which six separate rooms radiated out in a symmetrical manner—three to a side. Every square inch of surface—including the blue ceilings studded with five-pointed golden stars—dazzled.

On this otherwise pristine canvas, Sister Busby easily found the twelve erasures where the tomb owner's name once appeared. Frankly, they appeared to the nun as rude blemishes. Inwardly, Sister Busby felt outrage at the defacements. But in the harsh glare of the LED's beam, when tilted this way and that, she saw the damaged and fragmentary remains of the tomb owner's name in hieroglyphs. Out came her notepad, and as Sister Busby went from blemish to blemish, she began to piece together, much like a puzzle master, a name—*Sethi*.

She flushed with a sense of victory and vindication

for the tomb's owner as the lights of the tomb suddenly came on and in walked Inspector Ali Hassan.

"Sister Busby! How good to see you again!" and in a softer voice, "And I apologize about the antiquities guard and the lighting. Tomorrow he will be looking for a new job."

"Thank you, Inspector Hassan. It's good to see you too. And this tomb is simply breathtaking!"

"Indeed it is," the inspector replied while gazing about, "and the University of Milano people have done a wonderful job in finding it. Allow me to take you on a tour."

"I would enjoy that."

The pair spent the next half hour slowly wandering from room to room, from mural scene to inscriptional register. As for the six intrusive burials, Inspector Hassan explained that their burial shafts in the flooring had to be covered over with hinged steel plates and frames with heavy locks and lead seals. "Sister Busby, the shafts were clearly a safety issue, as all six had been placed precisely in the center of each of the six rooms."

Nowhere during this extremely detailed wandering did the nun detect in any of the walls the shadow of a hidden doorway. That troubled the powerful sensitive, because this was, after all, the tomb of a magician. Nowhere did she note any trickery, any subterfuge, like she remembered Erik Reissen had found with the magician's tomb of Djedi. Then it struck her squarely— *the hidden doorway must be at the end of the corridor!*

"So there you have it." Inspector Hassan said with considerable pride. "This is perhaps the best preserved tomb outside of the Valley of the Kings."

"Has the University of Milano team finished this project?" The nun inquired.

"Yes. They are currently working on its publication."

"Have they completed all the imagery?"

"As far as I know, yes."

"Okay Inspector Hassan, I want to show you something that you just might want to share with the Milano team."

"What might that be, Sister Busby?"

"Inspector, do you remember all the headaches that Dr. Reissen went through with the Djedi tomb?"

"Indeed I do! That tomb was a heart-attack almost every day! Acid traps, hidden entrance ways, walls that moved, you name it."

"Exactly. Now Inspector, this tomb's owner, while unknown, was a magician. What does that tell you?"

Hassan's eyes got wide. "That the University of Milano team may have missed something."

"Indeed. Was this the lighting that they used during their work?

"Generally, yes. But their photographic team also used other lighting."

"As I would expect. I would like to show you something, but first ask the guard outside to turn off the lights."

Now in the pitch black, Sister Busby again turned on her LED flashlight.

"That is indeed bright for such a small device!" Exclaimed the inspector.

"Yes, and its harshness tends to reveal far more than does the softer, yellower light of the floor lamps." The nun narrated as she walked to the end of the corridor.

"Inspector Hassan, please note that this floor-to-ceiling carving of Osiris is the only mural in this tomb with a carved frame." Passing the glaring light along the frame, Sister Busby continued. "Further, and it just may be my imagination, but I find the interior cutting of this frame to be incredibly precise. Not to mention, it has an exact copy in Tomb 5 of the Valley of the Kings."

"What!"

"Yes, Inspector. I believe that to be significant."

"Yes, I see what you mean, Sister Busby. Are you suggesting that this frame might be a doorway?"

"That is the only logical place for an additional secret chamber."

Ali Hassan rubbed at his chin in the shadow of the glare. "If this is a doorway, is there some kind of trigger or lever that will open it?"

Sister Busby panned the LED's beam again around the panel, but dawdled in her search on the deeply carved hieroglyphs that surrounded the image of Osiris. Finally, "I do not see anything. Do you Inspector?"

"Nothing obvious."

"Maybe that's the point, Inspector. What's not obvious?"

"Kindly illuminate the Osiride figure from several flat angles, then maybe something will stick out."

So the nun began to shine the beam from various perspectives. The Osiris figure was wrapped in a tight burial shroud, with crossed arms that held the royal crook and flail. Its head turned in profile toward the West and the setting sun—toward that divinity's home in the Netherworld. And ... lo and behold, the figure's left hand, unlike the rest of the carving, seemed oddly indented.

Sister Busby's heart rate quickened. "Do you see that, Inspector?"

"Indeed, I do. What should we do?"

"Press your palm against it, firmly, and let's see what happens."

"Might this be a trap?" The inspector asked. "Consider what happened to Dr. Reissen with the Djedi tomb."

"Inspector, we'll never know until someone pushes on that portion of the carving." Sister Busby said. "May I suggest that Dr. Reissen look into this architectural detail? This sort of thing is one of his specialties."

"A fine idea, Sister Busby."

"By the way, Inspector, the six burial shafts that are located in each of the six side chambers, did you notice how deep those shafts are?"

The man rubbed at the stubble on his chin. "As I recall, the Milano team surveyed them at five meters."

"Are they unusually smooth sided?"

"Why yes they are ... almost polished."

"Are there side chambers in them?"

"No. Just a shaft that bottoms out with jagged rocks."

"Do their openings have an edge?"

"I cannot recall. Let's check."

They entered the nearby, left-rear side chamber, and the inspector removed from his pocket a ring of keys and a small wire cutter. After cutting away the lead inspection seal and its wire, he applied a key, and the padlock clicked open. With a metallic screech, Hassan lifted open the hatch-like steel cover from its frame. As soon as he did, Sister Busby pointed the LED beam into the darkness.

"Inspector Hassan, kindly note two things. First, the carefully provided edge that surrounds the burial shaft's opening. It is," holding her fingers near it, "four finger-breaths wide. That is no coincidence. That is the proper width for a plaster false floor tile. Second, you remembered correctly. The four vertical sides of this burial shaft are indeed finely finished. So finely finished that I doubt anyone could climb out of it, much less if they were injured. I don't know about you, Inspector Hassan, but I have seen enough."

"What do you mean by that, Sister Busby?"

"These six burial shafts are anything but, Inspector.

I believe they were originally designed to be man-traps, which were only later reused for burial purposes."

"By Allah's gray beard!"

"May I make a suggestion, Inspector?"

"What might that be?"

"Seal this tomb until Dr. Reissen can inspect it, and in particular that Osiride panel carving. He'll know what to do."

CHAPTER 8

Five days after escaping the villa, Condé's body was in real trouble. Driven by two personalities—not to mention two different motivations—the senior security guard's physical body was experiencing a brutal toll. Sore and swollen feet, an aching lower back, an empty stomach, low blood sugar, and mounting dehydration rapidly ramped up to a crisis situation—not to mention the need of a shower.

Must rest. Condé begged his partner-in-crime.

"The witch is near! I can feel it." Sethi said. "We must press on!"

I'm sorry. But I must rest—right now.

"No, you miserable little worm. She is near. We must confront that bitch!"

Then the senior security guard practically crash-landed into the chair of an open-air, street-corner deli—conveniently one of Condé's his favorites.

"Ciao, Signore Condé," the expectant waiter greeted, upon seeing the distressed regular. "Are you alright?"

"A liter of water and the biggest salami sandwich you can make."

"Si, signore, subito!"

* * *

Sethi was right. Makris and Stone were very near,

strolling, arm-in-arm with shopping bags hanging from their free hands.

"Mel, I see a deli ahead at the corner with outdoor seating." J.J. pointed. "How about stopping to get something to eat?"

"Another gelato?" she said with a squeeze on his arm. "You eat another one of those, and you'll need to let out your UCS."

"I'm not talking about gelato, Beautiful, I'm talking about a serious sandwich of some kind."

"Okay, I give, just wipe off your chin. You're drooling."

Instead Stone froze in mid-step and stared in the direction of the deli. Its smells had reached the pair—onions, fresh breads, meats, and apparently something else.

Soul carrier! Beware! An old one lurks ahead. He seeks not you, but instead your wife. He holds great hate in his heart, for he is one of the resurrected. The First Soul alerted Stone, the First Soul of Creation that he had carried since birth.

"What's wrong?" Makris quietly asked.

"I'm getting this incredibly wrong vibe. Can't see anything yet. But you're the target, not me."

Looking quickly around, Stone led his wife by the elbow into a flower shop, filled with a riot of color and heady scents.

"Stay here. Hide among the flowers. They will mask your scent and presence."

"You're practically quoting from *Monsieur* Dexter's lecture on naturally occurring magical defenses."

"I'm happy you noticed."

"But …"

"No buts, Gorgeous. Stay here until I come back for you." He locked eyes with his Egyptian witch-wife. "Promise me that you'll stick *right* here."

"I promise." His wife answered, her eyes meeting his with concern. "But be sure you come back."

After a quick peck on her forehead, Stone sauntered out the open doorway. Makris knew better. There was now a cat-like signature to her husband's body language. His training had shifted him into another mode. He was now a predator on the hunt.

"Good day, pretty lady." The motherly, middle-aged shopkeeper greeted in passable English. "Is there something in particular that I can show you?"

"Why yes," she said absentmindedly, "do you have any chrysanthemums?"

"Oh my, yes, and you are in luck—red or white?"

*   *   *

Condé put down his half-eaten sandwich when his internal partner suddenly jerked to full alert.

What's wrong?

"We are in danger." The magician-priest declared.

The half-eaten sandwich in Condé's stomach began

to roil. Glancing around the senior security guard thought, *What kind? Which direction?*

"A powerful being approaches on the left … on foot."

Who?

"I do not know him. But he is extremely powerful … dangerous."

What about the witch?

"Strange, my inner eye can no longer see her."

*   *   *

Stone walked tight along the storefronts to his right. He knew his target was ahead, somewhere near the street intersection, perhaps even at the deli. He found himself slowing down, listening with his mind, and scanning for darkened auras. His hands unconsciously flexed in anticipation and readiness. Long-memorized defensive spells bubbled from his lips, forming a generalized warding sphere that could stop heavy rounds. Other spells, powerful offensive ones, waited on his tongue to be released.

*   *   *

Sethi sensed the stealthy approach of a powerful hunter. In response, Condé's body picked up the rest of his sandwich and left the deli, walking in the opposite direction from the threat.

Why are we leaving? Weren't we trying to find a

witch, instead of running from it? The security guard asked his traveling companion.

"What is approaching us is a powerful opponent. Find somewhere where we can observe this area safely. That way we will find out who is tracking us."

So Condé crossed the street, found a heavily-shadowed corner, entered it, and turned to wait. His heart was in his throat. The thought of taking another bite from his sandwich made him sick. Clearly, something or someone had really gotten Sethi's attention.

*　　*　　*

"Where is it?" Stone asked the First Soul.

It detected our approach and left in haste.

"So where was it?" Stone asked.

It sat at that table, the one with the chair askew and the half-empty water bottle.

Stone went to it and sat down. While doing so, the THIS Lictor of Magic placed his hand on the table and read the previous occupant's residual vibration. The subtle trembling of it spoke directly to the agitation of his quarry. Picking up the plastic water bottle, again Stone felt the same nervousness.

"What do you make of this, my old friend?"

Very little. Just that it left at our approach.

Frustrated, Stone was about to get up and leave, but the deli's waiter approached him.

"Ciao, signore."

"Do you speak English?"

"Si, signore, I do." The waiter said with swagger.

"Can you describe who sat at this table before I arrived?"

"Si, an older man. He was very hungry. He ordered a large salami sandwich and that bottle of water. Why do you ask? Are you a policeman?" He asked suspiciously.

"No," Stone said with a smile. Pulling his wallet, he extracted a twenty Euro bill and placed it on the table under the half-empty water bottle. "Could you describe this man? He has been threatening my wife." He said, this time stone-faced and without the smile.

The waiter sat down at the table, since it wasn't very busy, smoothly pocketed the Euro note, and proceeded to fill Stone in on his regular customer— *Signore* Condé.

Five minutes later, the two men shook hands, and Stone went back to the flower shop, only to find that his wife had created a magnificent necklace of bright and fragrant white flowers.

"Boy, do you look purdy!" Stone exclaimed in his best North Texas accent.

"Why thank you, Cowboy. Now would you please pay this kind lady?"

* * *

Condé and Sethi watched a tall and fit man sit down at their table, talk with the waiter, and then leave in the same direction he had come.

He looks military to me. American. Condé said on the basis of the short-cropped haircut and clothing.

"He is far more. He is a powerful magician. And one other thing, I just learned that the witch we seek is his wife."

What!

"Yes, my hungry friend. Our quest has become complicated."

Does this mean that we're finished chasing this witch? If so, when do I get my money?

"No. We are not finished. But now we know what he looks like. What we do not know is what she looks like. So we follow and see who he meets. And stop worrying about your rental fee."

CHAPTER 9

Bright and early Reissen arrived at his Pro Deo office. His assistant, Sergeant Agave, greeted him. "Boss, you have an important e-mail from an Egyptian inspector of antiquities."

"Thanks. I will look for it." He glanced at the man's half-finished Starbuck's paper cup. "And I still think that is swill."

Settled down at his desk, the Austrian noted the inspector's e-mail was sent late the previous evening. It read,

> Greetings from Egypt, Dr. Reissen!
>
> After an informative visit by your colleague, Sister Josephina Busby, I have decided your presence here at Sakkara would be much appreciated. I have ordered the tomb that she visited sealed until you arrive.
>
> Your reply is eagerly awaited.
>
> Sincerely yours,
>
> Ali Hassan, MA
> Inspector of the Sakkaran Archaeological District
> Supreme Council of Antiquities

Two minutes later Reissen's phone rang. It was from Sister Busby.

"Hello, my friend," Reissen said warmly. "What do I owe you for this wakeup call?"

"Have you received Inspector Hassan's invitation?"

"Yes, I have. What did you find that caused Ali to seal a tomb?"

"First off, my analysis of the twelve erasures points to Sethi as the owner of this tomb. Secondly, Erik, that tomb is another magical time bomb, much like the Djedi tomb. I strongly suspect that there is at least one secret chamber. I know that were once six man traps, later converted to intrusionary burials. In short, Inspector Hassan wants you here to assess the situation. How soon can you get here?"

The Austrian considered his immediate situation. Yes, he could catch a flight to Egypt that afternoon. Yes, it was important to maintain good relations with the Egyptian Antiquities Service and his friend Inspector Hassan. But he still had to manage the day-to-day running of Pro Deo's operations. Sergeant Agave could mind the store on a temporary basis. But to show up in Egypt, Reissen would need to bring along a photographer, at a minimum.

"Erik, are you still there?"

"Yes, I am. I have to think about this offer."

"You're kidding!"

"Sister Josephina. Let me get back to you in … about an hour. In the meantime, I will immediately respond to Ali's e-mail."

"Erik …"

"Patience my friend, it is a virtue."

The very next call the archaeologist made was to Father Richardo, who was his colleague and go-to source of tactical muscle from the Brothers of St. Paul.

"Ciao, Richardo."

"Father Richardo, this is Erik Reissen. Good morning, sir."

"Ah, Dr. Reissen. What a pleasure. What can I do for you?"

"I have just received a call from Egypt. The University of Milano's archaeological team may have found another magician's tomb full of booby traps. What I need is one of your colleagues who is good with a camera and military tactics."

For several moments the line went silent, while in the background Reissen heard the rapid typing of keys.

"I have on staff such a combination. When do you need him?"

"On this afternoon's flight to Egypt. We'll go together as a team."

"I can arrange that. I will also send you an e-mail about the man's qualifications."

"Thank you, Father Richardo. I knew I could count on you. I'll handle the airplane tickets from my end."

"That would be acceptable. And Dr. Reissen ..."

"Yes, Father?"

"Thank you for asking for our assistance."

*   *   *

The man from the Brothers of St. Paul arrived at Reissen's office an hour later. He was round-faced, with a big smile, a small wheelie, and a compact camera bag. He looked every bit the part of a tourist going on holiday. A blinding yellow Polo golf shirt and tan cargo shorts showed off the man's blocky build and bandy arms and legs. Reissen instantly liked him and his firm handshake.

"*Ciao,* Dr. Reissen. I'm Father Georgio Cardoza. Father Richardo told me that you needed a photographer. Well, I'm it."

"Thank you for coming on this adventure," the Austrian began. "I cannot guarantee anything. I just learned that we were going to Egypt this morning. By the way, what kind of camera are you carrying?"

"Cameras, Dr. Reissen. My main unit is a digital Canon EOS 5D. I also am packing two GoPros that we can mount on anything or anybody. I have a backup digital body, just in case the Canon craps out, and several sweet Zeiss lenses."

"Father Cardoza, excuse me, but you don't sound like a member of the clergy, much less than an Italian."

"Dr. Reissen, you're right. I'm the red-headed stepchild of the Brothers of St. Paul. I'm also from Camden, New Jersey, so that makes me an Italian-American by birth. But I have done a stint with the French Foreign Legion. Did some nasty things in sub-Saharan Africa, and then I found Jesus, as they are wont to say."

"So what else are you carrying, Father?"

"A Smith & Wesson MMP 9mm. with 145 grain hollow points. I realize that it's a pea-shooter, but it's compact, and the hollows pack a real punch."

"I see. As to what we will be doing, I will be playing the part of an Egyptian archaeologist and you my photographer. Are you comfortable with that?"

"Absolutely, Doc. What's the gig?"

Reissen had to think a moment about what "gig" meant. "We will be inspecting a recently opened tomb of an Egyptian magician. One of my colleagues suspects that there may be a secret chamber. My previous experiences with such situations caused me to contact Father Richardo for assistance."

"Fair enough. When do we leave?"

"Right now."

*   *   *

Firearm importation into Egypt naturally has always been an extremely sensitive issue that required special diplomatic processing of the airline passengers involved. Given the extremely short notice of their travel arrangements, the Holy See had to perform several miracles. But once Cardoza got through the necessary hoops, they hired a cab that took them to the south Sakkaran bus parking lot, where Sister Busby met them.

"Welcome back to Egypt, Erik." The nun greeted

sensibly dressed in a loosely fitting cotton shirt and tan slacks. She turned to Cardoza. "And who might you be?"

"Father Cardoza, ma'am, your photographer."

This statement caused the nun to raise her eyebrows as she took in the golf shirt and cargo shorts.

"So, Sister Busby," Reissen said while indirectly cluing in Cardoza as to her status, "would you mind leading us over to the tomb?"

"Absolutely. Please follow me, gentlemen."

While the nun led, Cardoza asked Reissen. "That red-head is a nun?"

"Yes, Father. And she is a top-notch Egyptologist, who specializes in dark magic. Beware—she can have quite a temper."

"Understood. Thanks for the heads up."

Upon reaching the tomb's entrance corridor, Reissen stopped and just took in the topographical scene. What he saw was a limestone outcrop with a descending passage gashed into its western margin. At the end of the artificial slope awaited the dark rectangle of the tomb's entrance.

"Father, capture this view, if you please." Turning to Cardoza, he saw that the man was already shooting.

"Got it, boss."

Next, Reissen descended the outside low-stepped portion of the corridor's ramp and stopped at the tomb's entrance. "You know, Sister Busby, there are forty-two steps to this entrance corridor, one each for the ancient

Egyptian districts and their gods." Then to Cardoza, "Father, when we are out of the way, kindly photograph this stepped ramp."

"Consider it done."

At this point, Sister Busby noticed that the tomb's antiquity guard had been changed.

"Excuse me," she asked the newcomer as she flashed him her site pass, "could you please turn on the lights?"

A single nod of the guard's head, and the illumination appeared.

It took only one look at the artistic grandeur all around him and Reissen declared. "This is a royal's tomb."

Finally arriving to the left-rear side chamber, the nun produced a wire cutter and key that successfully opened the steel hatch in the floor. Items that Inspector Hassan had kindly provided her as he was detained with other business.

Reissen gasped. "Remarkable. Just look at how smooth those walls are. There is no way that anyone could climb out of that depth. Father Cardoza?"

"Right here, boss."

"Shoot this, okay? And try to capture as best you can the smoothness of this pit's side walls."

"You got it."

Sister Busby pointed inside the tomb. "Erik, before we move on, check out these edges. They're perfect for supporting a plaster false floor tile."

"You're right. Good catch. Now, where is the location of that possible secret chamber you told me about?"

"Follow me."

Standing before the Osiride panel engraved into the main corridor's end wall, Sister Busby pulled out her LED flashlight and once again lit up the god of the Underworld from a variety of low angles.

"You're right about that left hand, Reissen said, studying the panel. "It does look suspicious."

"Before we do anything, we need some pictures." Sister Busby replied.

"On it." And Father Cardoza took about fifteen shots that ranged from the general to the specific and from several low angles.

Reissen moved forward. "Alright, everyone, stand back, preferably sheltered in the entrance of a side passage."

Reissen stood alone before the Osiride panel as he thought about what he was about to do. Placing one palm against the left hand that held the royal flail of punishment and judgment, the Austrian leaned in with his other hand atop. In one spasm of exertion and a grunt for good measure, the archaeologist pushed, hard.

A clear and audible *THUNK* emanated from deep within the wall.

Reissen quietly said. "Damn I am good."

CHAPTER 10

As Condé passed by the corner deli again, his friend the waiter saw him and waved to get his attention.

"People have been asking about you, Giuseppe. What have you been up to, eh?"

Confused by the question, Condé snapped back. "What do you mean?"

"A tall American told me that you were threatening his wife."

Now suddenly all contrite, "Who? Me? *Mio Dio!* Never would I do such a thing. He must be confusing me with someone else."

The waiter smiled knowingly as his patron seemed to protest too much. "That's alright, Giuseppe, I understand. A virile man like you might need an additional thrill or two. By the way, even your wife has been looking for you. She has stopped by twice. What have you been up to?"

The senior security guard did not answer, but instead glared back, and then abruptly turned on his heel, vowing to never return to this store.

So we have been noticed. We must proceed with extreme care. Sethi whispered in the security man's mind.

"So now we're following not only a witch but her magician husband. Before I move one more muscle, I want more money."

Sethi hissed with exasperation. *I will provide you with more riches than you can ever use.*

Condé smiled. He liked the sound of that.

*   *   *

Now in the role of the pursuer, Condé eased out of the shadows and slipped seamlessly into the constant movement of the passing crowds. Being short of stature had its distinct advantages, but sometimes visibility was reduced to quick glances. Still, the senior security guard had little trouble tracking the tall American from a distance. The man just stuck out. He entered the flower store halfway down the street and then reemerged moments later with a flower-bedecked woman. The pair then walked away in the other direction, hand-in-hand.

Sethi cursed under his breath.

"What's wrong?" Condé asked.

The witch is covered with flowers.

"So what?"

Sethi commiserated with himself. His "carrier" was ignorant of the ways of magic, and the *sem*-priest and master magician did not want to bother sharing all the details. The odds for his much-hoped-for revenge had been reduced—especially now that he was up against a formidable husband-and-wife pair.

Flowers, my dear friend, and their scent are protective barriers against many forms of magical attack, which I had intended to use.

"Flowers?"

Flowers, their scent and pollen, represent the very essence of Nature. Magic is generally powerless in their presence.

"What about honey bees?"

Sethi nearly choked at the senior security guard's question, for he had blundered into an impressive intellectual leap. Bees were the absolute bane of dark demons, souls unnaturally in possession of a mortal, and dark practitioners in general. Bees, Nature's natural defenders, made their food from nectar—the very essence of life. Their sting, while a form of suicide, actually represented the selfless transference of Nature's own life force—something totally anathema to any of the undead and dark demons. Sethi shuddered. Any random bee sting could utterly destroy his *ka*.

Why do you ask about bees?

"I dunno. It's just that I have always associated flowers with bees."

Where is the pair now? Sethi asked, to end this dangerous train of thought.

Condé craned his neck. "They are about a hundred meters ahead."

That distance is sufficient. Let us find out where they are going.

* * *

You know, of course, that our threat is now following

us, the First Soul whispered to Stone's mind.

"Yeah, I was hoping that would happen. I would love to confront this guy."

Remember, soul carrier, the threat is not with the mortal, but rather with the entity that is in possession of him.

"Any ideas, old wise one? Perhaps a good ambush point?"

Hmm, interesting tactic. I will think on this.

"Talking with yourself again?" Makris kidded.

"Yeah, the First Soul has informed me that our *friend* is again following us."

"Did I hear that you want to ambush him?"

"Yeah, and I'm open to any and all suggestions. Where could we trap an entity?"

"Well, certainly not on a busy street like this one," the Egyptian witch commented.

"Do you think a dousing of Holy Water would do it?"

"Probably not. We're talking about a resurrected soul, not a dark demon."

"Okay, then what would a resurrected soul fear the most?" Stone wanted to know.

"Actually, it's a resurrected soul in possession of an innocent mortal. It would fear without question a bee sting to its carrier, or lacking that, eating or inhaling flower nectar." She said, fluffing up her fragrant necklace of flowers.

"How about honey?"

"That would do, I suppose …"

"You sound doubtful."

"I am. A bee sting is the best, but the others will at least slow down the possessing entity's reaction time."

"Reaction time?"

"Yeah, Cowboy, its magical reaction time. Its ability to effectively counterpunch."

*   *   *

At sunset on the fifth day of Sethi's resurrection, he and Condé were in hot pursuit of the witch who had cast that disruptive resurrection spell. Moving forward through the narrow streets of a secluded Roman neighborhood, Condé, while peering around the corner of an alley, could not believe his eyes. Before a small *al-fresco* restaurant the witch sat alone at one of its three tables—the others unoccupied, as the hour was early. The cooking aromas of this evening's cuisine filled the air.

Their inviting target still wore a garland of white flowers, while sipping at a glass of red wine. The senior security guard glanced about and could not locate her husband, but knew without doubt he waited somewhere in ambush. Still, the bait seemed genuine. It was almost as if the witch was saying, "Here I am. Come, sit, and let us discuss the weather."

Sethi remained suspicious, while Condé was a mixture of eagerness to get paid and sheer curiosity.

Frankly, the old priest-magician was intrigued by the brave and brazen witch. In the end, the Egyptian overruled his qualms, entered the alley, and approached the seated witch from behind.

While still several yards away, the Egyptian witch loudly said, "Come, sit, and let us discuss the weather."

Sethi inwardly smiled at her boldness and sat down opposite. Now so close to her, the exotic natural beauty of the woman, the raven-black hair, brown almond-shaped eyes, flawless olive skin, and high cheek bones caused him to gasp in near-recognition. *So much like my own mother, Nefertari. Can it truly be?*

A clear and bell-like voice reached out and answered him. *I am flattered, but no. I am not the reincarnation of that famous queen, your natural mother, you of her body. But you must have been close—loved, for I can feel it in your heart.*

Condé/Sethi was twice stunned, one by the direct telepathic communication, the other by a paralysis spell that immediately took hold of the senior security guard's body. Condé attempted to move, but could not. Sethi attempted to speak, but he had been rendered mute.

Seeing the obvious signs of struggle, Makris said, *Gentlemen, becalm yourselves. Your paralysis is only temporary, but needful given your many abilities. I am here to offer you both a peaceful solution.* She gestured with her right hand. *You, security guard, wish to have your body's freedom returned to you once again.* Now indicating with the left, *While the other wishes to eventually return to his verdant and fragrant garden in the afterlife. Is this not true? Either nod your approval, or shake your head in denial.*

For a moment Condé's head struggled in muscular confusion, but did eventually nod.

This decision is good, for both of you. What I propose is that we, together, return to the villa. Once there, she gestured with her right hand, *you will be granted your freedom,* and then with the left, *while the nameless one will return his* ka *to his mummy. Is this agreeable?*

Again, a single nod.

I, however, wish to inform the other, the nameless one, that I know your name.

Condé's eyes went wide with alarm at this revelation, for with his name Sethi knew what the witch could potentially do.

Names are important as are their vocalization. I can assure you, nameless one, that I will employ your name in a powerful spell if anything untoward occurs on the way to the villa. Is that understood?

A single nod.

One other item before I release you from your paralysis. The flowers that I am wearing are most fragrant and are covered with pollen. Beware of this fact, oh nameless one, if you foolishly choose to act out of passion. I now balance your eternal existence upon the scale as did Ma'at upon your judgment against the weight of your heart, which so far have been benign. Is this understood?

A quick, eager nod.

Makris settled herself in her chair and sighed. *It is done.*

The numbness of Condé's arms and legs painfully began to reside. Once again his lips and tongue could move, but sluggishly. During this awakening process, Makris did not move a muscle, but instead concentrated on the short and disheveled man with the bushy moustache who sat across from her. He now shuffled his feet, rubbed at his hands, and grimaced at the prickly return of sensation. The senior security guard was not aware that Stone now stood silently behind him. For that matter, neither had Sethi as Stone had totally blocked out his mind.

The Egyptian witch suspected the worse, but prayed for the best. So she simply waited. Condé adjusted a stiff neck, worked his shoulders, and flexed his fingers.

The First Soul saw it first and screamed a warning into Stone's mind.

Then Condé *LUNGED* across the small table.

With fingers outstretched like talons, Sethi reached for the witch's throat. The priest-magician, now a missile of super-heated hate, sought only destruction, while mouthing the most horrible of death spells.

In response, several things happened at once. Makris triggered a warding spell as thick as a stone wall that Condé's hands could not penetrate. Stone grabbed the lunging man from behind by his shoulders, forced him back into the chair, and immediately began his ritual exorcism, which reduced the ancient's death spell to a single, surprised squeak. Finally, Makris stood up and placed the flowered garland over Condé's head and arranged it around his neck.

The senior security guard's eyes bulged out, mouth agape with a long intake of air, while his back arched grotesquely. His hands clawed at the air. Feet kicked. Stone hung on and continued his prayerful recitation. His eyes remained tightly shut and mind in full concentration, for never before had he expelled a *ka* from a mortal.

Two long minutes later, it was over. Condé's body, limp as a noodle, sat slumped in his chair. Stone, gasping and heavily perspiring from the effort, grunted out, "He's clear. His aura is a light green, but with muddy tinges of greed. Mel. You okay?"

She nodded, a little shaky. "Sethi had his death spell at the ready. But what happened to him? I saw no ectoplasmic emissions. Did you destroy it?"

"No, just displaced it. Was one hell of a fight." He panted. "But I just don't know where to."

Then Condé returned to the here and now. What he first saw were two strangers looking at him closely, one a man and the other a beautiful woman.

"*Signore* Condé, how do you feel?" the exhausted man asked with clear concern on his face.

"Like shit. I need a salami sandwich."

"Well, sir, you're in luck. We're right outside a nice neighborhood restaurant," the pretty lady said. "But the hour is still early. We just might have to drink a glass of wine before the kitchen opens."

CHAPTER 11

The interior of the Osiride panel moved inward fractionally, leaving a gap on its right side about a quarter of an inch wide. There was nothing to see but a limestone edge. Apparently, the heavy and thick panel rested on a left-handed door pivot of some kind.

Stepping away from his handiwork, Reissen waved Father Cardoza over to photograph his progress.

Meanwhile, Sister Busby was buzzing with excitement. "Let me see! Let me see!"

As the priest's camera strobbed out a flash with every exposure, the Austrian turned to his colleague in Egyptology. "At the moment, Sister Josephina, there is very little to see. However, before I push any further, I want the two of you out of the tomb. I am not going to take any chances."

Father Cardoza didn't argue with Reissen, but Sister Busby put her hands on hips and glared back. "I want to stay. You might need help."

"Sister Josephina." The Egyptologist pointed toward the tomb's exit. "Please wait at the entrance. It is not that far away."

The nun glared at him, then turned on her heel. Over her shoulder said, "We're supposed to be a team, Erik. You of all people should know that. Dead heroes aren't as valuable as live ones."

The Austrian did not comment. Instead, he waited

until she was safely away, then stood back from the panel several feet and took in the situation. To his best knowledge, the Egyptians only constructed traps that were in the flooring as false plaster plates or jars of toxic chemicals that could be triggered by a blundering footfall. So he got down on his hands and knees and began brushing the gritty floor with his gloved hands, sweeping the general area before the panel clean. Nowhere could he find any telltale grooves.

Next, while still on his knees, he carefully inspected the ceiling, which was painted a brilliant dark blue with golden five-pointed stars. *Is a cave in possible?* But again, he could not see any lines of a falling roof panel. *They could be plastered over, Erik,* his imagination told him, or was it his sixth sense talking to him?

In the end, Reissen listened to his inner voice and retreated.

Returning to his two colleagues, he said, "Let us call it a day. We have proven that the panel moves. Now I need to get some equipment, with Inspector Hassan's help." What the two compatriots did not miss were the huge sweat stains on the archaeologist's tan cotton shirt, front and back. Clearly, something had really spooked the Egyptologist.

*   *   *

The next day they returned, but this time with a full and

sealable biohazard suit, complete with its own air supply. Just where Inspector Hassan had acquired the insanely bright yellow garment, and on such short notice, no one knew for sure, but the Austrian was now in it, sweating profusely.

Another item that the good inspector provided was far more utilitarian—a six-foot plank of wood with a padded T-shaped attachment. That would be Reissen's battering ram, which, hopefully, would keep him out of harm's way.

As the Egyptologist placed the padded end of the ram against the Osiride panel, he gripped its opposite end, and began to push. Simultaneously, Father Cardoza digitally captured the moment of Pro Deo's operations director in action from the relative safety of the second side chamber's entrance. Using a two-hundred-millimeter lens, the priest quite literally captured the sweat running down the side of Reissen's face.

At first, little happened, but slowly the Austrian applied more pressure, to the point that he actually bowed the plank. Gradually, a grinding noise of stone on stone resulted, and something else. The gap widened several inches between the panel and its carved border. Reissen paused to inspect his progress before applying himself again. After two more expenditures of force, he had achieved some fourteen inches of gap. Next Reissen distinctly heard a metallic *PING!*

Then, all hell broke loose.

CHAPTER 12

Reissen found himself suddenly pinned to the ground in his bright yellow biohazard suit. And it was fortunate that he was, for he had air and containment. On the other hand, his head swam from an impact and consequently felt like a woozy ball of wool. His extremities were pinned down.

Laying there in the darkness, his head did a systems' check. Nothing seemed to hurt—other than his cranium, which he understood at a basal level as a good sign, so he began wriggling about to see just how much play he had. Very little was the answer. So he stopped struggling and took stock of the situation.

Okay, so I'm buried, but uninjured. A quick glance at the tank gauge at his collar confirmed that he had plenty of air. *Try to relax and wait this out. Help is probably already on its way.*

While that logical conclusion was indeed true, Reissen's pulse raced and he began to heavily sweat because of his latent claustrophobia.

After what seemed hours, but in actual fact was closer to fifteen minutes, his ears picked up the distinct sounds of shouting and the grinding of stone.

*   *   *

Father Cardoza, who had literally filmed the partial roof collapse, was the first on the scene shortly followed by

Sister Josephina, who presciently told the new security guard, a man named Jabari Khoury, to call in an emergency.

"Where is he?" Sister Josephina shrieked in the blinding tan dust cloud.

"My guess, buried at the end of the tomb's corridor. That's where he was last while I was filming. Start stacking rock along the sides of the corridor," the firm and calming voice of Cardoza commanded. "That way we can burrow in faster."

Working like frenzied bees, with nervous sweat streaming down their bodies, a nun and a priest made their grim progress as a two-man shuttle team.

Out of the sheer human need to let off steam during such a crisis, Cardoza narrated between pants of exertion. "The boss is a lucky man. Only about a meter of debris dropped in on him. He's got air. He's in a suit the lucky bastard. He's probably just stunned silly by some damn rock to the head. He'll be alright. You watch. He's a survivor. I know. I practically memorized his personnel jacket."

Sister Josephine said nothing, just piled rock as quickly as she could, while she silently prayed.

Rapidly the pair carved a path down the center of the corridor, but even though the air was clearing, there was still no sign of a yellow biohazard suit.

Then, accompanied by much shouting, six antiquity guards arrived and joined the fray. Under Mr. Khoury's direction, he formed them in a continuous conveyor-like line. Instead of measuring progress by inches, Cardoza now removed stone by the foot.

First a bright yellow glove appeared, then an arm, and before long, Reissen was carried out by Cardoza as if he weighed nothing.

Reissen looked into the priest's eyes. "Father Cardoza," he panted. "Please record what we have. I need a break."

"No shit, boss."

Now outside the tomb, Sister Josephina unzipped the bright yellow suit and found Reissen drenched to the skin. Rapidly, the desert's breezes chilled the archaeologist to the bone.

Shivering, Reissen looked up and said, "I need some water."

*   *   *

"So what do you think happened?" Cardoza asked the now sitting up archaeologist.

"While you were digging me out, I had time to ponder that question. Just before the cave in, I distinctly heard a metallic ring-, or ting-sound. When we clear all of that debris, I fully expect to find a piece of metal that was a trigger for that ceiling failure."

Sister Josephina couldn't believe her own ears. "Erik, look at yourself, you just survived intact from a roof collapse. Take a breather."

"You know, boss, the sister does have a point."

Cardoza agreed. "Why don't we call it a day and begin again tomorrow."

"I agree as well." Inspector Hassan chimed in, his face full of concern as he looked down at his old friend. "I will have my men clear the tomb. I will make a point to have them look for anything metallic."

"Well, clearly, I have been overruled." The Austrian drily remarked.

*   *   *

A heavily bruised Reissen returned with his team the next day to find Inspector Hassan waiting for them.

"How are you feeling, Erik?" He solicitously inquired.

"Stiff and sore, but ready to go." Looking around at all the neatly stacked piles of rubble next to the tomb's stepped entrance corridor, "And I see that your men have been busy."

But before the Austrian could proceed down the steps to the tomb's entrance, Inspector Hassan stopped him.

"Erik, look at this. The men found it in the tomb's corridor."

The object was a bronze bolt about six inches long. One end was abraded, while the other was smooth.

"Interesting." Reissen remarked. "Ali, come with me. I have a suspicion."

The Austrian found the tomb cleared and swept

clean. Only the odd looking gap in its ceiling hinted that something had occurred. Standing under it, Reissen looked up and could easily see its rectangular shape and how the cave in had been put into motion. A pivoting wooden beam had caused all the mayhem. In his hand, he held its trigger.

Reissen knelt before the partially opened panel slab and inspected the lower edge of the paneling.

"Ali, look here. See this semi-circular scrape on the stone?"

"Yes, Erik."

Then the Austrian reached his hand under the Osiride panel's lower edge.

"Ah ha. There it is! And the bolt fits in perfectly. Come here, Ali, feel."

And the inspector did. "What does this mean, Erik?"

"Once that bolt was freed, that pivoting beam above moved and broke the ceiling's plaster and rock mix to cause the cave in."

"By Allah's gray beard!"

"Indeed."

*   *   *

With the roof collapsing mechanism understood and photographed, Reissen found Sister Busby peering beyond the partially opened panel with her powerful LED flashlight. "Can you see anything, Sister?"

"Nope. But there seems to be a narrow passage beyond this panel. Thoughts?"

Reissen stood there, staring. Then he examined the panel itself and noted with satisfaction that the surface art had not been marred by either his make-shift ram or the cave in.

"Yes. The scrape here made by the bolt is fresh. That means that a ceiling collapse can be prevented by slipping in a short beam of wood, once the Osiride panel was open about four inches. That would stop the bolt from falling out."

Looking around meaningfully at Cardoza and Sister Josephina. "This level of devilishness I have never before seen on the part of the ancient Egyptians. We are in totally unknown territory with this tomb. From here on out, we must assume the worse. Is that understood?"

Two heads nodded.

"By the way, I wish to thank you both for all of your efforts yesterday. I can assure you that it was greatly appreciated."

"Alright, everyone, please get back to your places in the entrances to the side-chambers."

Reissen, sans the yellow biohazard suit, applied himself again, but this time from a more advantageous position of leverage. The Austrian reached out and grunted. The Osiride door panel fell almost completely open, revealing its secret passageway. The darkness now gaped two and a half feet wide.

Father Cardoza wordlessly moved forward and took several photos. Sister Busby stepped up with her flashlight and revealed what lurked in the dark beyond, which wasn't much. The secret passage opened up behind the panel's opening to perhaps a six-by-six-foot opening, chiseled out in a rough style. Its floor was suspiciously covered with sand.

"Sister Josephina," Reissen asked, "do you have a brush or sweep in your backpack?"

"Indeed I do." She produced a short-handled sweep.

"Thank you, Sister." The archaeologist smiled.

Kneeling before the open secret passage, Reissen regarded it like a basket full of pit vipers. Sticking his head into the gloom, looking this way and that, the Egyptologist very gently began brushing to one side the sandy layer. After several moments, a hard surface appeared that looked odd to the archaeologist, because it had swirling finger marks.

"There is a plaster floor tile here," he reported to his colleagues. "I have not yet found its outer dimensions. Allow me to clear away some more sand, and then, Father Cardoza, you can perform your magic."

As Reissen removed sand from the secret passage by the handful, the suspicious plaster tile gradually revealed itself. It extended to about three finger-widths from the vertical sides of the secret passage, which the archaeologist inferred, would be the width of its carved edging in the bedrock flooring. But he realized a problem—part of the plaster floor tile was overshadowed by the thick panel of the secret doorway. To remove the plaster floor tile intact, doing so would be an extremely dangerous trial of dexterity combined with strength.

Reissen cleared as far as he could reach, and Father Cardoza recorded his efforts.

"So what am I looking at?" the priest asked.

"If my experience with such things holds true, two things might lie beneath this easily breakable plaster floor tile. One option could be another deep and smoothly finished man-trap, much like what we encountered in the center of the six side chambers. However, there is another possibility. There could be a fragile and chambered amphora filled with caustic chemicals that, once mixed together, creates a highly explosive and corrosive cloud of fire and gas."

"You have to be kidding."

"Father, that was originally why we have that atrocious yellow suit on hand."

The priest just blinked. "So how big is that plaster floor tile?"

"I cannot reach in far enough to know. If the side chamber shafts are any indication, then I have brushed clean only about seventy percent of its surface. But what's really vexing me is how to lever it out."

"Doc, you have two choices. Either cut it out in pieces or just construct a bridge over it. The bridge's supports could use the stone floor edges as the plaster floor tile does itself."

"Damn, I like that idea." Reissen smiled with genuine admiration at the man's ingenuity. "But this narrow passage looks to be about thirty feet long before it 'dead-ends' at a sheer face. Then again, there may be a t-intersection, a turn, or side passage at the secret passage's end. But my point is, do you know how to devise such a bridging?"

"Yes I do, Doc, but we will have to deploy it in stages. Let's say we construct two platforms that can be easily leapfrogged forward and backward in tight quarters."

"Explain," the archaeologist said.

"Imagine two, narrow wooden pallets, with feet that spread the weight outward, in this case, on the edges of the secret passage."

Reissen nodded thoughtfully. "We might not need that second bridge."

"Why?" asked the priest.

"Because the odds of having more than one chemical booby-trap in such a space are quite low. I would be far more willing to bet on multiple man-traps." He thought for a moment, then nodded. "I am quite sure Inspector Hassan will be able to help us find what we need."

*   *   *

The next day, and after much measuring, fitting, refitting, grunting, and groaning, Reissen and Cardoza finally finished test-fitting the first bridging frame. Once in place, a short plank from the outer edge of the carved panel allowed someone to mount it.

Once there, the Austrian, again clad in the bright-yellow Big Bird suit—so named by Sister Busby, swept the secret passage's flooring about halfway down and found nothing to cause alarm. The archaeologist worked his way forward, now off the frame and on his knees, sweeping his way as he went.

Reaching the end of the secret passage, Reissen found not a T-intersection, nor another turn, but rather a blank wall. As he tapped it with the back of the wooden sweep, the resonance sounded dull, while the ceiling overhead and nearby side walls had a distinctive *CLINK* to them. Reissen, with extreme care, scrunched up his longish frame and, after some swearing, turned around, and worked his way out.

Standing once again out in the desert breezes and out of the Big Bird suit, he told the others of his findings. "We have a plastered-in plug to dig through. This reconnaissance is fast evolving into a full-blown excavation. We need to report back to Inspector Hassan, make some recommendations, and hand off this investigation."

"What?" Sister Busby exclaimed in shock.

"Sister Josephina, I cannot be in two places at once."

"But for only a week?"

"A week is a bureaucratic eternity. I have responsibilities. The operation of Pro Deo depends on me."

"That's what your assistant is for, Erik," the redheaded nun countered. "Learn to delegate."

"There are many archaeologists in this country who can take over this project. And as for my assistant, Sergeant Agave, he is a young man who does not have my administrative experience. "

"Erik, give me a break, how many of your colleagues have the guts to crawl over a booby-trap?"

Standing nose to nose with Sister Busby, Reissen got the last word in. "It is time we visit Inspector Hassan."

Cardoza, mute, shrugged at the fuming Sister Busby as Reissen turned to go.

*   *   *

"Welcome, Erik! How goes the investigation of Sakkaran Tomb 707?"

"Is that what you designated it?"

"Yes, remarkable, is it not? The Sakkaran archaeological preserve is a prolific one and growing day by day! Now, my good friend, what news do you bring me?"

"First off, Inspector Hassan we did indeed find a booby trap in the tomb's secret passage. We have circumnavigated it for the moment, but it will require investigation in the near future to ascertain precisely what it is. Second, today we detected at the end of the secret passage a plastered-in blockage. What's behind it is unknown.

"Now, to appropriately undertake the removal of that blockage, and then investigate, and potentially conserve the cultural artifacts behind it will, I estimate, require the time and resources of a full excavation and restoration effort."

At first Hassan didn't understand what the Austrian had said. "The permit for this project is yours, Erik. The formal paperwork for this concession will only be a formality." He finished with a dismissive wave of his hand.

The Austrian took a deep breath. "Inspector Hassan, Ali, sadly, I cannot undertake this project. I am needed back at the Vatican. My presence here for the past days was a personal favor to you and only as a consultant." A deep sigh. "Sir, I have delivered my report. Now, it is up to you to assign the appropriate team to undertake this project."

Inspector Hassan's face fell a mile at Reissen's answer.

"I see. Thank you, Dr. Reissen, for your report and your team's time. I appreciate your prompt arrival and assessment. I am grateful for your assistance." The inspector rose from behind his desk, circled around it, and stiffly extended his hand.

The Austrian took it and thought it was like holding a long-dead fish.

*   *   *

After the Austrian left his office, Ali Hassan, the director of the second largest archaeological preserve in Egypt, had already made up his mind. Reissen had extensive experience with such hazardous archaeological sites. Hassan had himself witnessed the man's archaeological and management brilliance. Somehow, someway, Hassan was going to get his way.

CHAPTER 13

Upon Reissen's return to Rome the next day, he found at his Pro Deo office, as suspected, a mound of correspondence on his laptop and desktop. Other than that, Sergeant Agave had done a fine job of "minding the store" during his absence. Then three unexpected visitors appeared—the American J.J. Stone, his striking Egyptian wife, Dr. Melaina Makris, and their society's President, Betsy Silver Moon.

Quickly shifting mental gears, the Austrian rose from his desk and greeted the trio. "Betsy, Melaina, and J.J., come in and sit down, please."

Once everyone was settled, the archaeologist asked, "So why are you here?"

The threesome looked at each other and Makris spoke first. "We've had an interesting turn of events."

"Oh?"

"Yes. That at-large CMES security guard who was possessed, attempted to kill me over his resurrection."

Reissen sat back with a frown. "Chairman DeSalvo shared a photo of that unfortunate and I passed it on to my Vatican superiors. Both CMES and the Vatican were looking for him."

"Well, yesterday," Makris continued, "we confronted the possessed unfortunate and J.J. exorcised from him the resurrected *ka* of an Egyptian priest-magician. He claimed that his mother was Nefertari, who I apparently reminded him of, the chief wife and first queen of Ramses the Great. After a brief meal, I removed from him all memory of me, while J.J. escorted the guard back to the coven's villa headquarters."

At this news Reissen went silent.

"I take it that you did not know of this development?" Silver Moon said.

"No, I did not. I just returned from Egypt. But I have just begun to catch up on my e-mails since I got back. I suspect that this subject was covered."

"Erik," Stone added, "our visit today is only to inform you of what we have been up to, in your jurisdiction, so to speak."

A nod. "Understood. I appreciate that you stopped by to fill me in."

The Egyptologist paused, sighed, and looked at his colleagues. "Now brace yourselves. I was just in Egypt at the behest of an archaeological inspector, who wanted me to look over a newly discovered tomb. That tomb belonged to a priest-magician named Sethi, a son of Ramses and Nefertari. Do you think that your priest-magician might be the same individual?"

The three TIIIS representatives looked at each other. "I suppose it's possible," Makris finally said.

"This story gets better. Right this moment, we have a Turkish scholar working in the Vatican library preparing a translation of a papyrus for publication. I have seen his work, and it is first class. It's a biography of a priest-magician named, believe it or not, Sethi. He also is purportedly the son of Ramses the Great."

"This is getting weird," Stone breathed.

"Indeed, J.J., I agree. But there is even more. In this papyrus, it is stated that this Sethi was the first voice or leader of a council of Egyptian magicians. Does that sound familiar to anyone?"

"CMES," Silver Moon said with certainty. "So how did Sethi's mummy get to the Roman villa?"

The Austrian shrugged. "Unknown. But my guess is when CMES evacuated Memphis and moved to Rome, they brought him as a totem of some kind."

"That means this Sethi is very important to their history," Stone offered.

"Indeed." Reissen agreed.

"But what about this tomb you mentioned, Erik?" Makris asked.

"That tomb is the problem. I have seen its inscriptions, its murals, and they are of high quality. It is, from an artistic standpoint, a royal commission suitable for a prince of the Nineteenth Dynasty. Furthermore, it is located in the neighborhood of the magicians Djedi and his father Imhotep's tombs—the most famous magicians of Egyptian history."

Once again Makris' hand raised to her mouth in shock. "A cemetery of magicians …"

"Yes, a cemetery of magicians." The Austrian Egyptologist said slowly, as the import sank in for him as well.

"But you said that the tomb was the problem," Stone said. "What did you mean by that?"

Reissen sighed. "I have been invited to investigate it by the Inspector of Sakkara. However, I am also the research and operations director of Pro Deo." He emphasized with upraised hands that took in his office. "In short, I am being torn between my first love and the responsibilities of my current position."

Stone cleared his throat. "Only one of those positions can take precedence right now. So just make your choice, Erik."

*   *   *

Before Reissen had to answer that difficult question, his phone rang. Looking down, he could see its number originated from within the Vatican.

He raised his index finger to his guests to stay and automatically answered, "*Ciao*, Reissen." At first he listened intently, frowned, and then said, "*Subito*, Cardinal Bonaventura."

The Austrian hung up and apologized. "I must go immediately. I am sorry, but my superior has just requested my presence."

After seeing his guests out, Reissen wished them all a good flight back to the States. Then he strode out of the Gregorian Museum toward the Civilian Administration Building, where the cardinal's office was located. During the brisk walk along the Via del

Governatorato, the Austrian ran a string of scenarios through his mind, but nothing seemed to click as to why his superior needed such an immediate meeting with him.

He entered the peach- and cream-colored palatial edifice by its main entrance, and mounted its staircase two steps at a time, en route to the third floor.

Pausing a moment to collect himself at the top of the staircase, the Austrian then approached the cardinal's suite and announced himself to the seated priest.

"*Bene,* Dr. Reissen. You are here so soon. The cardinal will see you presently. Please take a seat."

Reissen sat and waited. He took the opportunity to soak in the palatial ornamentation of the suite's reception area.

High above, towered a twenty-foot ceiling decorated with white plaster architectural details. On its cream stuccoed walls hung tapestries that the Austrian judged were older than the building itself. The receptionist's desk was a wooden relic from a distant monastic past, incongruously adorned with two flat screens and flanked by two luxuriant plants. At his feet lay an intricate Asian carpet that reminded him of his late predecessor's taste in décor.

"*Scusa*, Dr. Reissen, the cardinal will see you now."

Out of habit, the Austrian laid his hand on the heavy wooden door before entering. Strangely, his sixth sense told him nothing of its occupant. Then he knocked, entered, and found himself in either an ultra-modern or purposefully Spartan environment of bare walls and shellacked wooden flooring. Three putty-colored metal file cabinets and a matching desk completed the scene.

Cardinal Bonaventura stood up behind his desk as Reissen entered his domain. Stocky in build, much like a wrestler, the man seemed wider than tall. "Thank you, Dr. Reissen, for coming so quickly. Please sit." The clergyman pointed to the visitor's chair. "Do you know why you are here?"

"No, Your Eminence," said Reissen as he sat.

"I have just gotten off the phone with three high officials of the Egyptian archaeological service. It seems that they need you and you alone."

Reissen turned suddenly cold.

"Now do you have an idea why you are here?"

Reissen could not lift his head to face the cleric. "Your Eminence, because of my service to the Vatican, in particular—as Pro Deo's head of research and operations."

"Most astute. Where do your true passions lie, Dr. Reissen?" The cleric's tone was not unfriendly, only official. The inner turmoil within Reissen began to calm down.

"I have an idea, Your Eminence. Demote me to a field researcher for Pro Deo, and I believe that the problem is solved."

The cardinal with a bowling ball for a head smiled a Cheshire grin. "You're good, Dr. Reissen. I like that. But I have a better idea. Recently you worked in concert with the Brothers of St. Paul, is that correct?"

"That is correct, Your Eminence."

"Why did you do so?"

"Because as a research resource I knew that I needed experienced military and paranormal backup—in essence, muscle."

"And how did that work out for you?"

"Your Eminence, Father Cardoza and I worked seamlessly together, although I have yet to review his photographs."

"Trust me, Dr. Reissen, I have reviewed them, and they're quite revealing."

"How so?" The Austrian asked more than a bit curious and taken aback at the cardinal's inside knowledge.

"The architectural imagery is clear and well-composed. But you, Dr. Reissen, are truly a wasted resource sitting behind a desk. You're a field man through and through. Under no circumstances will I 'demote' you, sir. But I will promote you to an acting liaison position that reports both to me and Father Richardo. Come to me for funding." The cardinal indicated with a fat thumb to his chest. "Go to Father Richardo for that 'muscle' you mentioned."

Reissen let out a breath he hadn't realized he'd been holding. "Thank you, Your Eminence! And I have another idea for your consideration. The late Cardinal Alberti selected me to be his successor. I wish to do the same."

Chuckling, the cardinal rubbed at the bridge of his pug nose. "Why am I not surprised? So who do you have in mind for your successor, Dr. Reissen?"

"Sister Josephina Busby. She has all the in-house credentials, knowledge, and spirit for the position."

The cardinal folded his hands before him and blankly stared back at the Austrian. "Your request is denied. I have already signed the promotion papers for someone else to fill your old position—a Vatican cleric well known for his efficiency and thoroughness. A piece of advice, Dr. Reissen. As a member of the laity, you should know better than to involve yourself in Vatican internal politics. As for Sister Josephina Busby, she too will join you in the field. It seems that the two of you make a good team."

Clearing his throat into his fist, the cardinal continued. "Contact Inspector Ali Hassan immediately so he can prepare for your arrival at Sakkara. I do not want to disappoint our Moslem brethren in Egypt. The Vatican needs to nurture its relations with all religions and nations and this is a classic instance. Get in touch also with Father Richardo as to the type and specialty of personnel that you require.

"Now, Dr. Reissen, I am a busy man with not enough time. Congratulations on your promotion. Remember to stop and speak with Father Simon on your way out. He will provide you with your new office location and any travel arrangements until your assistant is assigned."

"Your Eminence, may I make another request?"

"No, you may not. Sergeant Agave has already been transferred and reassigned to you as your office assistant. By the way, do you know the reason why Sergeant Agave wants to be your assistant?"

"No, Your Eminence."

"Because he thinks, in his words," the cardinal's eyebrows rose, "*you're one bad-ass vampire killer.*"

"Good day, Dr. Reissen."

CHAPTER 14

That afternoon following his meeting with Cardinal Bonaventura, Reissen sent an e-mail to Inspector Ali Hassan. He outlined his availability to undertake the Tomb 707 investigation. Within the hour, Inspector Hassan responded and informed the Austrian that the wheels of bureaucracy were furiously turning. The inspector's closing line was, "It would be a pleasure to see you next week." Reissen was in business again.

Next, he contacted Father Richardo.

"Congratulations on your promotion, Dr. Reissen. It seems that we will have the opportunity of working together quite closely. This development, I applaud."

"Thank you, Father."

"How may the Brothers of St. Paul be of assistance?"

"I need two resources that I hope you can supply—a photographer and a surveyor. If Father Cardoza is available, I would readily welcome him aboard."

"Father Cardoza is available. In fact, he is eager to rejoin your archaeological expedition. A for the surveyor, I currently do not have anyone with that skill on staff. Allow me to work on that requirement."

"Understood. And Father, thank you very much for your help."

"Dr. Reissen, be assured that the Brothers of St. Paul are steadfastly behind you."

Before leaving for Egypt, however, Reissen finally got his hands on Cardoza's photographic imagery. While excellent, many, if not most of the photographs, would have to be redone with a meter stick included for scale and a message board for context and recordkeeping purposes. That fault was Reissen's, as the first "visit" had been only for investigative purposes, not archaeological excavation or publication.

Yes, he admitted to himself, as he perused through the many frames, he did bash his way through the Osiride panel's doorway much like a Hollywood tomb raider. But it could not be helped. Inspector Hassan needed his assessment. Now the Austrian was tasked with dealing with it.

*   *   *

This time Father Cardoza left his side arm in Rome, which simplified considerably their travel arrangements. Reissen, who traveled light as a matter of course, ended up carrying one of the photographer's loaded-down bags of equipment.

Their lodging had been provided by the Holy See in the nearby city of Memphis, coincidentally in the same hotel as the team from the Austrian archaeological institute, who were still working at the Temple of Ptah. Father Cardoza was oblivious to Reissen's *déjà vu*, as the Austrian had been that excavation's past director for some time. It was then and there that the Egyptologist decided to make his mini-team's presence scarce to that excavation's current archaeological director, Dr. Gretchen Gunner, his former assistant at the Temple of Ptah. He thought it best to do so.

*   *   *

The shoals of academic politics can be often jagged and treacherous. It was well known Gunner held a grudge against Reissen, first for taking on the wildly successful emergency excavation of the Djedi tomb, and second for leaving the university outright for the Vatican. In his absence, Gunner firmly suspected that her promotion to director of the Temple of Ptah excavation had only been a matter of convenience, and not granted in recognition of her scholarly status. Any other Egyptologist would have been overjoyed at the promotion, but Gunner thought otherwise. She saw it as more of a "hand-me-down" assignment, the cleanup of an unfinished project that her roguish colleague had abandoned for the far sexier tomb excavation.

Moreover, Gunner's professional relations with the late Inspector Dr. Hussain Kama had been rocky—even as Reissen's assistant. They were not much better with his successor, Ali Hassan. Bluntly, Gunner wanted to be respected and treated the same way as Reissen, and that was where her rigid and overly defensive personality squarely got in the way. And there was another thing—Reissen was well-liked by the students and staff. Whenever he asked for volunteers, both formed a line. It was the same with the Egyptians. When both Kama and Hassan had come to Reissen for assistance, he had the gall to accept, and then perform brilliantly—while borrowing four of her archaeological staff.

But there was even more. Reissen had become Austrian television's darling, and that had really chafed Gunner. In her mind, since when did one's photogenic qualities trump solid scholarship? The problem was Reissen's work was flawless, much like his video persona. Gunner was fit to be tied over it. But now that Reissen was a member of the Vatican, she couldn't even snipe at him at university departmental meetings.

*   *   *

Reissen struggled with how to diffuse this situation. He knew that Gunner's teutonic and highly territorial personality could turn volcanic. He had seen it himself during departmental meetings. He also knew that inevitably word would get out that he was staying at the hotel, and then his former students and colleagues would want to say hello. Gossip would flow.

As convenient as the hotel in Memphis was, that city had others more devoted to tourism instead of an academic budget. Reissen saw, here, an opportunity to sidestep a landmine. He canceled his team's hotel booking and made other arrangements.

But as he hung up the phone, grabbed his bags, and turned to leave the hotel lobby, Gunner appeared before him as if out of nowhere. In fact, she practically ran him down.

"Why, *Frau* Professor Dr. Gunner, what a pleasant surprise," Reissen said through gritted teeth.

Gunner's shock at her former colleague's presence was complete. "Why yes, Erik, yes indeed."

"How is the work at the Ptah Temple?"

"Progressing smoothly. Its entire foundation has been exposed…"

"That's wonderful news. But my party is waiting for me." He nodded toward the overloaded Father Cardoza, attired in an electric green golf shirt and tan cargo shorts.

"Are you just passing through, or working in Sakkara?"

Reissen could hear the hope in her voice, but could not lie either.

"Working in Sakkara."

Her face twitched. "Where?"

Reissen sighed. "Tomb 707."

"What! That's the University of Milano's concession! How—"

"—Gretchen, it has been a pleasure to see you again." Reissen said as he maneuvered past her and kept his eyes trained straight ahead.

*   *   *

Once safely in the taxi, en route to their new hotel, Father Cardoza commented. "That was one tightly wound woman. Who is she?"

"My former assistant archaeological director."

"Holy shit, Doc! You must be some sort of saint."

"So I have been told," the Austrian drily said.

"So what's the plan?"

"We will keep our distance from the entire Austrian archaeological team."

"Gotcha."

*   *   *

Settled into their new accommodations, Cardoza eyed the pool and its flora and fauna.

"Later," Reissen said. "Our next stop is Inspector Hassan's office." He turned to face the priest. "Father, I need you to be my assistant. That means you see everything that I do. Can you do that?"

"Absolutely, Doc. That's why I'm here. I'm your cook, chief, and bottle washer."

"Oh?"

"Yeah. And your photographer, too."

"Thank you for telling me."

"Not a problem, boss."

The cab ride to the government office of the Egyptian Antiquities Service in Memphis did not take long. Arriving ten minutes early for their appointment with the inspector, Reissen took the opportunity to explain to the good priest what they were potentially up against.

"Father, we might have to request help from the Egyptian military to clear Tomb 707's booby-trap."

"Why?"

"Because at another Egyptian tomb, I found several caustic chemical bombs. They were nasty things that spewed acid, fire, and toxic gas. We got lucky with one that sort of fizzled. But when we encountered another, Inspector Hassan pulled some strings and had their military remove it."

"Interesting. By the way, Doc, did Father Richardo brief you that I have ordinance and sapper experience?"

"Ordinance and sapper?"

"A combat engineer, someone who blows up stuff and disarms others."

"Really?"

"Yeah."

"Father, why didn't you tell me this before?"

"Because I was under orders to keep my mouth shut and observe."

"Does that mean that you are no longer under such orders?"

"That's correct, Doc. Now I'm an open book."

"Dr. Reissen! I am so happy that you have reconsidered!" An ebullient Inspector Ali Hassan said as he walked through his wide office doorway. "Please, gentlemen, come in!" The inspector held the door and shook his visitors' hands as they entered.

Following a flood of effusive pleasantries, the inspector got down to business.

"Erik, I have spoken with the director of the University of Milano archaeological team, and he is very happy to assist you as needed. In fact, given your experiences with the Djedi tomb, he believed that would be 'most helpful,' once I explained to him what we have thus far found in Tomb 707."

"May I ask, Ali, what precisely did Professor Dr. Gomas offer in the way of assistance?"

"Clearance, conservation, and restoration mainly. But if required, I would imagine he would take on some photography and survey work as well. It all depends upon what is needed."

"What about publication rights?"

"Do you want them?"

"No, I do not," Reissen firmly said with a shake of his head. "The pressure to publish has been lifted from me. But I am willing to bet that Dr. Gomas will want those rights. So I suggest, Ali, that you offer them to the man now. That would allow him to better plan ahead and set up his budget."

"I agree. Anything else?"

"Do you still have the telephone number of the Egyptian Army's demolition squad?"

"Indeed I do," the inspector said with a smile.

"I just hope that we will not have to use it."

* * *

The next day, Reissen and Cardoza returned to the tomb site bright and early. Approaching the new antiquities guard on post, a man named Jabari Khoury, the Austrian greeted him in his native language, struck up a conversation, and only then identified himself. While the guard had seen Reissen before in the company of Sister Busby, he didn't know who he was. But at hearing Reissen's name, Khoury jerked to attention. The Austrian told the man to relax, and then introduced Father Cardoza. Khoury, a Coptic Christian, kissed the priest's hand and asked for his blessing, which Father Cardoza delivered in Latin. When Reissen translated the blessing, which not only included the guard but also his family, the man simply beamed.

"Mr. Khoury," the Austrian asked, "do you smoke cigarettes?"

"Oh yes, Dr. Reissen. But my wife says that I should not."

"I see. Well, Mr. Khoury, let us not tell your wife." The Austrian slipped the guard a fresh blue-and-gold hard pack of Dunhill's.

With that important ritual completed, the guard opened the tomb and turned on its lights.

All was as Reissen remembered it.

"Father Cardoza, we need a fresh set of images of the entrance corridor and tomb, but this time with a meter stick and message board. Let's get started while it is still relatively cool."

"Will do, boss."

CHAPTER 15

"*Signore* Condé, tell me again about your experience," said William DeSalvo, the chairman of CMES.

The senior security guard sighed and shrugged. "The first thing I noticed on Level Four was the sudden appearance of dust clouds that seemed to be everywhere. Even during earth tremors, I have never before seen such an amount. My flashlights could not cut through it. I stumbled around because of all the bones and mummies on the floor. Then my foot got stuck, I felt a stab of pain in my lower leg, and that was all I remember until I was returned to the villa by an exceptionally tall man."

"I see. Thank you, *Signore* Condé for your service. I see that on your contract you have two years left before your pension. With your permission, I will waive the remainder of your contract."

"Thank you, *Signore Presidente*. But I wish to finish out my contract before my retirement. I believe that to be the honorable thing to do."

"As you wish, *Signore* Condé. And welcome back."

As the senior security guard left to return to his shift, he felt cheated. *That damn notable promised me riches beyond imagination! And what do I get? The offer of an early retirement with a wife that I dread coming home to.*

*   *   *

While Condé simmered over his situation, DeSalvo did as well, for he still did not know who had caused the mass resurrection in the first place. More vexing, he did not possess one scintilla of evidence to pursue. And that blundering security guard only recalled being escorted back to the villa by a tall man. "How can that be?" he murmured to his desk blotter. Thoroughly frustrated, he called over his favorite security officer.

"*Signore* Gnotti. Kindly make a visit."

Such a request Matteo Gnotti knew was a direct if not stern order from the chairman. Rising from his cubical, the middle-aged veteran jogged over to his chairman. He arrived cool, calm, and collected, a testament to his daily exercise regime.

Knocking on the top of the chairman's barrier, he announced, "*Si, Signore Presidente*?"

Unlike Paul Kiel, Gnotti's superior, DeSalvo liked Gnotti's style and his ability to read his needs. It saved so much time.

"Please, sit."

The chairman steepled his fingers before he began.

"My request is simple, Matteo. Who cast the resurrection spell? That is what I want to know."

Gnotti went through a checklist in his head.

"*Signore Presidente*. We have already checked the videos, checked the security tapes. I don't understand what you are looking for."

DeSalvo leaned forward in his chair and locked eyes with his security officer. "Matteo. What I want you to pretend is that this investigation is an academic exercise. Return to examine the videos and tapes with a clear mind, open to the most outlandish and outrageous of possibilities. To cast a spell of that magnitude means that the conjurer *had* to be present before our villa. Detect that person. Check every possibility."

"*Si, Signore Presidente*. I agree. Someone ... or something ... had to be present. We will redouble our efforts."

"Thank you, Matteo. Now, do not disappoint me."

*   *   *

The president's office in Old Main was a musty and airless wood-paneled chamber from another time. It was used only when the president visited the Old Oaks Academy's campus, which was not often. Since President Betsy Silver Moon was a native of New Mexico, with its bright, warm, bluebird-blue sky, why would she want to live in western Pennsylvania, given modern-day telecommunications? Yes, the campus was nestled within a magnificent oak forest, caressed by early morning fogs, surrounded by luxuriously green lawns, and dotted with manicured flower gardens. But no, Betsy Silver Moon was a Navajo through and through, who loved the desert, its breathtaking stone formations, and pine-covered mountains.

But on this particular day, Silver Moon sat behind an early American antique desk with her laptop before her. To her surprise and great pleasure TIIIS' international network was quiet, meaning no crisis had broken out that would upset her ulcers. Ever since the Farce in the Desert several years back, CMES' reputation continued its downward spiral, while paranormal societies and enclaves around the world flocked to TIIIS' banner. By the droves they broke their treaties with that hateful coven. Yet, perhaps strangely, Silver Moon had to admit that helping CMES twice— first with the felling of a vampire and second with the death spell—suggested the possibility of a *détente*, or at least the formation of a working relationship between the two paranormal powerhouses.

She had the personal phone number of CMES' chairman in her device. That, in and of itself, represented a diplomatic step forward. Silver Moon mused on that possibility. *Could a cooperative treaty be crafted with the* Consilium, *much like the one we enjoy with the Vatican?*

But Silver Moon was not on campus to think about the unthinkable. She and two of her society's most creative resources had just returned from Rome. She awaited their arrival. She smiled. *Imagine a more capable husband and wife team? I, frankly, cannot.*

The president heard a soft knock on her door. She glanced once again at her personal device. It said ten o'clock sharp. Again she smiled. "Come in."

J.J. Stone, the society's Lictor of Magic, and his regal wife, Dr. Melaina Makris, entered and took their seats.

The debrief ended up talking for a full hour, far longer than Silver Moon had expected. The initial resurrection casting they discussed in detail, noting the need to delimit such spells in the future. As for the subsequent death spell and Sethi complication troubled the powerful sensitive, but her team's on-the-spot solution had been a good one. The safe return of the security guard was a nice diplomatic touch. She made a point to remember it for future use.

"Who escorted the security guard back to the villa?" Silver Moon asked.

"I did," Stone confirmed. "Mel stayed at the hotel."

"Good. They know you, but not your wife."

"Precisely."

She was also pleased the pair had brought her along to pay a visit to Reissen. Vatican contacts were invaluable assets that required polishing from time to time. All in all, the initial adventure and its solution had been a success, meaning, of course, that CMES had been humbled, rendered briefly powerless, and off-balance. Frankly, that was precisely where she wanted them, feeling vulnerable and uncertain. And in her eyes that made CMES more predictable.

"One other thing, Betsy," Melaina said.

"Yes."

"We're expecting."

"What! When is it due?" Silver Moon said as she nearly levitated from her chair.

"Seven or eight months, give or take." Makris simply glowed. Stone just sat quietly, supremely pleased with his wife.

"This is extraordinary! Seldom does our faculty have children running about. I must make preparations, a nursery or daycare, then a school for the tyke. This is all so exciting!"

"Breathe, Betsy." Stone said.

"Yes, yes, you're so right. It's just such wonderful and exciting news!"

The president took a deep breath and looked toward the ceiling. "Imagine, if you will, a child born and raised on this campus. What could that child accomplish?"

*   *   *

"Was our infrared video surveillance operational prior to the Resurrection Incident?" Gnotti asked his colleague, a woman named Lucia, who was in charge of the villa's many security cameras and weight-sensing devices.

"*Si, Signore* Gnotti. We had full surveillance."

"Has anyone thoroughly gone through the infrared video?"

"*Si, Signore* Gnotti, I did myself."

"Did you detect any anomalies?"

A shrug. "Certainly I did, *Signore*. We have bats at night, and flying insects, but not much else."

"I see, but what about during the day? Did you find anything then?"

Lucia blanched. "*Scusami, Signore* Gnotti, but the infrared videos only run during the evening hours. During daylight hours there are too many hot spots and false shadows."

"And, *Signora* Lucia, when did we first detect that the Resurrection Incident was taking place?"

"Around noon, *Signore*."

"*Precisamente, Signora* Lucia. Now use your imagination. An adept is standing before our headquarters, let us say in the street, and releases the rabbits seen in the video, which appear seemingly out of thin air. How would you detect and find that individual?"

The woman frowned. "Allow me to look into this, *Signore* Gnotti."

"Thank you, *Signora* Lucia."

*   *   *

Lucia was an old soul—literally. She estimated her birth took place sometime during the Medici rule of Florence, so about 1550, give or take a decade. During the course of Lucia's long life she had seen her fair share, which made the eidetic vampire a perfect security resource.

Pleasant in appearance and docile in nature, of average height, with brown eyes and hair, the native of Florence had been made a vampire on a Sunday evening, in a driving rain storm, in the year 1566. Her brutish attacker had left her torn body in a roadside ditch. She had been en route to her Servite Order's convent on the outskirts of Florence when her assailant attacked her.

An outstanding student who could memorize practically anything, Lucia, by the age of fifteen, had mastered Latin and Greek and had even been trusted to begin copying manuscripts. Her sudden loss had been a blow to her religious order, not to mention their coffers, as literacy was highly prized.

Initially Lucia did not take to her condition well but soon learned. As the hunger took hold, she found that wild animals could satisfy, because her vampiric powers allowed her to catch them. Quickly, she developed a taste for squirrel, rabbit, fox, and deer—especially deer. Filthy, smelly, homeless, with a gaunt look and parchment-white skin, the young virgin was ashamed, and firmly believed that for some imagined reason, a divine curse had been cast against her.

Wandering widely away from Florence, she soon fell in with another of her kind in the hills of Tuscany. Disgusted by his taking of human life, she dedicated herself, instead, to the blood-letting of animal kind. During this time, Lucia was introduced as a rare white vampire to a minor coven of the *Consilium*.

Initially sneered at and jeered, once her linguistic skills were discovered in that predominately illiterate region, Lucia's station was quickly secured. She sat in on the coven's inner council, recorded their decisions, and composed many communications with the mother coven in Rome. By the fourth year of her making, Lucia had become a council member, mainly because of her sound and reasoned logic, learned from Greek manuscripts.

Inevitably, given the circumstances of the times, maker met the made. In this instance, the maker had broken several cardinal rules regarding human predation and its proper disposal. Such carelessness was not tolerated by the coven for reasons of their much-feared discovery and survival. Upon his capture, he was brought before the council for a judgment. Lucia, one of his creations, sat in council that day and spoke to those who stood as witness.

"I cannot judge with logic and sobriety as this awful wretch made me. I am consumed with emotion, the desire for vengeance, and thus must remove myself from his judgment. That is my hallowed promise. But, if I were not so conflicted, I would bind him to the judgment tree and allow Sol to do his worst."

The other members of the council, six in number, listened to her sagacious words and found themselves in agreement. That very evening, the felon was so bound and survived the first day as the weather had been intolerant. However, on the second, by mid-day, the careless vampire had been fully reduced to ash.

That was then. Now the white vampire applied her formidable memory and logic to the challenge made by her colleague Gnotti. The discovery of absolute proof, the vampire outright dismissed. Lucia instead focused upon probability. She asked herself a simple question: "Who would profit most from CMES' discomfiture?"

Given the recent exodus of once treaty-bound and tribute-paying paranormal societies and covens, following the Farce in the Desert, Lucia's needle pointed toward TIIIS. From her perspective, she saw the slow unfolding of a strategy that began with the elevation of TIIIS' current president. Its former president, P. I. E. Smithers, she considered an overly ethical and doddering fool, even if he was a quaint nineteenth-century gentleman. But CMES had seriously underestimated the ability of the new president, that Native American Indian, to lead and marshal her international membership.

Further, Lucia believed she detected a subtlety that only a few would appreciate. "If TIIIS originally caused the Resurrection Incident, then how delicious would it be to offer a fig leaf solution to it?" This Lucia firmly believed based upon sound magical convention—*that if counter magic is to be effective, it must address the original conjuring in every respect.* So, Lucia considered quite likely the probability that TIIIS was responsible for the Resurrection Incident.

So who was the conjurer within TIIIS capable of

performing both the original spell and its counter? Even more importantly, who possessed the will and motivation to cast such a powerful spell?

Lucia smiled because she held in her hand the unraveling thread. Little did she know what she would discover once she tugged on it.

CHAPTER 16

Reissen sat in a tight crouch on the back of his knees. With handpick at the ready, safety goggles on, and a dull green plastic bucket and whiskbroom before him, the archaeologist took stock of the plastered-over blockage at the secret passage's dead end. After several swings of the small pick, huge chunks of the whitish binder began to fly. Beneath it the ends of bread-loaf-sized blocks began to appear, which had been laid wet in regular courses. The Egyptologist stopped to clean up the plaster debris, turned in place, and made his way back to the passage's entrance. Once there, the meaty hand of Father Cardoza reached in and took the filled bucket outside to empty it.

Returning with an empty bucket, Cardoza asked, "How's it going, boss?"

"Slow, but predictable. I want you to crawl in and take some pictures. Don't forget the scales." Reissen said as he stood up and stretched outside of the passage.

"I'll get my gear."

While the Austrian guzzled a full bottle of water, the priest crawled in on the plank, crossed over the bridging frame, and got to work.

"Sure seems tight in here," the priest said as he frog-walked to the dead end.

Only then did Reissen grimly suspect that he too might be claustrophobic.

Finished with his camera work, Cardoza emerged through the panel's gap, dripping in nervous sweat.

Reissen handed him a bottle of water from their cooler. "Are you alright, Father?"

"Yeah. Now I am."

"Claustrophobic?"

"A tad, but I cope real good after a bit," the man said defensively.

"You're sure?"

"Yeah."

Reissen nodded, made a mental note, picked up his excavation gear, and returned to his digging. After some minutes, the archaeologist began carefully prying away his first bread loaf-shaped block of limestone. Coming from an upper corner, its extraction caused a small cascade of falling grit. Peering with his headlamp into the gap, Reissen sighed as he saw only more stone. And with that known, he began tearing away at the layer of blocks with abandon. As with everything in archaeology, demotion is the easy part, while the cleanup was pure drudgery. More than once, as he lugged out the blocks, he thought about how he could rig up some sort of a conveyor system. To his credit, Father Cardoza labored on without a word, hauling away debris to their designated dump site.

By noon of day one, both men were spent. Two full layers of blockage had been removed—two and a half feet of penetration into what they now called the secondary passage. Fortunately, its rough-hewn walls were the same dimensions as the secret passage—a reasonably comfortable six feet square.

Passing out his final bucket of the day, Reissen wiped his forehead. "Father, I do not know about you, but I need a beer." The sweat-soaked and dusty Austrian admitted. "You drink?"

"In this particular instance, absolutely boss. After all, you can't be seen drinking alone. Someone might think you're an alcoholic."

*   *   *

Day two at the tomb began much as the day before had. Mr. Khoury, their antiquities guard, greeted the pair like long-lost friends, and then they got down to the clearance of the secondary passage. This time, however, Reissen thought to bring along three more plastic buckets. Somehow, the clearance proceeded in a more efficient manner, something that his colleague *Frau Professor Dr. Gunner* would undoubtedly have approved of.

Half way through the fourth layer of blockage, Reissen stopped cold. He had partially exposed the rounded form of a jar's body. All of his six senses went on high alert. Gently brushing at the object, the Egyptologist could clearly see the painted glyphs of a hieroglyphic curse text.

He called out, "Father Cardoza. I found a booby-trap."

"Describe it."

"It looks like a sealed ceramic pot, much like that others that I have encountered before. They are covered with magical curse texts, and to back those up, they have several delicate chambers within them. Breaking those chambers causes a nasty chemical reaction."

"How 'nasty'?"

"A chemical ignition accompanied by fire and toxic gas."

"Let me in there, boss. This is what I'm paid to do."

"Okay, but allow me to clean up. Also, bring in your gear and record this before it is extracted."

*   *   *

It took the priest thirty grueling minutes to successfully "clear" the device. Now resting within one of the plastic buckets, he carried it outside the tomb proper and into the glaring sunlight.

"If what you say is true, this is one dangerous item, boss."

"How so?"

"Well, I've been doing some thinking. This one is relatively small. How big were the ones that you found?"

"You're right. They were large *amphorae*, easily fifteen liters in capacity. This one is maybe only two liters maximum."

"Yeah. My guess is that over the ages they became cagier and downsized their surprises. Besides, this sucker would be one hell of a handful in those tight quarters."

The Egyptologist could only nod in agreement at that assessment. "What should we do with it?"

"I say we walk it off into the desert and set it off."

"Why would you want to do that?"

"A number of reasons, boss, but first and foremost, we need to know if it is still live, as in dangerous. Then any others that we might encounter can be dealt with accordingly. Plus, it's better that we set it off on purpose than have someone else stumble on it by accident."

The Austrian grunted in understanding and turned to their curious antiquities guard. "Mr. Khoury, could you arrange for a guard who has a rifle and is a good shot?"

Blinking at the request, "I will call my superior, Dr. Reissen."

"Have the guard meet us over there." The archaeologist pointed toward a desolate area.

"Yes, Dr. Reissen."

"And, Father Cardoza, bring your all your camera gear. I want to record the jar's painted spells before you video its detonation."

*   *   *

A good half hour later, Reissen, Cardoza, and a video camera on a tripod were joined by no less than three armed guards who practically marched in formation to their chosen "ignition" site. Mr. Khoury led them. Seeing the comical sight, the priest hid his mirth behind his hand. The archaeologist stared in disbelief at the entourage.

The men stood in a position down wind and thirty yards away from their target. When the delegation arrived, Reissen said to Mr. Khoury, "Have your detachment shoot at that pot over there."

The target in question they had placed on an elevated flat rock so that Father Cardoza could record its curse texts before its destruction. The three men took aim and fired.

At first they heard a distinct hissing sound. Then a loud pop was recorded as the pot exploded in a column of flame that disbursed its contents in all directions like a hand grenade. The armed delegation scattered like a flock of doves. All that remained was a thin whitish gas cloud that slowly drifted off and disbursed in the desert.

"Thank you, gentlemen!" Reissen announced. "You have just saved the life of an archaeologist!"

"What just happened?" Father Cardoza asked from behind the video camera.

"Basically, Father, an energetic hydrogen chloride reaction caused the initial explosion. Then a secondary chemical reaction produced the flame and the toxic phosphine gas cloud. Did you smell anything odd?"

"No. Should I have?"

"If you had, you would have smelled garlic and dead fish—the bomb's principle ingredients. The gas is highly corrosive and burns the skin. If inhaled, it attacks the central nervous system, initially causing numbness, and then death."

"Holy crap!"

"Now getting back to what you said earlier. Imagine such an explosion in that tight passage."

"Not good."

"Not good at all." The archaeologist repeated.

So ended day two.

*　*　*

Day three began as before with the morning greeting ritual with Mr. Khoury. Reissen had no doubt that Inspector Hassan had been fully briefed on the previous day's events.

"Father Cardoza, let's go out to the ignition site."

"Why?"

"I would like to collect any of the surviving pottery, and perhaps, just perhaps, recover some of its magical decoration. Would you like to join me?"

"Absolutely, boss."

The flat stone that once served as a base was now heavily pitted and covered with a whitish powder.

"Don't touch that stone," Reissen warned. "That powdery glazing is toxic."

As for the ceramic pot itself, they found precious little left to recover.

Returning to the tomb, Father Cardoza asked the obvious. "How much farther?"

"I figure that we have progressed half way. I base that estimate on the ability of the remaining blockage to withstand a similar explosion."

Near day's end, and after having removed another two layers of stone blocks, Reissen heard a distinctly hollow sound. Smiling to himself, he meticulously cleared away all the debris and requested some photos to record their progress.

At that night's dinner and beers, Reissen shared his thoughts with Father Cardoza. "Tomorrow we will break through."

"Really!"

"Yes, of that I am quite certain. But as to what awaits us on the other side, I do not know. So in anticipation of the breakthrough, we will need to somehow extend the electrical power and lighting into that part of the tomb. Which means that we will also have to visit Inspector Hassan first thing tomorrow."

"Why?"

"Father Cardoza, it is considered good form to invite Egyptian officials of the Antiquities Service to any momentous event or discovery made. Besides, I suspect that he also has the electrical equipment we need."

"Understood."

CHAPTER 17

Lucia selected the surveillance video of the recent TIIIS death spell ceremony. The first thing she noted was that the individuals involved were camouflaged in light-bending uniforms. This she already knew about because of her coven's request for the TIIIS Lictor of Magic's slaughter of the ancient vampire Sigmund. But what the security officer wanted was to listen to the audio portion of the ritual. Using headphones, much like a submarine's sonar man, she concentrated on the first thirty or so minutes of the security video. Even with her vampiric ears, she could detect precious little. Then during the dramatic blood-letting of the goat, she distinctly heard something, several phrases grunted out with extraordinary will and purpose. She made a note of the time hack on the utterances.

Having finished with the audio file, Lucia returned to that sector, adjusted several audio slide bars, and focused again. She still couldn't place what she heard, but her ears said it was definitely not Latin or Greek, and certainly not any dialect of Italian that she knew. It possessed a guttural quality with odd sound values that stumped her. So she made a copy of the audio passage, to pass around among the coven's more linguistically gifted. She targeted those with a Near Eastern background based upon a hunch. She flagged the e-mail as URGENT.

Over the next three hours, replies from her in-house resources trickled in, most apologetically clueless. Apparently several of the more enterprising had shared the file with their colleagues out of sheer curiosity. That was when someone helpful entered the conversation.

It's Demotic Egyptian, this new email said. *And a serious curse to boot.*

The best part was that this individual provided a translation.

> Allow this innocent's blood to spread within the *pomerium*.

> Allow this innocent's blood to bring a swift death to all living *things* within this *pomerium*.

I apologize that I cannot make heads or tails of the rest. A breeze garbled it. But regarding these two lines, I am quite certain.

At this news, Lucia was ecstatic. The translation's context fit seamlessly with the video feed of the goat's sacrifice. She had her marker, and that meant whoever cast the Resurrection Incident's spell had to be a Demotic Egyptian speaker as well.

"So, who in TIIIS can speak Demotic Egyptian?" she absentmindedly asked her laptop's screen.

Lucia went for broke and initiated a global search of the entire CMES database for anyone that could speak the language. In forty-three seconds the security officer had her shortlist. Seven members of CMES, two currently available, knew the language—which included the individual who had provided the translation.

But significantly, one non-member of CMES appeared on her list, a certain Demotic Egyptian scholar by the name of Dr. Melaina Makris. Wonder of wonders, this individual had once been a card-carrying member of the failed CMES North American recruitment project called *The Gathering*. Her membership file said that she was a research scholar at the Metropolitan Museum of Art on sabbatical from Berkeley. This Dr. Makris was a witch. Her file indicated so on her initially measured psychic profile. A subsequent one showed an astounding leap in her abilities that went almost off the charts. Even the then director of membership, a Ms. Jennifer Sauerbrünn, had commented on this performance uptick as "she must have kissed a ley line."

Fascinating ... and the audio's intensity reveals so much power expended in the casting ...

Makris' membership file from *The Gathering* also contained several high-quality images that depicted a beautiful and exotic-looking face. Continuing to follow her hunch, Lucia downloaded the three images and ran them through the in-house image-recognition software. That done, she fired off another global database search.

Thirty-four seconds later the security officer almost choked. Makris appeared in a security video dated to the very day *The Gathering* building succumbed to its disastrous fire, which eventually condemned the entire building, and signaled the marginalization of CMES' North American zone.

Lucia paused at the brink of an incredible revelation.

Why had this powerful witch walked the perimeter of The Gathering *building on that momentous day? Unfortunately, there was not an audio feed on this surveillance video tape, but the imagery did clearly show that Makris was moving her lips, perhaps speaking in a conversation. Or was she caught in the act of casting a spell around the stricken structure?*

Lucia reran the tape. *No. She was walking alone, and I do not see any evidence of a cell device. So Makris must have caught in the act of casting a spell!*

Lucia wanted more, so she constructed a detailed search request that cross-referenced Makris with her home of Alexandria, Egypt—a critical detail that she had let slip on her membership application.

Sixty-seven seconds later, Lucia had Makris' motivation. Both of her parents had been taken from her by CMES personnel. Her father, Ahmed, had been murdered by the Dark One, William Alexander, while he sat as the CMES *consul* of the region of Alexandria, Egypt. Her mother, Fatima, was also murdered by a CMES member—a senior gynecological physician, who consequently had died under mysterious circumstances by an unknown form of magic! *I wonder who did that—Makris?*

Lucia didn't need to confirm Makris was a member of TIIIS, for she personally knew that the Egyptian was. Routinely, CMES made it a practice to penetrate the Old Oaks Academy in western Pennsylvania. A recent student-plant had spent a semester at the campus and taken a class from the woman on spell casting.

With the circle now complete, the vampire treated herself to not one, but two plastic bladders of Type O blood from her personal refrigerator. Finished gorging herself with the luscious liquid, her still-virgin body writhed in ecstasy. The pupils of her eyes dilated with pleasure. Her back arched, arms outstretched, fangs and claws extended. Her face smoldered a flushed and ruddy red as if in full organism—which, for her, the meal had been.

After an hour, Lucia was once again herself and under tight control. She knew that she now had to devise a solution for Makris—a plotting and dangerous woman who had practically destroyed CMES North American zone on her own. The security officer knew that her colleague Gnotti wanted her report and would pass it off as his research. But Lucia was ambitious and instead decided to approach the chairman directly about this. So she concocted an *elegant* plan of retaliation. After all, she was not about to disappoint her *Signore Presidente*.

CHAPTER 18

"Erik and Father Cardoza!" Inspector Ali Hassan greeted them with open arms. "I hear that you two have been very busy. Please come in, sit, and tell me all about your adventures."

The inspector lifted his office phone from its cradle, spoke briefly with his assistant, and ordered some tea. This told Reissen several things—all good.

"My guard, Mohammed Khoury, tells me that you made an explosion yesterday. Was it another of those traps that magicians like to make?"

"Yes. Would you like to see the video of it?"

The inspector's smile took on a hint of excitement. "Why, yes I would."

Reissen nodded. "Father, would you please?"

The photographer fumbled out his pad, turned it on, and then placed it horizontally before the inspector. Its volume was on max. The inspector watched the video four times, exclaiming his surprise each time, clearly impressed by his forefathers' ingenuity.

"Most impressive," Inspector Hassan said while rubbing his hands together with pleasure. "But why have you stopped by? Surely not to just show me this entertaining video."

The tea arrived on a silver tea service. Once everyone had been served, Reissen answered the inspector.

"Ali, we are here for several things. First, to invite you to witness a breakthrough into a new chamber."

Ali grinned broadly at that news.

"Secondly, that new chamber will require its own electrical power and lighting. Can your administration provide this?"

"Absolutely. But before I send the electricians, is it safe for them?" The inspector asked with raised eyebrows.

"They will have to carefully crawl a portion of the way."

The inspector waved the issue aside.

"When do you want me on site Erik?"

"What would be most convenient for you?"

"How about eleven?"

"Perfect."

"And, Inspector, please bring a headlamp and a pair of safety goggles."

* * *

Even at six by six, it was tight in the secret passage with three men in it. Reissen moved forward and knelt within the blockage's passage and faced the last layer of stones. Inspector Hassan did the same at the start of the blockage some eight feet back, while Father Cardoza squatted behind them both with all his camera gear. The priest sighted a video camera mounted on a monopod over the inspector's right shoulder. The head lamps of the three men made for a surreal confusion of shadow and light in the tight confines. Some scenes from the *Blair Witch Project* would have looked stabilized and stage-produced comparatively.

With his handpick and four plastic buckets lined up before him, Reissen took a deep breath. "Here we go." He pulled out the pre-loosened upper-most right-hand block. With it came a shower of grit and plaster in a fluffy cloud. Father Cardoza silently cursed at the ruined visibility. Inspector Hassan just sat there breathless, like an expectant father.

Once the archaeologist had removed the entire top row of limestone blocks, he paused and shone through the gap with his head lamp.

"What do you see?" The video captured Hassan voice filled with anticipation mixed with excitement.

"Not very much, Inspector. My helmet's beam is not strong enough. That means the chamber must be large." Reissen said as he passed back buckets of debris before he started muscling out the next course of stone.

In truth the situation became comical, as the other two men did not want to move, but the buckets had to be emptied. Eventually the entire blockage was cleared, because the inspector ordered Mr. Khoury to take them at the Osirian panel's entrance and empty them out.

The air was thick with dust and made worse with the escape of the unbreathable stale air. Reissen reluctantly ordered everyone out in the hopes that it would clear.

With everyone now standing in the tomb's central corridor, the secret passage indeed began to slowly clear. The inspector went out to talk to his guard. Father Cardoza fastidiously cleaned his video camera and its lens. Reissen retrieved from his small backpack an LED flashlight. Then the archaeologist crawled back in, leaned into the secret passage, and turned it on.

"That air went entirely to shit when you started your break through," Cardoza said without looking up from his equipment.

"I know, but you kept filming, right?"

"Sure did."

"Good. Perhaps you captured something. Now come over here."

Peering down the secret passage and right through the blockage passage, the pair clearly saw what lurked beyond, in the clearing air.

CHAPTER 19

"What is your recommendation to punish TIIIS Lucia?" DeSalvo asked his security officer.

"That depends upon what you believe to be their most important asset. Is that Makris? The witch who first initiated and then ended the Resurrection Incident? Or their Lictor of Magic, who somehow managed to defeat our three champions, a sniper team, and evaded a bomb run during the Contest in the Desert? Or do you wish to again attack their Old Oaks Academy? *Signore Presidente*, I require distinct parameters before I can form a suitable punishment."

DeSalvo, who was quite familiar with the white vampire had read her personnel jacket, liked her reasoned answer. Her request for limits. In fact, he found her quite attractive, given her current vampiric flush. "Lucia, what would hurt them the most?"

"Again, *Signore Presidente* that is a statement devoid of direction or specifics. What is your pleasure, *Signore*?"

"I wish an end to our current international decline. I wish that the paranormal community would again quake in fear at the mere mention of our name. That is my 'pleasure,' *Signora* Lucia."

"That is quite a pleasure, *Signore*. We are now discussing our society's global policy and the world's perception of us. I fear that I cannot deliver your 'pleasure' without the appropriate authority."

DeSalvo inwardly smiled. "You will have it. But first, present your plan. Then we will talk about granting you 'the appropriate authority'."

The chairman was impressed with this security officer. She had spunk, ambition, and obviously long experience in making life and death judgments as a regional council member. After all, she was a vampire, even if a white one. Besides, she made his loins groan with desire.

*   *   *

Stone nervously sat in the waiting room of the obstetrician-gynecologist's office. Big as he was, he filled the ergonomically shaped plastic chair and then some. The reading materials available were not exactly his taste. He could only look at his device so many times. He had deleted all of his recent phone calls. His e-mail was similarly cleansed. But what really got to him was the size of some of the pregnant women who were there. They looked seriously uncomfortable, sometimes planking in their chairs, or standing, or just getting up and walking around.

"Mr. Stone," the receptionist called out, "the doctor will see you now. Proceed to Room Three."

The *doctor* was Dr. Marcia Samuels. Her family was long-time members of TIIIS and she a powerful psychic healer in particular. He'd checked.

Walking to the sacred door which provided access to the almighty "doctor," Stone felt the heat of ten sets on eyes on his back. He could just imagine what was running through their minds. He didn't bother to listen in on them either.

Passing through a sterile-looking corridor adorned only with images donated by big pharma, Stone approached the open door of Room Three. Standing within its threshold he saw the ubiquitous stirruped examination table, upon which his beaming wife sat in a paper examination gown.

To one side, on a low-wheeled stool, sat the "doctor." Samuels was a crisp, all-business, no-nonsense woman with reading glasses that hung on a golden chain. Presently, those half-glasses were perched on her pug nose surrounded by freckles. Wisps of auburn hair peeked out from under her green surgical cap. She held a digital medical chart in her hands.

"Ah, Mr. Stone," the doctor said while standing and removing her half-glasses. "I must say that you have quite the reputation." She said extending her hand. It was cool and firm, but tingled with a warm psychic tremor. Her timbered voice was a mixture of genuine interest and professional protocol. "Your wife is progressing nicely, as is your child. Do you have any questions for me?"

"How long has she been pregnant?"

"Best guess," she shrugged with a tilt of her head, "six weeks. Her breasts are well on their way to becoming milk bottles. They are tender, their nipples highly sensitive. Be gentle when you hug her. By the way, she is in remarkable physical condition. Whatever she is doing, please help her maintain this level of conditioning. It will only help the baby. Sexual intercourse is permitted until it is uncomfortable for the mother."

Stone listened carefully to the instructions, blushed, and mutely nodded.

"Anything else, Mr. Stone?"

"No, doctor, but I'm sure that I will in the future."

"No doubt." She curtly said as she stood to leave, then stopped. "Congratulations are in order. I simply can't wait to have little ones running about the Old Oaks campus." She then left the couple alone and knocked on the door of the next examination room.

"So how did it go, honey?" Stone now took the roller stool and his wife's hand.

She rolled her eyes, "Very interesting."

"Ready to go home?"

"Yes, please, and one other thing."

"Yes."

"I would like to stop at Tastee Freez."

Stone smiled. "Another chocolate milkshake?"

"No, this time I think I'll have a strawberry banana split with extra nuts."

*   *   *

"*Signore Presidente*, the only appropriate response to TIIIS' desecration of our dead is to kill those who did so."

"Specifically?"

"We outright kill the witch *and* her husband. For good measure, we also eliminate as many of their leadership as possible. In short, I wish to decapitate TIIIS."

DeSalvo leaned forward against his desk with his elbows planted. "And how, Lucia," the chairman asked in disbelief, "would you go about doing that? Perhaps your formidable memory has *failed* you. You speak of killing their Lictor of Magic, who bested our three champions, a sniper team, and a bombing run. I seem to be hearing an echo, repeating your own words. And as for the witch, you yourself read her psychic profiles from *The Gathering* membership files. Are you going *daft*?"

Lucia could endure many things, but not a challenge to her intellect. She bridled at her superior's words. Her fingernails drew bloody wounds in her clenched fists. But what hurt the most was she realized he was right. TIIIS had truly positioned itself in a nearly impregnable position. Nearly...?

Lucia sympathized. She well knew that DeSalvo had the misfortune to occupy the chairmanship during much of CMES' recent decline, and that he had made several disastrous decisions. This white vampire desired decisive, bold action. Wanted CMES feared again.

What was holding him back?

"I apologize, *Signora* Lucia. That was rash."

DeSalvo paused. The next words he would utter would either make or break CMES's future. "If we are again to be a feared coven, then that fear must be earned with lurid violence. The killing of two people will not be sufficient, but the sudden and global assassination of their leadership will be a good beginning. Right now," he said, his finger stabbing into his desk. "TIIIS is basking in a confidence it does not deserve. Lucia, drive them cowering back into the shadows!" He snarled with an upraised and clenched fist.

The sudden force of her superior's emotion swelled Lucia's chest. The prospect of releasing such carnage caused her nipples to harden like cherry stones and her face to glow with desire.

DeSalvo sensed her arousal. "There will come a time, Lucia, when I will take a mate. Please consider this my first overture."

"Si, Signore Presidente." Lucia glowed.

CHAPTER 20

With the stones of the blocking plug removed, the darkness ahead beckoned like a foreboding cave. As before the threesome formed up, with Inspector Hassan behind Reissen. Father Cardoza had his camera at the ready and video up and running. Kneeling at the end of the inner threshold of the blockage's passage, Reissen said, "Okay, ready, everyone? I am going to turn on the LED. Shield your eyes."

The effect of the blue-white light was astounding. It revealed a single chamber with four square painted columns supporting its ceiling. Between them lay an open rose granite sarcophagus with its heavy lid discarded to one side. The floor was a litter of cultural artifacts and fallen chunks of painted stone from the blue and gold-starred ceiling overhead. Panning the light revealed plaster-smoothed walls painted white and covered with beautifully painted hieroglyphs and murals.

"Why aren't we going in?" Inspector Hassan urged from behind the archaeologist.

In response, Reissen panned the floor carefully and it was good that he did. "Ali, you will not believe this, but I am looking at ancient footprints on a dusty floor. All of them are clearly following a specific path. That tells me that there are booby-traps in this chamber. Still want to rush in?"

As far as Father Cardoza was concerned, the video he was getting was golden, but Reissen's commentary was priceless.

"Okay. Ali, squeeze in next to me so that you can see what I'm seeing. Sorry, Father Cardoza, but we are about to eclipse your view. You and your camera will be next for an exclusive."

After some shuffling, grunting, and squeezing about, the archaeologist and inspector knelt side by side. "Ali," Reissen said while panning the LED's beam low across the flooring, "can you see the footprints?"

"Yes, yes I can."

"See how they all suspiciously snake around. It is almost as though their owners knew where to step—where not to. So before we enter the tomb, we must back out to allow Father Cardoza to document this evidence."

Once back in the secret passage, Inspector Hassan wore a concerned look, and Reissen saw it.

"What's wrong, Ali?"

"I'm confused. This appears to be a robbed tomb, yet it was sealed so well. I don't understand."

"Well, Ali, even though we have yet to step foot into this subsidiary chamber, what I am seeing has gotten my suspicions alerted. Regardless of what we will find, I think there is plenty to keep the University of Milano team busy for several years. In fact, I am willing to bet that some of these finds will find their way to the new Grand Egyptian Museum."

Hassan brightened noticeably. "I certainly hope so."

"Only time will tell."

"Okay, everybody, I'm finished. Come on through," Father Cardoza said as he backed out of the passageway.

Squeezing past the stationary priest and all his equipment, Reissen took the first step inside. "Ali, when you follow me, be sure to step on my boot prints."

"Yes, Erik, I will."

Having carefully followed the Austrian's suggestion, the inspector was soon standing next to him and near the wide-open sarcophagus. Meanwhile, Father Cardoza was recording everything from the relative safety of the chamber's threshold.

"It's empty," the inspector said looking into the stone funerary container, noticeably deflated.

"Yes, but if you look carefully, the lid was removed with care. I see no cracks or hammer-marks on it."

Reissen then panned the LED light around the centrally placed sarcophagus. "Interesting. Ali, look over there. The deceased's case of canopic jars was left intact and untouched."

Then, "What is missing Ali, other than the tomb owner's mummy? Here, take my flashlight."

After several sweeps of its blinding glare, Ali said, "I see no gold or jewelry. All the damage to the trunks and furniture seems superficial. Look there, Erik. They didn't touch any of the ivory inlays. This is odd."

"I agree." Now taking back the flashlight, "And I note that there are no erasures anywhere in this chamber." Panning the flooring, the archaeologist carefully made his way around, following the others' prints while Ali wisely stayed put next to the sarcophagus.

"I read ... Sethi ... *sem*-priest of the great god Set of Tanis ... first magician of *Userma'at-re' Setepenre* ... son of his body ... first voice of the great council of magicians ..."

"This is a tomb of a prince of Ramses II!" Hassan breathed in awe.

Reissen carefully returned to Hassan's side. "Seen enough for today?"

"Yes, my dear friend, I have." The inspector beamed.

"Alright, now retrace your boot prints back to Father Cardoza."

As the inspector did so, he frankly misstepped as his head was on a swivel as he took in all the burial goods, his mind a million miles away, instead of focusing on his feet. The sound of the failing plaster caused the man to freeze in place.

"Ali, look down and check your feet." Reissen tensely said. "What do you see?"

"Some big cracks in the flooring."

"Shift your weight away from the cracks." The

Austrian coached. "Then take one step back."

Inspector Hassan did so and then stood ram-rod straight and still as a statue.

"Ali, it's alright to breathe. I will come over to you and we will together navigate our way out."

Trembling, "Thank you, Erik."

The Austrian archaeologist now stood behind the nervous Egyptian.

"Ali, look down at the footprints. See them?"

"Yes, Erik."

Gripping the inspector by his shoulders. "Okay. I am going to guide you out." Slowly turning the man to the right and away from the cracked flooring, they shuffled their way forward and reached the subsidiary tomb's entrance.

Father Cardoza, with his eye pressed against his video camera's viewfinder, had captured the entire scene.

When Hassan next turned around, he saw that Reissen was no longer behind him, but instead was back in the chamber, on his knees, and rapping on its floor with his knuckles.

THUMP.

THUMP.

CLINK.

CLINK.

Then Reissen took the end cap of his LED light and rammed it firmly amid the cracks. The result was spectacular as a three by three foot hole suddenly opened up. Peeking his head over the edge, he said with a bit of an echo. "Damn, this one is deep."

Then looking up directly into Cardoza's lens, "This is definitely a man-trap. It has smooth-sided walls and is about thirty feet deep. Its jagged rocky bottom would definitely twist an ankle or break a leg. Neither a good thing."

Having returned to the chamber's entrance, Reissen took the opportunity to take several more looks around with his LED light. A professional pang of regret gripped his chest at having to walk away from such an extraordinary find.

*　　*　　*

The next day Dr. Luigi Gomas, the archaeological director and discoverer of Tomb 707 from the University of Milano, paid a visit to Inspector Hassan's office. To the Italian's surprise, he was led to a conference room where two other men sat with a laptop, a projector, and a screen.

"Dr. Gomas, allow me to introduce you to Father Cardoza, of the Vatican, and Dr. Erik Reissen, also of the Vatican. They wish to brief you on the latest developments regarding Tomb 707."

Clearly blind-sided, Gomas numbly shook hands with the pair and then came to. "Dr. Reissen—*the* Reissen?"

"*Si, profesore*. I am Reissen."

"Why are *you* here?" the astonished man asked.

"*Profesore* Gomas," Reissen began, "we wish to share with you a video that we believe will explain much. Father Cardoza, if you please."

During the screening of the five-minute video, Gomas gasped several times. The Italian was initially quite incensed about what he was seeing until the video came to the part about the cave in, the discovery and detonation of a bobby-trap, and the man-trap in the subsidiary chamber. *Father Cardoza has done a brilliant edit*, Reissen thought.

At the video's conclusion, a wide-eyed and shocked Gomas just sat staring at Cardoza's video screen.

When he found his tongue, he asked. "Is this real?"

"I can assure you, *Profesore* Gomas, that it is. If you do not believe me, then ask Inspector Hassan. He almost fell into that man-trap."

The inspector stood there with his arms crossed and soberly nodded in confirmation.

Then Reissen made several remarks.

"*Profesore* Gomas, this tomb potentially contains several dangerous and as yet to be found booby-traps and man-traps that need to be immediately addressed. They, however, are now your headache. I have been assured that Inspector Hassan, and perhaps even the Egyptian military, will assist you and your team with them. We," he indicated Father Cardoza, "have removed only one chemical booby-trap and have successfully disposed of it. It was covered with curse texts using the formulaic style of the well-known *Execration Texts,* but modified to protect a tomb from unwanted intruders. Again, Father Cardoza has fully recorded the spell's text in a digital medium, and we will give these to you, as well as this video. Unfortunately, the jar itself was totally destroyed in the explosion."

The Austrian paused to swallow.

"You and your team are now free to clear this subsidiary chamber, conserve and restore as necessary, and publish its contents and inscriptions, along with the outer portion of the tomb. But please be careful. There may be another man-trap in it."

Gomas defensively folded his arms over his chest. "So, just like that, the contents, inscriptions, and art of the subsidiary chamber are to be handed over to my archaeological expedition?"

"Si, profesore."

Still the Italian archaeologist grumbled. "And what of the discovery of this subsidiary chamber and its passages? Who receives the credit for that?" Gomas retorted with a glance toward Inspector Hassan.

"Your archaeological expedition, of course." Reissen answered flatly.

The man sat back in his chair stunned. Reissen knew what he had just offered was unprecedented, and he gave the Italian some time to think about it that fact.

When Gomas finally found his tongue, he stood

and shook the men's hands. "*Grazie*," was the best he could do.

"*Profesore* Gomas," Inspector Hassan added, "I have some paperwork for you to sign. It is an addendum to your previous archaeological permit, which now includes the clearing, conservation, restoration, and publication rights for the subsidiary chamber."

*　　*　　*

That evening, during their last dinner before returning to Rome, Father Cardoza asked, "Erik, just what was the significance of what we found?"

Reissen smiled. "What we found will require the perspective of time to fully appreciate. It seems that someone wanted the prince's mummy quite badly. Why? For what purpose? Who knows? But I did note that there were only three sets of footprints. Who were they?

"The main clue is the prince's canopic jars. What fascinates me is that the would-be thieves didn't take them along with the mummy. That tells me that they were not out to destroy the man's *ka,* or perhaps that they were in a hurry. Perhaps the removal of the sarcophagus' lid took longer than they had estimated. Removing and then replacing the booby-trap took perhaps even more. Or, perhaps they had another agenda entirely. Yes, they were greedy. They stripped away Lord only knows how much portable wealth, but they were also very selective in their plundering. That suggests to me that whoever took Sethi's mummy were most likely jaded priests of high station. Gold and jewelry they could readily carry, keep, or fence, but to them the rich ivory inlays in the funerary furniture was just—ivory. Why bother? True grave robbers would have been far more thorough.

"But there is a far deeper purpose here, and the untouched canopic jars are again the clue. In the mind of the Egyptian several things are vital for one's survival in the afterlife. First and foremost is the mummy, in which the individual's heart is itself entombed."

Reissen paused to take a long pull from a liter bottle of Stella Egyptian beer. Finishing it, he waved to the waiter for another. Between Reissen and Cardoza, a skyline of bottles had formed that evening on their dinner table.

"Now, Father, think on this. The tomb owner's name was erased in the outer tomb, but preserved intact within the subsidiary chamber. What does that give you? The tomb owner's soul or *ka*'s survival in the afterlife. Granted no one would see it and speak it aloud, but the name remains preserved. That issue aside, someone made doubly sure of the survival of this individual's *ka* by leaving behind his canopic jars within a secret and hidden chamber. That suggests to me a knowledge and appreciation of Egyptian funerary magic. If you think about it, it is really a quite beautiful plan."

Cardoza took another swig himself. "Ah, boss, so what do the jars contain?"

"I am sorry, I thought you knew. These four jars contain the mummified internal organs of the individual. To have them intact means that you can use them in the afterlife, which directly translates into how well you can enjoy and partake of the afterlife. So the lungs allow you to breathe. The stomach so you can eat. The livers so you can drink. The intestines so that you can eliminate. The all important heart remained in the mummy with an amulet to protect it. As for the genitals, another amulet made sure that it was functional. The Egyptians were truly a practical culture, even in their use of magic."

The Austrian took another drink, this time from his fresh bottle.

"But there is more. Usually, secreted within the canopic jar chest is a copy of a magical document called *Going Forth By Day*. This text is a magical insurance policy for its owner, who is specified by name in numerous places, to successfully pass the Last Judgment in the Underworld."

By the dubious look on the priest's face, Reissen could see that he still had his doubts. "So, Father, in essence, that subsidiary chamber became for Sethi a cenotaph."

"What's that?"

"A funerary insurance policy. It is a secondary burial, separate from where his mummy is or was. Basically, his mummy and his bodily parts were spread around to absolutely ensure his survival in the afterlife. As of now, that is my interpretation, and I am going to stick to it." Then the Austrian gracefully burped into his fist.

CHAPTER 21

Stone's exorcism had forcibly expelled Sethi's *ka* from Condé's body. It was not destroyed—just displaced. The question was—displaced where? From the priest-magician's point-of-view, his *ka* was tumbling, adrift, and without a rudder in a turbulent river, whose inhabitants bit and snapped at him, but never quite touched him. It was maddening, struggling to breathe, fighting off dark things, and all the time not knowing where the river bank was—not knowing in which direction to swim to safety.

The priest-magician didn't know it, but his *ka* had been sent to the Dark Realm, as described in *The Knot of Eternity*.

So did Sethi perceive his new reality after being cast out of the senior security guard's body. Without doubt, his plight was serious, one filled with fright, uncertainty, and repentance. He called out his beloved wife's name into the muddy void without echo. He cried openly for a final moment with his children. The wailing was such that it reached many places. The sheer will, desire, and love expressed to return to the verdant garden paradise from which he was torn became a spell of unheard of power. And so Sethi's ka rose up from the fearsome depths of the Dark Realm toward the beckoning light and entered the Light Realm.

This occurred because Sethi's *ka* had sufficient

moorings—his preserved mummy, canopic jars, and name. That his righteous existence had occurred, that his heart had been weighed by Ma'at herself, and recorded by Thoth in the Great Hall before all the gods, there could be no question. His guide, *Going Forth By Day*, lay unmolested within the canopic case. Within that magical papyrus could be found his *Declaration of Innocence* that stated his righteousness in every regard before all forty-two of his judges, each whom he addressed by name. Here listed is but a sample.

Hail, *Usekh-nemmt*, who comes forth from *Anu*, I have not committed sin.

Hail, *Hept-khet*, who comes forth from *Kher-aha*, I have not committed robbery with violence.

Hail, *Fenti*, who comes forth from *Khemenu*, I have not stolen.

Hail, *Am-khaibit*, who comes forth from *Qernet*, I have not slain men and women.

Hail, *Neba*, who comes and goes, I have not uttered lies.

Hail, *Utu-nesert*, who comes forth from *Het-ka-ptah*, I have not uttered abominations.

Hail, *Qerrti*, who comes forth from *Amentet*, I have not committed adultery.

Hail, *Ta-retiu*, who comes forth from the night, I have not attacked any man.

Hail, *Tenemiu*, who comes forth from *Bast*, I have not slandered anyone.

Hail, *Sertiu*, who comes forth from *Anu*, I have not been angry without just cause.

Hail, *Tutu*, who comes forth from *Ati*, I have not debauched the wife of any man.

Hail, *Maa-antuf*, who comes forth from *Per-Menu*, I have not polluted myself.

Hail, *Nekhenu*, who comes forth from *Heqat*, I have not shut my ears to the words of truth.

Hail, *Kenemti*, who comes forth from *Kenmet*, I have not blasphemed.

Hail, *An-hetep-f*, who comes forth from *Sau*, I am not a man of violence.

Hail, *Nefer-Tem*, who comes forth from *Het-ka-Ptah*, I have done no evil.

Hail, *Tem-Sepu*, who comes forth from *Tetu*, I have not worked witchcraft against the king.

With such a *Declaration of Innocence*, the *ka* of Sethi found the strength and was granted the divine guidance needed to reach the river's bank, where because of his great yearning, he rejoined his family in the verdant garden paradise from which he was so unjustly torn.

*　　*　　*

Sethi stood arm in arm with his much-beloved wife within the shade of a many-columned porch. They, together, took in their wheat field, which stood tall and ripe to the height of a man. He gazed upon the stand of date palms heavily laden with overly-ripe fruits. His chest swelled as he breathed in the heady sweetness of ever-blooming stands of papyrus and lotus. Within their home, the sounds of grandchildren playing tickled their ears with joy and mirth.

"I have missed you, my husband."

"As I have missed you, my wife. You have my hallowed promise to never again leave your side."

Now playfully tugging at the front of his freshly starched ivory white kilt, "Prove to me, my husband, just how much you have missed me."

"I shall."

And with that, Sethi and his wife turned and disappeared into the solitude of their eternal household.

CHAPTER 22

So many targets ... so little time.

Lucia decided to form a team of coordinators, each responsible for several assassins and their targets. Each coordinator would be a native of their designated region, who would know intimately the cultural landscape and necessary details. Seven coordinators in all, assigned by geographic region, were made responsible for the US, Canada, the British Isles, India, the Near East, the Far East, and Eastern Europe.

Lucia chose the date of execution several months into the future, to make sure that the many assets were in place and ready. She devised a contingency plan. The precise time of the assassinations would be at fifteen hundred hours, forty-three minutes, Rome time. 15:43—because she believed it to be her birth year. Once simultaneously initiated, the grand plan would trigger a baptism of blood that would harken the rebirth of CMES as a much-feared coven of immense influence and power. Lucia firmly believed that as each and every one fell, former treaty allies would take note and once again flock to the protective embrace of the CMES banner. Once leaderless, TIIIS would again become a cowering rabble.

* * *

Andy Grissom was a likable young man born, raised,

and educated in the northeastern United States. With a well-placed corporate lawyer for a father and an oral surgeon for a mother, their family's standard of living had been quite comfortable. For Grissom that meant swimming and playing squash at a posh athletic club and attending the finest urban prep schools.

That young Grissom was quite bright hadn't hurt. He landed a full-ride scholarship to Brown University. Majoring in history and pre-law, the young man saw himself following in his father's footsteps.

Neither of Grissom's parents possessed a psychic profile worth a damn, but their son did—hence their membership in CMES. As Grissom's father would often say of that expensive decision, "It's the best damn down payment on Andrew's future." Testing well early on, the boy developed during his high school years into an adept with a rating of a Class Two out of six. Ever the source of parental pride, Grissom entered Brown rightly feeling his oats.

Then came the collapse of *The Gathering* building in Manhattan, and with it, his father lost his high-paying and equally influential position within the CMES hierarchy. Grissom's scholarship became a godsend, allowing him to continue on pretty much as before. The Grissoms for their part scrambled, righted themselves, and marched on with the failure relegated to a financial blip on the family's radar. But Grissom took the collapse personally. An inbred, deep, and abiding hatred of TIIIS now became an obsession, for who else could have done such a thing? No, Grissom reasoned, *they* must have done it. His carbon-fiber membership card, emblazoned with his holographic image, no longer was worth a damn. Before *The Gathering*'s fall, it guaranteed him and his friends *carte blanche* entry into any of Manhattan's most exclusive restaurants and clubs.

Filled with the hot zeal of a young and entitled zealot, already CMES-groomed, was easily recruited to infiltrate the TIIIS stronghold located in western Pennsylvania—Old Oaks Academy. His marching orders were straightforward—pretend to be a college freshman once again, absorb all the damning or interesting scuttlebutt that you can, and periodically report back about what you found. For Grissom it was a grand game, where he was a young Daniel Craig taking on the evil SPECTRE. For CMES he was just a useful tool.

Unfortunately for Grissom, his young indoctrination by CMES' emotional paeans of "slash and burn," and "attack and devour," didn't hold a thimble of value at Old Oaks Academy. He discovered, much to his dismay, that CMES' approach was irrational and not at all intellectually satisfying. This internal revelation was caused by an ancient text that his entire class had to study and analyze. It was called *The Knot of Eternity*. Never had he once heard it mentioned within CMES during his youthful training. Now, when it came to the casting of magic, restraint and logic were counseled by his instructors, instead of being the mindless tool of raging emotion and revenge.

And as for the lecturers, their matter-of-fact approach instilled a sense of responsibility for one's actions. Two in particular stood out in Grissom's mind. One was Mr. J.J. Stone, the society's Lictor of Magic, who had taught Grissom's class on demonology. An imposing and absolutely no-nonsense man, Stone was TIIIS' guardian of the good and destroyer of evil. He openly admitted that he had blood on his hands, had gotten lucky, and had made dire mistakes. The scuttlebutt was, he was the victor at the Contest in the Desert, an event never once mentioned during Grissom's former life. His only recollection of Stone's name from those days was one associated with mindless derision and damnation. And yet, Grissom found himself respecting the man for who he was—a battle-proven warrior who had remained true to his fundamental principles.

The other lecturer who had made a lasting impression on Grissom was an Egyptian witch, Dr. Makris, who, in spite of her tininess, inspired a fear Mr. Stone could not. Smooth and polished in manner like a piece of granite, this brilliant and demanding woman allowed nothing, absolutely nothing, to slip past her. Quick with smiling praise and devastatingly brutal when presented with bullshit, her class on spell casting and the role of personal responsibility transformed Grissom's worldview. On top of that, a delicious rumor circulated that this witch-tigress was Mr. Stone's wife!

In the late fall, the young CMES implant was assigned a narrow plot of garden to prepare for the spring. In his opinion, digging in the ground and getting dirty was something only people called "farmers" did, not a certified Second Class Adept. Yet, Grissom eventually found something satisfying about breaking up the soil, removing weeds and their long root tendrils, working in the fertilizer, and completing the task. Perhaps it was the pretty girl named Amy, who worked side by side at her plot, quietly humming and singing to herself as she did.

All in all, the Old Oaks Academy campus had been a shock for Grissom. He had never been in Pennsylvania before, much less *western* Pennsylvania. Grissom had never before seen such vast and perfect lawns of green, much less dense old oak forests dark with mystery. Nothing here was crowded. Instead, all of the stately architecture was spaced out in a serene circular setting, divided only by the gurgling waters of the Jordan River that bisected the campus. There were no vast seas of concrete here. Rather, neat and rolling lawns dominated, broken only by beaten footpaths and flower gardens that student's fussed over in hopes of winning the Spring Prize.

This was a different view of the world—one vastly at odds with his urban and CMES upbringing. But something else troubled the young man—how devoid of substance his former life had been and how hungry his spirit was for nourishment. Nourishment he found here, amongst the peace, beauty, simplicity, and intrinsic logic of Old Oaks Academy.

He began to excel in his classes, take pride in his work, and make friends with his fellow students and professors. He found himself breathing differently, thinking differently. The thought that his parents would not approve, that his passion for CMES had fallen flat, couldn't stop him from basking in this way of life, this way of magic.

During his Christmas break, his superiors at CMES called him in.

*   *   *

"Mr. Grissom, thank you for coming." The CMES Director of North American Membership said. "I much appreciate it. Time is after all—money."

Grissom noticed just how artificial, no brittle, the Manhattan woman's appearance truly was. She was too blonde, her figure too perfect to be real, her clothing too tight, and her makeup way to severe—and those candy red lips... Grissom caught himself thinking of Amy and the other, more wholesome women at Old Oaks Academy.

The Manhattan woman's voice interrupted his thoughts. "My records say that you have successfully completed your first semester at Old Oaks Academy with two A's and a B. Not bad for a second-time freshman. What are your impressions of their campus?" Her grotesquely made up eyes looked at him as if he was a bug on a slide.

Careful, here. "It's a weird place full of priorities that don't make any sense." *Don't give anything away.* Now was not the time. He took a breath. *Something else for good measure.* "Frankly, it's painful."

Her eyes now glistened with interest. "How so?"

Grissom shifted in his seat. "Well, they have this ritual of dumping the entire freshman class into this cold stream that runs through campus. They called it our 'baptism.' Then, later on, they make you dig in the dirt and plant flower bulbs. You'd think that students would have better things to do, like reading assignments, and studying for tests."

The Manhattan woman smiled just a little so as to not crack her makeup. "Do I detect revulsion from you, Mr. Grissom?"

Good, she's going for it. "Absolutely, Director Sauerbrünn."

The director's eyes dilated when he used her title.

Then she sighed. "Well, Mr. Grissom, you'll just have to tough it out." She glanced down at a piece of paper before her. No doubt a pat list of questions. "Tell me about your instructors."

"Well, Mr. Dexter is an odd, old Frenchman. I had him for Offensive and Defensive Magic."

"Yes, that was the class that you earned a grade of 'B' in. Why so?"

"I was protecting my Adept Second Class status, Director. I didn't want to come on too strong."

Again that slight smile. "Clever, Mr. Grissom. What about the others?"

Grissom wetted his lips a little. "Mr. Stone was flat out a nut case. Pure US Marine hard-ass who is in love with himself. He is a dumb weapon. Point and shoot."

"Interesting characterization, Mr. Grissom. I agree with you. Any others?"

"Dr. Makris, frankly, is one scary witch."

"I note that you earned A's in both Mr. Stone's and Dr. Makris' classes. How come?"

"Because the students there are dumb as rocks, and both professors grade on a steep curve."

"Interesting. Anything else?"

At this point, Grissom knew that he had to throw her a bone before she sensed his outrageous lies. "Yes, there is this rumor that Stone and Makris are married."

"You ... don't ... say?"

Much to Grissom's surprise, Director Sauerbrünn's face became a stiff mask—like those he'd seen girls put on in high school and college when they encountered the guys who had jilted them. Grissom also began to notice his damp armpits. He had said the wrong thing.

The Manhattan woman was quick to transform back into a smile, though...albeit a slightly murderous one, Grissom noted. "Well, Mr. Grissom, keep up the good work! Have a happy holiday!"

Two days later, Grissom was contacted by a

security officer with a name he didn't recognize—Lucy, Lorrie, something like that. When the young man realized the e-mail originated from "Mother Rome," he was floored.

The missive requested that he track three individuals at the Old Oaks Academy—President Betsy Silver Moon, Dr. Melaina Makris, and J.J. Stone. Any specifics about their whereabouts were requested. Such updates he should send periodically to the e-mail's sender. As flattering as the e-mail was, Grissom had a better idea. *Yeah, now I'm Daniel Craig, double-agent!*

CHAPTER 23

In all, Lucia targeted twenty-three individuals from the TIIIS leadership, including its international president, regional governors, and sub-governors. Among that number she also included Makris and Stone. Realistically, the white vampire didn't expect to get them all. But that didn't mean she wasn't motivated to try. From her viewpoint, even the assassination of half that number would cause a disruptive ripple-effect throughout TIIIS, at least long enough to initially topple it from its lofty position. Such a blow would also leak out to their allies, which would create disquiet as to whether TIIIS could protect its treaty-bound brethren from similar attacks. If executed, TIIIS couldn't recover from such a loss of leadership. Lucia was sure.

The load placed upon the seven coordinators was unevenly distributed. The US coordinator had the most targets on its list, with eleven, while the coordinators of the British Isles, Canada, and Near East had three each, and the coordinators of India, Eastern Europe, and the Far East had one a piece. Lucia understood that a much broader net of informants would be required to track the targets of the US territory.

With so many resources in play, Lucia held a conference call with her coordinators to kick off the mission.

"Fellow brethren, this is Lucia, Security Special

Projects Coordinator in Rome. Our *Signore Presidente* wishes to send a distinct message to our paranormal colleagues that the *Consilium* is to be respected and feared. As a consequence, the seven of you, divided by geography, will eliminate the following targets in your region.

"In the United States, the international president of TIIIS, Betsy Silver Moon; regional governor Klara Kotula; and sub-governors John Running Deer, Deirdre Meier, Clarence Ott, Phillip Gregory, John Strong, Jeremy Shott, and Kevin Reiss—nine in all. In addition, J.J. Stone, their Lictor of Magic, and Dr. Melaina Makris are to be assassinated. Because of the great distances involved, I encourage you to create a broad net of informers to track the whereabouts of these individuals."

Murmurs of approval emanated from the line, along with several gasps of disbelief at the audacity of the list and the magnitude of the undertaking.

"In Canada, the sub-governors Nathan Fournier of Halifax, Sir James McElhinney of Regina, and Liam Gagnon of Vancouver.

"In the British Isles, the regional governor Sir Kyle Simmons of London, and sub-governors Niall Ryan of Dublin and Logan Robertson of Edinburgh."

"Here, here, kill the bloody bastards!" Bubbled forth from her audience.

"On the Indian subcontinent, regional governor Paanan Reddy of Mumbai.

"In the Near East, regional governor Demetrius Skuria of Nicosia, and sub-governors Yosef Hamdan of Amman and Ariel Ohavon of Tel Aviv."

"May Al-Shaitan claim them all!" Others chanted.

"In Eastern Europe, regional governor Kemel Kartel of Ankara.

"And finally, in the Far East, regional governor Rissa Koh of Singapore.

"If you have been counting, that is twenty-three targets in all, who must expire on the same day and at the same time around the world—hence our need for tight coordination."

*   *   *

Andy Grissom, upon returning to the Old Oaks Academy campus after his holiday break, was one very torn individual. On the one hand, he now held a special e-mail address along with several pictures that he was to use if he ever caught sight of TIIIS President Betsy Silver Moon. He knew by sight Dr. Makris and Mr. Stone. If these individuals appeared at the campus, he was to immediately report the fact—a simple enough task for a Second Class Adept.

But on the other hand, Grissom wondered about the "why" behind the need for such information. Not being a dolt, he suspected nothing good. And there he ran squarely into his quandary. Why would he want harm to come to these people? One that he had never even met?

Yes, Silver Moon was the president of TIIIS. He got that. But did TIIIS deserve such injury to Dr. Makris and Mr. Stone, especially in light of his current on-campus experiences?

Grissom's actions had consequences. TIIIS had taught him that. He no longer felt like Daniel Craig fighting SPECTRE. Instead, he felt a sure and building sense of guilt associated with such treachery, which naturally led the young man to ask the pivotal question—who was he really?

Even though it was January and cold, he needed to dig in the dirt and get his fingernails filthy. There was not any snow on the ground, so he grabbed his gardening tools and bucket and set off. To his surprise and relief, Amy, his gardening neighbor, was busy at her plot too.

"Hi there," Grissom found himself saying to avoid any awkwardness between him and the pretty auburn-haired woman, who he considered as Irish as a bright green four-leafed clover. "Have a good Christmas?"

Amy lifted her head to smile back at him. "Hi there, yourself! And yes, I did. How 'bout you?"

"It was good," Grissom said as he knelt down to break up the soil, looking for errant weeds.

"So what are you doing here in the dead of winter?" Amy said with a conspiratorial grin.

"I'm trying to cheat. And you?"

"The same. But actually, I'm really here to blow off some steam."

"Really?"

"Yeah, I have some tough decisions to make, and working with my hands helps. If that makes any sort of sense. Sort of loosens up my brain to think deep thoughts."

Grissom felt his shoulders sag. "I know what you mean. I'm going through an existential crisis of my own. That's why I'm here. To lose myself."

Amy quirked an eyebrow at him. "You're not suicidal, are you?"

"Nothing like that." He waved his trowel in dismissal. "I just have to choose whether to follow in the footsteps of my parents or strike out on my own."

Amy pulled her own trowel out of the dirt and sat back on her heels. "If this means anything, I'd vote for myself. It's that skin thing. Because I'm the one who has to live in it and with it."

Grissom found Amy's offhand snap analysis accurate and to the point. He looked over at her. "Thank you, Amy. That was just what I needed to hear."

She rocked on her heels and began working again. "Not a problem. If you want, we can talk anytime, and it doesn't have to be on our knees." She grinned, wrinkling her freckled nose. "Hint, hint, I like beer."

Grissom for the first time in a long time actually smiled a genuine smile. "I like beer too." And with that he got up, brushed off his knees and hands, gathered his tools and bucket, and left his flower garden plot behind, feeling that he had crossed an important threshold.

As he walked off, Amy watched him carefully. She had been assigned to him at the start of first semester. Amy, hardly a freshman herself, was a powerful empath and telepath, who tracked imposters, interlopers, and the like for the campus' security force. As appropriate, she would even tap into their thoughts, but only if necessary. She had some serious ethical standards about that.

Returning to her plot, Amy spoke softly into her hidden mic. "Andrew Grissom is struggling with his conscience. We're getting through, but he's under considerable pressure to perform or provide his minders with something. Just what that something is, I don't know, but it has something to do with President Silver Moon, Dr. Makris, and Mr. Stone."

"Good job, Amy!" babbled out Joshua Remington, the newly promoted head of the campus' IT and Security Department. "We've been tracking his e-mail traffic, and some of it is extremely 'exotic' of late."

*   *   *

The chess match between the forces of intelligence and counter-intelligence has been ongoing for millennia. The leveraged ingenuity, subterfuge, and dishonesty can dizzy the mind. Now imagine the arcane and subtle world of the paranormal, where technology is augmented with so much more. As many times as CMES has sent its "emissaries" to infiltrate the Old

Oaks Academy, TIIIS has countered in multiple ways to assess the threat and disarm it if possible. The age-old adage, "Fight fire with fire," was the iron-clad standard, where most times there was no black and white. And, to be frank, to expect to find such absolutes would be going on a fool's errand.

Andy Grissom was just the latest example. His detection began with his application to the academy. His *normal* parents represented the first red flag, as latent sensitives or even highly-gifted ones were typically the product of good genes. This made TIIIS consider the possibility that Grissom was adopted, and after some investigation, found out that was indeed the case. Andrew Grissom turned out to be none other than the bastard scion of the Dark One, William Alexander. Even better, his authentic birth certificate as Andrew Alexander revealed that his true age and the one entered in his application did not match. Digging a bit deeper, TIIIS discovered that the young man had attended and matriculated from Brown University.

The second red flag on Grissom was based upon his northeastern upbringing and the prep schools he had attended, many of which were known CMES recruiting bases. Peer pressure is a powerful thing.

But even more damning, TIIIS security pulled up the membership records purloined from *The Gathering*'s own database. Here, Grissom's adoptive father and mother appeared not only as members in good standing, but also as donors. That his father had represented *The Gathering* in several legal cases involving black market and counterfeit membership cards to that exclusive coven only closed the book on Andy Grissom's background and upbringing.

Still, TIIIS accepted Grissom's application and allowed him on campus. Why? To turn the man into a double agent. But before that could happen, Amy O'Rourke was assigned to monitor his state of mind and his movements. Meanwhile, his instructors and lecturers had been alerted about him as well. Why? So they would be sure to engage him in classroom discussions, thought exercises, student activities, and *indirectly* inundate the young man with ambiguous experiences that would *directly* challenge his initial brainwashing. To date, the TIIIS IT and Security Department had a ninety-three-percent success rating at turning infiltrators into allies.

*   *   *

Joshua Remington, or Josh, was a befreckled, red-headed IT maven and security veteran who had survived the CMES attack on the Falls Church, Virginia, technical facility three years back and the Christmas Eve helicopter raid on the campus chapel the year after. During that last event, he was wounded several times, while defending the campus' staff and student body, whom he considered his own family.

Skinny, brilliant, and creative, Josh was amazed by

the bold stupidity of CMES—and Andrew Grissom was only the latest case. For a Second Class Adept—that is by CMES standards—Grissom was dumb as a stump when it came to IT security and cell phone awareness. He might have made sure to be off campus when his handlers contacted him, but the IT department easily monitored his communications 24/7 ever since the first red flag appeared. And when Grissom's minders asked him to report on Silver Moon, Makris, and Stone, alarm bells went off. Josh sent Amy into action.

*   *   *

Two days later, Amy spied Grissom walking toward his dorm after his last lecture of the day and decided to collect.

"Say, hey der', farmer," she greeted with her best smile.

The opener stopped the northeasterner dead in his tracks, whose mind had been a million miles away.

Grissom stared blankly at the attractive woman with auburn hair. "I'm no farmer."

"Could have fooled me. Why just two days ago we were up to our elbows in garden mulch."

Recognition flashed on his face. "Oh, I'm so sorry, Amy. I didn't recognize you without your head bandana."

She played along, crossing her arms and putting on a pout. "Boy you really know how to sweet-talk a girl."

"I'm sorry Amy. It's just that I have had a lot on my mind lately."

"Well, I have an idea. It's Thursday, it's five o'clock, and I'm thirsty. How about you joining me for a beer at the pub in Old Main?"

He smiled. "You mean the Acorn? Great idea!"

"Do you have an I.D.?"

"Uh, uh yeah, I sort of do," he said sheepishly.

"Then let's go. Time's a wasting, farmer."

After their third mug, Amy began steering the conversation toward Grissom's existential crisis. After the fourth beer, Grissom, a bit bleary-eyed, opened up.

"My folks are country-club wannabe snobs."

"Wow! That's a mouthful. Say that ten times fast," Amy goaded.

"No! I really mean it," he said darkly.

"And you don't want to be that? A 'country-club wannabe snob'?"

"No, that's not for me. Ever since I arrived here, I have been doing a whole bunch of thinking about things, especially after studying *The Knot of Eternity*."

"Such as?"

"Who I am and what I *really* want to be." He said tightly gripping his mug.

"That's some pretty heavy-duty thinking there, farm boy. We all go through that, ya' know."

"Yeah, I suppose. But I'm adopted, Amy. I checked. And what my folks want me to be, I don't think I can do."

"Like?"

Grissom now glanced about furtively. Seeing that no one was in ear-shot, he leaned forward over the small table and confessed. "Amy, I have to be true to myself. Not to be … is … well … an awful thing."

"So what's this 'awful thing'?" Amy said while leaning in too.

He swallowed. His eyes were swimming in beer, but she caught his sincerity in there too. "Betray a good and decent people."

Amy blinked in surprise. "Betray whom?" She dared to ask.

"Our president, President Silver Moon for one. Dr. Makris and Mr. Stone for another."

Amy grabbed his forearm. "Our president, Andy, is a good woman. Anyone who would want you to betray her is just, flat, wrong. As for the other two, well, don't get me started. They're the salt of the earth."

"That's how I feel too," he slurred, speaking a little too loudly.

She hushed him. "Are your parents paying for your education here?"

"No. Other folks are."

Amy let go that murky detail. "So if you decide not to betray these fine people, you get to live in your own skin."

"Yeah."

"Do you feel better?"

"Yeah, I do. As far as I'm concerned, I'm over

with trying to be my parent's lap dog. 'Our son did this, our son did that.' I'm sick of it."

"Have you ever met Betsy, or Makris, or Stone?"

"I had a class with both, but who's Betsy?"

"Why Betsy Silver Moon, farmer."

"No, I haven't. What's she like?"

"I thought you would never ask."

*   *   *

"Jesus, O'Rourke! Do you know what time it is?" A groggy Josh Remington breathed hard into his phone.

"Yeah, Remington, I do. Now listen up. I think Andy Grissom's ready to be brought into the barn."

Josh was now fully awake, "What do you suggest?"

"A visit from Mr. Stone. He has this way about him. Grissom respects quiet, no-bullshit strength. Points for him."

"Understood. Anything else?"

"Yeah, I think I need another beer."

"Have one on me!" And Remington killed the connection with a laugh. *Who would ever believe that Dr. Amy O'Rourke was perhaps the best psychoanalytical interrogator in the country, much less a Class Four Adept?*

CHAPTER 24

Grissom nervously made his way toward the student mess hall for lunch, his head in a whirl. Last night's drunken talk with Amy had caught him short, and he feared he had said too much. Not that anything he had said was a lie. Actually, it was the whole truth. But he'd told her that he was adopted, and that was just too much to share. He should have known better.

The northeasterner's stomach grumbled for the third time and he picked up his pace, head down, frowning, and more than a bit embarrassed with himself.

As Grissom reached out to grab the stout door handle of the mess, its bronze shiny with use, another hand beat him to it, opening the heavy oak portal.

"I got it," a deep voice said.

Looking over his shoulder and up, Grissom blanched as he caught himself staring into a pair of older, wiser eyes. "Oh, thank you, sir … ah, Mr. Stone."

"Not a problem. I'm starved. Mind if I join you?"

"Uh, sure…"

"You're Grissom, isn't that right?"

"Yeah."

"I remember now, you always sat in the back near the wall. Good defensive choice. Are you former military?"

"Nope."

Minutes later, after both men had worked their way through the lines. They sat down at a table near a quiet corner—Stone's favorite. He and the venerable Mr. Henry, his mentor, had often sat here to commiserate about a beer's quality or how best to deal with CMES.

Grissom looked around, unsure by this turn of events. "Uh, you eat here often?"

"Believe it or not, this is the best grub around." The Lictor of Magic took a massive bite out of one of his two loaded-down cheeseburgers. Instead of a side of fries, to please his wife, he had selected a Caesar salad.

Grissom had opted for a bowl of chili smothered with onions and cheese, several slices of black bread with butter, and an apple. Noting this, Stone commented, "You eat too healthy. Life is short. Cheeseburgers are the way to go." He took another bite.

The northeasterner couldn't help but smile at that revelation from a man, who, in his mind, had seen it all. With his face in his chili, he felt Stone's eyes on him and a curious warmth tickling the back of his mind.

"Just how old are you?" his former instructor pointedly asked.

Surprised by the sudden question, and almost snorting chili through his nose, Grissom slipped and said, "Twenty-three."

"I thought as much. So this isn't exactly your first rodeo, is it, Mr. Grissom."

Grissom wiped at his mouth with a brown recycled

napkin. "Uh, I don't know what you mean, Mr. Stone."

"Yeah, and virgins always remain virgins until after their wedding day." The big man smirked from across the table as he stabbed at his salad.

The warmth left his mind. Grissom grew suddenly cold. "You just scanned my mind, didn't you!" he furiously whispered.

"Yep."

"Ethically, that's a form of rape, Mr. Stone!"

"Yep."

"I could press charges with the dean." Grissom threatened with his best glare. He was intimidated by Stone's off-handed coolness.

"Yep, you could. So what's your next move?" Stone now leaned in on his elbows, over his empty plates. "By the way, your chili is getting cold. You might want to go over there and microwave it."

Grissom did, more to reclaim his composure than to reheat his meal.

Upon returning, he found Stone munching on a third cheeseburger. "Damn, I just love these." He chewed from the corner of his mouth so he could speak. "They put garlic, pepper, and onions in the meat. Makes all the difference in the world."

Grissom stubbornly focused on his chili.

"So you think Daniel Craig, an actor, playing a fictional character, is 'way cool'?"

The northeasterner almost choked a second time. "You bastard!"

"You'll have to do better than that, Mr. Grissom. I have been called far worse by quite frightful entities more times than I can count." Another bite.

"Why are you doing this?"

Stone wiped the mustard from the corner of his mouth and looked the young man square in the eyes. "Because, sir, you are a potentially hostile intruder on this campus, and I am its guardian. I don't need a reason."

Grissom began backpedaling in his mind. "But …"

"No buts, Mr. Grissom. You're too old to be a freshman. In addition to protecting this campus, I am the guardian of the good and the destroyer of evil. You know this. You sat in my demonology class last semester. When it comes to evil, I'm all over it. By the way, I witnessed the death of your natural father."

Grissom's face turned a pasty white, but curiosity got the better of him. "You knew my … father?"

"Yes. But not as a friend."

Grissom leaned forward. "Tell me about him!"

Stone considered for a minute. "Are you absolutely sure?"

"Yes … please."

Stone rose and moved their food trays over to an empty table and returned. Grissom hadn't moved a muscle. He just sat there with his hands tightly folded in front of him, almost like a choirboy waiting for his blessing.

"As best as we can tell, you were born in

Manhattan while William Alexander was the regional director of CMES North America. He ruled his region from the penthouse of a building I helped destroy."

"*The Gathering* building?"

"Yes."

A flood of mixed emotions ebbed and crested within Grissom, and Stone kept his silence to allow it.

After several moments, Grissom said, "That explains a lot, why my *step*-parents stayed in the northeast, my father's job at *The Gathering* ... But what about this William Alexander, my natural father? My step-parents never mentioned him."

Stone looked down at his massive and callused hands. "Where to start?" Now looking deeply into Grissom's eyes. "What I am about to tell you will be difficult to hear, but I know that you can handle it. I also know that you have it in you not to follow in your father's footsteps, that you can be your own man."

Stone took a deep breath. "William Alexander lived a long, long life—as in, centuries long. His original name was da Ziliolo. His place of birth was Renaissance Venice. He sold his soul to a demon for the ingredients of a magical draught that extended his life. In time, he became quite a wizard, gathering demonic spells in an awesome and frightful book, which he then used against his enemies. With it he built a reputation and earned the nickname The Dark One."

Grissom quietly sat, holding his head in his hands, listening, but not believing what his ears were telling him, for nowhere had he heard any of this before.

Stone rubbed his thick thumbs over each other. "Mr. Grissom, I realize that this is a lot to absorb in one sitting. But you do not have to be like your natural father. Far from it. You can be your own man. Follow your own drum, your own dreams."

Grissom didn't look up from the table. "How did he die?"

Stone's face twisted with regret and horror at the memory, but had to tell the young man, as there was a powerful lesson to be told in its telling.

"Your father, when he made his pact for the immortality ingredients, was tricked by the demon. Only after he began using it did he find out about its pitfalls. Things such as fresh water, which he could no longer drink or use; direct sunlight which he could no longer tolerate."

Grissom's blood chilled. "Had he become a vampire?"

"A reasonable assumption, but no, not quite. Do you know anything about auras and what they mean?"

"Yeah, I do."

"Can you see them?"

A shake of the head.

"Well, seeing them is a learnable skill. I would encourage you to pursue it. You're more than capable of doing so. When I encountered your father, at his death, his aura was the darkest, blackest that I had ever encountered with a mortal. His death ... was by immersion in Holy Water ... blessed by the Roman pontiff himself."

Grissom's jaw sagged open, and his eyes glazed over.

"I don't want to make that kind of mistake. I don't want to be like my father," Grissom choked out, his throat tight and dry.

"Frankly, Mr. Grissom, I am very pleased to hear that. Today, you possess a marvelous, light green aura, but when you first showed up in my class, it had a distinctly muddy quality to it. Apparently you like being here at Old Oaks. Our oak forests and gardens have worked their magic on you, eh? They often have that effect on folks. We try to intercept interlopers like you and convince them of the quality of our way of life. But in so many ways, you have achieved this on your own. You possess characteristics and virtues that your true father did not, and for that you should be congratulated." Stone reached over with his open hand.

Grissom took it and squeezed it back along with several tears. "Thank you for lunch and the talk, Mr. Stone. I appreciate it."

At that Stone generated his warmest of smiles, accompanied by a gentle psychic nudge to further buoy the young man's spirits.

"So, Mr. Grissom. The name my friends use in my company is J.J." He caught Grissom's gaze and held it. "Please use it."

Something passed between the two of them, and

Grissom slowly nodded. Then he smiled. "And mine's Andy."

Stone broke the grip and kicked back into his chair. "Well, Andy, tell me about what you want to be. You never know, I might be able to help out some."

CHAPTER 25

Betsy Silver Moon sat in the morning sun on her veranda with her favorite blue coffee mug. Fragrant vapors wafted as she scanned through her e-mail, erasing this and reading that. But today one communication, heavily encrypted, commanded her attention.

> Be advised a threat is underway. CMES-Rome has designated twenty-three members of our leadership—including you madam—for assassination. When, where, and how is not known. Seven independent coordinators have been tasked to execute this operation. More to follow.

After several rereads and a couple of deep breaths, Silver Moon stared off into the distance to compose herself, while her coffee went stone cold. She knew this source, personally.

A seasoned and experienced warrior of the Cold War, Duncan Hicks could speak five languages in various dialects. His face was unremarkable, his stature slight, and he was easily lost in a crowd. But Hicks possessed a Class Four Adept rating. Best of all, he held a part-time supernumerary position within CMES-Rome. The irony was, that while CMES had infiltrated the Old Oaks Academy many times, the coven never seemed to consider that the same might happen to it. Although it would perform sweeps for electronic probes, spend an inordinate amount of money on external security devices and sensors, they believed themselves to be arrogantly immune to organic intrusion. This is why the recent resurrection of their own dead so befuddled them.

Twenty-three, and Silver Moon began ticking off in her mind just who that might include.

My God, that's all of our top leadership! That would hamstring TIIIS and cause our allies to flee. How should I deal with this without showing our hand?

Within minutes she ran through a laundry list of options, she discarded them all, and decided to fly to Old Oaks Academy. Once there, she had three individuals to talk to. She needed counsel from her experts face-to-face. And then she had to consider a similar, and perhaps confirming report, from a CMES plant within the student body.

*   *   *

Amy busied herself in the flower garden, turning over the soil, removing nascent weeds and anything else that offended her eye. With her bucket half-full, she sensed a presence, stopped, sat back on her heels, and saw Andy Grissom smiling down at her.

"So where are your tools, farmer?" she asked with a genuine smile.

Walking over to his neighboring plot, the northeasterner squatted down. "Amy, I don't know who you are, or what you are, but I want to thank you nonetheless."

"Huh? For what?"

"I just got through having lunch with J.J. Stone. He's a real keeper."

"So?"

"So, I figure you talked to him about me. And for that, you have my thanks."

Amy went back to her gardening, furiously thinking about how to deal with this awkward moment.

"Have I said something wrong, Amy?"

She looked up again and smiled. "No, Andy. You didn't say anything wrong. I'm just happy for you."

Amy got back to her gardening, looking down to hide her tears of joy.

*   *   *

"Betsy," Stone said over the phone, "we just might be in luck."

"How?" Silver Moon flatly asked.

"Because the campus IT and Security Department has just identified another CMES plant within our student body. This young plant, however, we have turned. When all of this is said and done, by the way, we will have to provide him with a new identity and location."

"Consider that done. But what can this plant do for us *now*?" Silver Moon's voice was all business.

"In the past, he was contacted to report in specifically about your whereabouts, mine, and Melaina's. He has an e-mail account with which to do this."

Silver Moon understood and smiled. "Have Remington vet that e-mail, even ping it if necessary, in order to access its veracity. When I am on campus, I want to meet this young man."

*   *   *

The meeting took place in the president's temporary on-campus office in Old Main's tower. Silver Moon wanted to have her discussion with Grissom there for several reasons, not the least being privacy. Stone delivered the young man to the unmarked wooden door, knocked twice, turned, and said, "Go in, Andy, kick ass, and make some history." He then walked away.

Tentatively Grissom held the door knob and then turned it to enter.

Inside he found a tiny Native American woman, middle aged, typing rapidly on her laptop.

"Come on in and sit. I'll just be a moment," she told him, not looking up.

After several stabs of her keyboard, which Grissom recognized as a shutdown, she closed the device, turned, and said, "You must be Mr. Andrew Alexander-Grissom. Is that correct?"

Grissom jerked at hearing the hyphenation of his

name. "That is correct. Who are you?"

"I'm Betsy Silver Moon, the international president of this society. I believe that CMES has asked you to report on me and two others."

The northeasterner blinked at her directness and all that it represented.

She eyed him for a few moments. Then, when he didn't say anything, she continued. "Are you going to report my whereabouts to your minders, Mr. Alexander-Grissom?"

Grissom had felt the fire in her gaze, but also a strange confidence about her. He could look her in the eye. He shook his head. "No, ma'am."

"Why not?"

"Because I have decided to live in my own skin, be my own man, and follow my own path."

"Pretty words, Mr. Alexander-Grissom. Pretty words. But that's all they are. There is a saying, 'Once betrayed, twice betrayed.' Are you familiar with it?"

"Yes, but I think it goes, 'a man who betrayed you once would betray you twice.'"

"Yes, thank you. So why should I believe you?"

"Only my actions will serve as proof."

"Huh. Good answer, but once again, a pretty one. But given that my life is potentially on the line, I require more ... proof. Are you willing to provide it?"

He suddenly felt less confident. "Sure ..."

"Mr. Alexander-Grissom, in our business, nothing is ever 'sure.'"

"Yes, ma'am."

Silver Moon rubbed at her chin. She leaned forward against the office desk, her fingers lightly intertwined before her. "Andrew, have you ever consciously allowed someone to scan your mind?"

"Not to my knowledge."

"Have you ever been hypnotized?"

"Don't think so."

"Would you allow me, trust me, to do so?"

"Sure—," just catching himself—"Yes, ma'am."

The president got up from behind her desk and stood behind Grissom. "I am going to place my fingertips on your face and forehead."

"Just like Spock does with a mind-meld?"

"Just like that," she said with a hint of bitter humor in her voice. "Now close your eyes and relax."

Silver Moon's cool fingertips felt wonderful, restful, and strangely warm and comforting. Grissom's breathing became shallow, his pulse dropped into a resting state, and he began to lightly snore. Six minutes later, Silver Moon, still holding his head, gently shook him awake.

"How do you feel, Andy?"

He blinked. "I feel great, rested."

"Good."

The president sat down once again with a sigh.

"So, how did I do?"

"Andy, you don't recall it, but you have experienced more than most mortals deserve."

"Like what?"

"You certainly *deserve* to know the full story, but now is not the time. Right now your ... spirit, for the lack of a better word ... is healing itself. Allow that natural process to continue and complete its course, and then take on 'the rest of the story.' I know my answer does not satisfy you right now, but it is the best answer for you in the long term. But for the moment, you are healing well. Take heart in that."

"You make it out as if I'm some sort of tortured victim."

Silver Moon smiled. "Nice try at phishing, Mr. Alexander-Grissom. For the moment, that's all you're going to get from me."

*   *   *

Later that evening, at the Stones' on campus faculty residence, Betsy Silver Moon and *Monsieur* Henri Dexter joined the couple for a traditional, homemade, Egyptian dinner. Melaina had gone all out, with a multi-course banquet, plentiful wine (that she did not partake in), and good conversation.

"My dear friends," Silver Moon began, "I asked J.J. and Melaina to host this meal so that we may talk about something that has come to my attention."

The president looked down into her lap and then continued. "There is a tangible threat to our society. In all, some twenty-three of us have been targeted for assassination—in essence, our entire international leadership, including you Melaina and your husband. In addition, there is a similar report from a CMES plant, which while not as detailed, also threatened the three of us. What should I do about it?"

Dexter was the first to comment. The well-seasoned Frenchman, expert in offensive and defensive magic, he was one of the few chapel survivors of the Christmas Eve Raid. "Cut off the head of the snake, and the snake's ability to bite withers."

Silver Moon nodded. "Brilliantly put, Henri, but to do that would mean that we have targets—which we don't."

"Pull those threatened and hide them in The Vault." Stone suggested, referring to the secret underground chamber beneath the Old Main building on the campus.

"A sound suggestion, J.J., but by doing so, we would tip them off that we are aware of their plan. And then there's the sixty-four-dollar question, when would we release that haggling bunch?"

"Where did the news of this threat originate?" Melaina asked.

"CMES-Rome."

"Those ungrateful bastards," the Egyptian witch muttered. "We should have left them to stew in their ancestor's hatred."

Silver Moon nodded. "Personally, I had sincerely hoped for some sort of *détente*, but I was wrong."

"Can we warn those on the list without having a leak?" J.J. asked.

"Doubtful. Right now, only you three and one other know of this threat."

"Then you need to bait the assassins." Stone suggested. "When the attack comes, the assassins are discovered."

Stone's comment seemed to jar something loose in *Monsieur* Dexter's mind, as he began unconsciously tapping his front teeth with one of his long, boney fingers. All noticed this tick and waited quietly for the man to speak.

After several sips of wine from the others, the Frenchman finally said, "Perhaps we should look at this problem from an aggressive point of view, instead of being just reactive."

Makris said, "How can we target the assassins before they commit their murders? What specifics about these murderers can we gather to magically and perhaps remotely stop them?"

"Could such a thing even be done?" Silver Moon asked.

Makris nodded. "But we must know the identities of the assassins. We need specifics."

"*Madam* are you referring to voodoo?" Dexter bluntly asked Makris.

"Yes, Henri, but a much more ancient variety."

"Ah … that would be delicious." The Frenchman nearly swooned.

"Honey, what kind of specifics would you need?" Stone put to his wife.

"Authentic names and mailing addresses so we can send a small parcel or letter." Makris stopped for a moment, biting her lip. Then she smiled and looked up. "In fact, Henri, we just might be able to cut off the head of that snake you mentioned. One target would be infinitely easier to deal with than a list of assassins. So who is this attack's organizer?"

"I have some homework to do," Silver Moon quietly said. "I believe I can get that information. Now, for the rest of you, continue thinking, but keep your thoughts close."

Three nods.

CHAPTER 26

What is the birth name and p.o. address for this leader of surprises?

That is all Silver Moon wrote in her encrypted return e-mail to her CMES-Rome mole. She kept it short, sweet, and also purposefully vague just in case it was intercepted. Given the importance of the initial communication, she fully expected to hear back within the next forty-eight hours.

In the meantime, she fretted briefly about Mr. Alexander-Grissom. In many ways, he was a threat, a ticking time bomb of sorts. If only they could get past this Rome threat, she would personally cut all those fusible bomb wires in his head and set the young man free.

*   *   *

Birth name was difficult to come by:

LUCIA d'SANTA FLORENCIA

Address:

C.A. Lucia
Via Frascati 33
00078 Monte Porzio Catone RM
ITALY

*   *   *

Given the engrained proclivities of expert spell whisperers and extreme forensic psychics, Melaina had to fashion her special mailing with the greatest of care. Of concern was that not a trace of her DNA could be resurrected, so she made a visit to a local hardware store and grocery to gather her supplies.

Her preparation was key. Melaina made her kitchen into a witch's laboratory by thoroughly washing and wiping down all of its surfaces with paper towels dripping with apple vinegar. When finished, the room glistened and smelled divine.

She then sterilized the containers and mixing implements she was going to use. As for her purchased ingredients, she washed or placed them in Ziploc bags until needed.

The Alexandrian witch performed this entire process while wearing a disposable paper painting suit, a filter-paper mask, latex gloves, and disposable booties. Dripping wet from sweat within this near-surgical containment, Melaina wondered what her colleagues might think if one stopped by for a visit—that perhaps a large white marshmallow had sprouted arms and legs.

Once her preparations were complete, Melaina went to her bathroom, stripped, luxuriated in the shower, and got dressed in fresh protective gear.

The computer generated letter stated that the bearer had won an all-expense paid vacation to the French Rivera. She treated the letter as if it was highly contagious, which it was. She wore surgical gloves when she printed the letter and its envelope at her department's office. These she placed within an extra-large Ziploc bag. She had bought a ream of printer paper and box of envelopes from a common office supply instead of using the academy's supply—to remove herself as far as possible from detection.

Next, the Egyptian carefully applied to the letter a variety of layered spells and enchantments. To do so, Melaina concocted a goodly amount of lemon ink, which, while not totally invisible, is not readily noticed. This medium she made unique by affixed a spell to the liquid that further hid her identity as the conjurer from even the very best of spell whisperers. Now she could write with total anonymity.

Melaina's next task was to apply a trigger spell, written in ancient Egyptian Demotic, using the lemon ink, to the inside flap of the paper envelope. This tedious work she performed with the sharpened end of an easily disposable chopstick. With a care that she had learned from her school days at Oxford, and perfected throughout her research career, Melaina slowly wrote out the needful characters without one smear. She then placed the envelope on the kitchen counter to dry.

The envelope's trigger spell would remain inactive, dormant, and thus undetectable by any sensitive worth their salt. But the moment someone tore open or cut through the envelope's flap, the spell's words would be rent, and the mechanical energy imparted would awaken the spell and make it effective. At this point, the trigger spell was capable of doing something, and that special something was to summon another spell.

Melaina's final step called for the precise application of the actual death spell that would be invoked by the envelope's trigger spell. Here, the Egyptian witch labored over the reverse side of the congratulatory contest letter and produced it without blemish, all while within her confinement clothing. This conjuring, also written in Egyptian Demotic, she wrote out four times along the four edges of the letter's backside. This ensured that the spell would come into direct contact with the letter's recipient, a critical detail for the casting's success.

> I invoke you today, *Syrokkata.*
>
> You who dissolve the sinews, the ligaments, and the joints, you are to dissolve the sinews of Lucia d'Santa Florencia for all time.

Melaina included an additional phrase that would remove all evidence of her witchery. Given where this letter was to be sent, she felt the need for extra precaution.

> Once your dreadful task is completed, allow your breath to pass over and char these words beyond all recognition, and only then banish yourself to back from whence you came.

But Melaina's deadly post was not yet complete. She decided to introduce further camouflage to confuse any potential forensic investigators. The addressed envelope and its letter she slipped within a commercial mail carrier's rigid cardboard jacket. But even that jacket she made special by affixing the return address as that of the CMES-Paris coven and impressing on its back upper left-hand corner that coven's secret, uninked mark—a tiny *fleur-de-lis*.

Melaina then placed the completed mailing jacket and letter within a sterile plastic slip of its own. The only thing left now was to deliver this deadly missive to a commercial drop box in Paris, France. This the Egyptian witch would accomplish upon her arrival at the main terminal of Charles de Gaulle Airport. The flight there and back, just to send a letter, seemed silly and a colossal waste of resources, but Melaina's society must survive. That, alone, made the lengthy roundtrip worth it.

*   *   *

In this age of electronic communications via the Internet—e-mail, Twitter, Snap chat, Messenger, what have you—Julio still marveled that he held his job as a mail sorter. Apparently, some people had never heard of a *fax*. But he shrugged it off and didn't care when the post arrived each day in its large brown burlap bag. In many ways, the near-retiree welcomed the moment to chat with the postal carrier, because once he closed and locked the tall vertical receiving door, he would be sitting on his backside for the rest of the day sorting and assessing for potential threats.

Julio, while getting on in years and stooped with an arthritic back, nonetheless possessed decades of experience psychically touching the post, looking for suspicious or threatening clues, sometimes even smelling them out. Every piece he handled, he did so with care, because Julio considered himself CMES' postal gatekeeper for "Mother Rome." In his mind, there was no greater honor.

This day's postal allotment he considered relatively light—maybe a kilo and a half total in weight. That meant the promise of a long lunch. He dumped the bag's contents onto his large stainless steel examination table—letters of all sizes, shapes, and colors. His arthritic hands began their sorting almost as if they had a mind of their own.

Julio's methodology was to initially touch everything and feel for that funny tingling sensation that signaled to his brain the presence of magic. When asked what his fingertips told him, he just smiled and snorted. "Doesn't your nose tell you what you smell? The frying of garlic and onions, the baking of bread, the roasting of sausages, the musty reek of fresh manure? My fingers feel magic, in all its varieties and kinds. Some smell good, others not."

On this day, nothing from the pile felt bad or

dangerous, and that was good. For the "bad," he had a special container that went directly to the incinerator. For the "good," that he sorted by department first, and then by individual, and here came into play Julio's second greatest asset—he was a gifted detective with an impeccable memory for detail.

Rapidly reading through the address headings, he began flipping the postal pieces into departmental piles. Some departments received practically no mail, while others seemed to thrive and depend upon it. Organizing further, Julio broke down each department's pile according to individual and once again, some never received anything, while others did.

Julio was far more than an experienced, latent sensitive. The man had an extraordinary sense for ferreting out the odd and out of place. It was said that Julio's hunches were better than some people's facts. And after handling and sorting the day's mail delivery, one packet just didn't feel quite right to the man, and for several reasons. Only rarely did any of the security staff receive physical mail, because they communicated exclusively via technology. Secondly, Lucia, that odd white vampire, never received anything. So he carefully examined the commercial mailing packet. It originated from the CMES-Paris coven. That prompted him to check the packet's back side. And yes, there was the enclave's impressed mark. Finally, he scrutinized where the packet had been picked up—the Paris airport. That, too, made sense. In fact, everything about this packet made sense, which caused the man to doubt himself.

"Julio, perhaps you're just getting old," he murmured as he returned the packet to the sorting table. As far as he was concerned, the entire lot could be delivered. He loaded up the four-wheeled cart for tomorrow's morning distribution.

CHAPTER 27

DeSalvo picked up the white vampire precisely at ten that evening from her flat with his convertible Ferrari Testarossa. Dressed casually in slacks, a silk jacket, and open-collared shirt, she wore bright red heels with a black tube dress and nothing more. With the top down, the howl of the shiny liquid-black vehicle's motor filled the couple's ears with a relentless, throbbing, spitting mechanical snarl. With each gear change, Lucia felt herself melting away into seat, wanting to mount the gear shift lever, and hammer away her virginity forever.

DeSalvo, sensing this, only drove the car harder and harder, taking *Autostrada* 24 east toward Tivoli, and before long, Rome was far behind them. Behind his seat, the chairman had thoughtfully placed a small cooler of "refreshments" for this evening's adventure, along with four long silk scarves.

"*Signore Presidente*, you drive so well," Lucia leaned over and cooed in his ear, as the wind whipped her auburn hair.

"*Si*, I used to be a race car driver. Lucia, did you know that?"

"No," the white vampire lied, but her eyes dilated nonetheless with excitement as her vampiric senses reached near-overload. The rich smell of the leather seats, the reek of the exhaust's unburned gasoline and motor oil, the luscious and urgent sound of that V-12 motor's high-RPM scream, William's heady papyrus body oil … she realized that all of this was just a prelude, a tease, for what she knew was coming. And Lucia dreamily welcomed it all.

DeSalvo drove for several more miles before turning off onto a secondary road that wound through hills covered with fragrant vineyards.

"Where are we?"

"On my estate. Patience."

The white vampire no longer had any "patience" after over some five hundred and twenty-odd years of existence.

Then the chairman pulled his vehicle onto a leveled area covered in white limestone gravel. It was an overlook with a magnificent view of Rome in the far distance to the left and Tivoli directly in front of them. All of this was framed in God's own universe clear as the eye could see.

"We have arrived," DeSalvo unnecessarily said.

"By the ancient gods, this is so beautiful."

"As are you, Lucia." The driver said huskily as he reached behind his seat and pulled out a bottle of wine and two glasses. "This is from my own private stock. It's a hearty red. I hope that you will like it."

Once he worked the cork free, he filled the glasses half-way and said. "A toast, to us."

They drank as one, eyes locked. "Why me, *Signore*?"

"Lucia, my name is William. Please use it."

"I shall … William. But why me?"

"Because I have watched you long enough from afar. Because you're beautiful, brilliant, and I want us to have a baby."

"That is all?" The white vampire said with a sultry tone.

"Oh no, Lucia. My estate needs you. It sorely needs a woman's presence to make it a home. With you, I have a brilliant partner with whom I can talk to, argue with, pour out my heart to, my frustrations. I need a woman to love, and raise a family with. Lucia, that is 'why' … you."

"But *Sign* … William, you know nothing about me. How can you make such a rash decision?"

DeSalvo smiled. "Listen to us, Lucia. I know all about you, I have studied you, and best of all, I have watched you in action. And just recently I overheard *Signore* Gnotti bitching about how you stole his ideas. What utter nonsense. That man cannot do anything but delegate. Am I right?"

A quick nod from behind her nearly emptied glass.

"And, Lucia, you are a unique, strong woman. And when you feed, the flush that comes to your face overwhelms me with passion. No one has ever had that affect upon me, ever."

"William, it is I who is overwhelmed. I do not know what to say."

"This is my second and final overture, Lucia. Will you be my mate?" And with that, DeSalvo took out of his jacket's side pocket a small black velvet box. He opened it and the ring inside glistened in the starlight.

Lucia held a hand to the side of her face in silent, open-mouthed wonder at the sight.

"Lucia?"

The white vampire, reach out and casually dropped her wine glass outside of the vehicle, sprang over the consol and landed on top of him, held his head, and smothered his smoothly shaven face with kisses. Her own face damp with tears of sheer joy.

DeSalvo kissed her back, hard. Then, finally coming up for air, "I guess that was a 'yes'?"

"Indeed it was my husband," a husky voice replied as she removed the heavy gold heirloom from its box and slipped it on.

"It fits my hand … perfectly."

Looking up into her shining face, "As I said, Lucia, I have been studying you for quite some time."

"I see, my husband. Now, do you have any plans for ridding me of my current affliction?"

"Affliction?"

"Yes, my husband … my virginity." Her voice smoldered.

Discarding his wine glass as well, "In fact, Lucia, I do have a remedy for your 'affliction.' But I believe its sacrifice should be celebrated with something special. Let's get out of the car."

*   *   *

At first Lucia thought his idea curious, but soon came to understand its own kind of logic. Having been effortlessly picked up and carefully placed upon the center Ferrari's hood, DeSalvo gently secured her arms and legs in a most lascivious fashion, spread-eagling her lean and taunt body across it with four silk scarves bound to the spokes of the front wheels.

Giggling, "Now pray tell my husband, what do you have in store for me now?" As DeSalvo rustled away in the cooler behind his seat cushion.

Now holding up her head with one hand, "I offer you nourishment, my wife, one of your favorites I believe." As he pressed to her mouth a liter bladder of Type O blood.

Surprised, overjoyed, and yes always hungry, Lucia bit into the bladder and drank deeply. Never once did her eyes leave his as they dilated into solid black orbs in the evening's darkness.

The back-arching pleasure of being fed in such a loving way hit the white vampire like a wave. In near frenzy at the feeding, her canines extended, her nails became long claws—another reason for her binding.

Once she had sucked the bag dry her skin flushed pink. "More, I must have more ..." And once again her husband offered another bladder of the red liquid, supported her head, while gazing upon her face that now had become a ruddy red blush. Finished, Lucia's eyes closed, one hunger sated, and moaned, "Take me now, my Willi. Please take me now ..."

DeSalvo, upon hearing his childhood name, instantly conjured the memory of his German-speaking mother, a loving Jew lost to the Holocaust, and tears freely streamed from his eyes. *Yes*, he thought, *she is indeed the one.*

He gently settled back Lucia's head upon the hood, and walked over to the front of the car. His hands slid up his bride's legs, thighs, and pushed her tiny dress up to her waist.

"Please my Willi, now …"

And Willi did, carefully, slowly, rhythmically. His wife's vocal encouragements only prolonged the journey that they both had been denied, but now so thoroughly enjoyed.

CHAPTER 28

When Melaina returned home from her first trimester physical, she found her husband laying in wait. He greeted her with a bunch of black-eyed Susans in a glass vase.

"So how did it go, Honey?"

"Everything went just fine. But Dr. Samuels was disappointed that you were not there. She firmly emphasized that we're a team. So next time, no excuses, Cowboy."

"Yes ma'am. You have my hallowed promise, so help me God." Then with a look of lechery, "Besides, I so love it when you-all go into witchy-mode." He said with a thick north Texas accent.

"Witchy-mode!"

"Yeah, that. When your eyes get all wild and frisky lookin'." Stone declared as he effortlessly scooped up his wife into his arms.

"What are you doing, Cowboy?"

"I'm fixin' to get all frisky, Gorgeous. How's about you?"

* * *

Grissom was right in the middle of a heady lecture in Ancient Religions when his device vibrated in his shirt pocket. He ignored it. Then it hummed once again like an angry bee. Checking it, he gulped when he saw the address—CMES-Rome. Surreptitiously, he withdrew the device and thumbed the needed keys.

> Must have all locations of all parties for two weeks
> hence. Respond immediately upon receipt.

A small trickle of sweat coursed its way down the middle of his back. *What am I to do? I have no idea where she will be two weeks out, much less where Makris and Stone will be. Will they accept that answer? They'll have to. Besides, if I did know, I would never tell them.*

Touching the "respond" icon, Grissom told the truth that he couldn't say whether or not any of the targets would be on campus. Touching the "send" icon, he felt relieved, but also a bit dirty. He needed to tell someone, but who? Then he had an idea.

*   *   *

After lecture, Grissom made his way over to Meyers Hall, a stout, thick fortification of a building faithfully constructed in the Romanesque Style. On its second floor he found the faculty office that he was looking for. He knocked twice on its heavy wooden door with a sealed metal grate and was rewarded with a voice from within, "Enter at your own risk."

Opening the door with a theatrical creak, he found Mr. Stone surrounded by open books, some piled upon one another. Looking up with a pair of reading glasses on, he greeted, "Andy, come on in and sit down. Glad you're here. I could use a break. What's on your mind?"

Nervous to be sitting in his office, but even more jittery about what he was about to divulge, Grissom instead asked, "What are you working on?"

Stone sensed the young man's heightened state, and answered his question. "Believe it or not, I'm working on an ancient Sumerian demon text, and try as I might, its translation eludes me. But I'll eventually break it." Taking off his glasses, the north Texan asked a second time, "So why did you climb all of those narrow stairs to visit me?"

Grissom answered by getting up, and closing the office's heavy door. Once reseated, "I just received an encrypted e-mail from CMES-Rome. They wanted to know where our president, you, and Dr. Makris would be in two weeks to today. That was the sum of it."

Stone rubbed at his forehead, "And what did you reply?"

"That I didn't know."

"Good answer. And, Andy, I'm really glad you came to me with this. When did you get the e-mail?"

"Less than an hour ago."

"Good." Then Stone reached for his office's landline and made a call. "Hello, Josh, how are you doing today?

"Great. Did Andrew Grissom get a suspicious looking e-mail in the past hour?

"Uh-huh. Yeah. Could you break its encryption?

"No? Well, don't bother. Grissom just told me what its content was."

"Yeah.

"Best brother."

"You know about my e-mails?"

"Absolutely Andy. We have to. Don't take this personally, but it's a dog-eat-dog world out there. So what did you make of the meaning behind it?"

"That someone at CMES-Rome is about to do something in two weeks."

"Yeah, that's my read as well. Something in two weeks. Damn that's a long time to worry." Stone said as he gazed off into the distance.

"Andy, you did the right thing. Anything else?"

"Nope."

"Then get the hell out of here. I have this Sumerian demon to beat."

As soon as Grissom closed his office door, Stone paused thirty seconds before he made another call.

"Hey Betsy. It's me.

"She's good. Got straight-A's on her first trimester exam." He paused, "Grissom just delivered us a timeframe.

"Two weeks. His minders wanted to know if you were going to be on campus two weeks out.

"Under no circumstances do I want you here.

"My suggestion? That beautiful meditation spot in the hills near the rattlesnake mound.

"Yeah.

"Bye. Will do."

Stone sat back in his office chair with a squeak. He hadn't lied to Grissom about the stress of worrying for two weeks. He also had this gut feeling that the entire "two week" thing might also be a ruse. After all, the "two" in the message could just as easily mean "two days." There was just no telling. Then, "what do you think, First Soul?"

I sadly must agree. 'There is no telling,' but I would counsel immediate preparation, heightened watchfulness, and the exercise of patience, as vexing a course as that might be.

* * *

Lucia was in a deep dive coordinating her e-mail messages and their returns with a complex Excel spreadsheet. It was the only way she could grasp the big picture on twenty-three targets. She was so deep that the white vampire hadn't heard the first knock on her cube's framing. Turning away from her task with a bit of frustration showing, she saw who it was. "*Signore Presidente*. What a surprise." She somehow managed to professionally say, but the softening of her eyes would have given her away to anyone who would have noticed.

"I thought that I would stop by and inquire about your latest special project and how it is progressing."

He said with a relaxed and boyish grin.

Without skipping a beat, "As well as possible. It is becoming obvious that it is hard to predict where twenty-three people will be at any one given moment."

"Of that I have no doubt. I was wondering are we being too ambitious?" As he glanced down at the golden object that dominated her ring finger.

The white vampire frowned. "No, I do not believe so *Signore*. We have discovered that well over one half have extremely predictable schedules, while a quarter we can relatively well predict where they will be. But as for the remainder," she shrugged, "they are indeed a challenge."

"So, at this moment, you believe that roughly seventy-five percent can be erased with one stroke?"

"Yes … I believe that, *Signore*."

"Excellent. Carry on Lucia." DeSalvo said with a roguish flip of his eyebrow he left his wife to her duties.

"Always, *Signore*," Lucia replied while flashing an errant tip of her tongue.

Turning back to her laptop, the newly promoted head of special projects dove once more into her coordination efforts. Probabilities and possibilities danced in her head. Her laptop chimed again, announcing a reply, and it was a good one. With a sick sort of glee she ticked off one more highly probable kill.

And then there came another, annoying knock on her cubicle's frame. *What does my adoring husband want this time?* But rather this time it wasn't him, but the distribution cleric with a piece of mail—for her of all people.

CHAPTER 29

Lucia sat in her cube in total astonishment. No one ever sent her physical mail. The consummate loner, she knew of no one to even correspond with. *Is this from my Willi?* Suspicious, just like the mail sorter had been, she checked all the commercial packet's details. Then she asked herself, *who knows me in the Paris coven?* As she spun the stiff packet by its opposing corners, causing it to become a twirling blur.

Who ... do ... I ... know? Then her curiosity got the better of her. *Time to find out,* as she grabbed the packet's tab and ripped out its reinforced string. Peering inside, the white vampire found a richly textured, cream-colored envelope with her name and address crisply typed across its face.

C.A. Lucia d'Santa Florencia
Via Frascati 33
00078 Monte Porzio Catone RM
ITALY

She paused to read, and reread the envelope. It had been so long since she had seen her full name printed out in such a manner that she caressed the type with her fingertips. Inundated by a flood of old memories, Lucia's eyes watered. Not enough to tear, but just enough to show that she was touched by the formality. Then and there she thought, *I am going to save this for*

another time, as she carefully placed the envelope on
the shelf before her, arranging it just so, where she
could enjoy its presence. And with that she returned to
her coordination tasks.

*   *   *

Silver Moon could take it no longer. An hour after
Stone's phone call the president placed all of TIIIS'
leadership on an unofficial notice of an unspecified
threat. Rationalizing to herself, it was the very least that
she could do for them. Then the dawn broke. *Our
society needs an emergency code for such situations.
Something innocuous, like a birth announcement, or the
celebration of someone's birthday.* She called Joshua
Remington and communicated her idea, which he
whole-heartedly agreed with. That done, she still felt
empty, lost, and at odds. *Damnit Betsy! You're the
president. Get a hold of yourself!*

Most of her colleagues around the world, however,
understood their president's vague warning, because
they knew her as not an alarmist. Almost as one, each
consulted their calendars and circled in red three days,
two weeks out, as being potentially hazardous to their
health. Several even cryptically replied, wished her a
fine vacation, a happy birthday, and the like, letting her
know that they understood. But as with any group, even
with everyone's e-mail address listed as a hint of
exclusivity, several could not make heads or tails of the

message. Of them, three actually called Silver Moon for clarification as to what her transmission meant. Yes, they were that dim.

Finished with those calls, Silver Moon bowed her head. *Most understood, thank God! Yet, a few apparently couldn't find their way out of a wet paper bag. Well, that's what Darwin Awards are for.*

*   *   *

After two hours of coordination, Lucia finished the update to her Excel spreadsheet that the white vampire had named "The Kill Sheet." Closing her laptop with finality, the mystery envelope above beckoned to her. With her curiosity now totally out of control, she could no longer resist its temptation. She reached up and tore open the linen envelope and opened the two folds of its contents, which she read once, twice, thrice. As she did the giggles began and built into snorting laughter.

This is good! She concluded. *Someone with an immense sense of humor has given me an all-expense paid vacation on the French Rivera! Imagine me, a white vampire, out in the bright Mediterranean sunshine! This is hysterical! This just must be from Willi.* Searching, she found no name, just the name of a well-known travel agency, its contact information, and the vacation award code.

With her tears of laughter still wet upon her face, the white vampire noticed that she was having an odd difficulty with her hands and so she put down the vacation award letter to rub them. But even that simple motion became challenging, as her wrists seemed to go numb and then limp without any control.

*   *   *

Four minutes later the in-house medics arrived at Lucia's cubical. They had to fight their way to get past all the rubber-necking staffers. Among them was DeSalvo.

What Dr. Andrea Gomez-Ortiz found shocked him to the core. His patient was flat on her back, motionless, with a strangely whitish-blue pallor that he identified as extreme hypoxia. His confirmation came from the patient's chest, which was not moving. Looking directly into the patient's stationary eyes, what he saw was silent horror and pure fear. She was still alive, but just barely.

Taking an arm to check a pulse, Gomez-Ortiz encountered something that he had never before seen— an arm that didn't seem to have any internal structure. Quite literarily, the arm sagged as if a boneless appendage like an octopus' tentacle. Quickly examining the woman's other limbs only confirmed the same observation. Tearing open the patient's shirt only revealed further horror. His patient couldn't breathe because the ribs and diaphragm had been reduced to a sagging gelatinous mass of organic material. Then, he distinctly heard his patient's death rattle—the final escape of air through her nose and mouth.

"*Dio mio*," the physician whispered. By his own reckoning, he had literally watched his patient expire within mere moments. Even worse, whatever had done this only continued as the woman's form horizontally sagged into the flooring.

"Get everyone back, now!" He ordered. "We may have a HAZMAT emergency here!"

While everyone scattered to save their skins, the physician attempted to get his patient onto a gurney lowered to its maximum. The only way that he could transfer the victim, was by carefully lifting her fast deteriorating remains with his open hands.

As Gomez-Ortiz struggled with his patient, no one noticed that the open letter and torn envelope on Lucia's desk had charred beyond recognition. The head of the snake had been dispatched.

*   *   *

Lucia's sudden demise absolutely crushed DeSalvo. But one action captured it all. For after Lucia had been removed from her cubical by the medical team, DeSalvo stood before it helpless, and freely tearing.

Then he saw it. A shiny thing lay next to her waste basket. Getting down on his hands and knees the chairman retrieved it—her wedding ring. It had fallen off her finger, a finger without substance.

* * *

Suffice it to say that his senior security man Kiel, who stood before him, was positively terrified by both what had happened to his staffer Lucia, but even more by his society's chairman, whose stony face glowed a ruddy red.

"I want an explanation *Signore* Kiel right *now*." DeSalvo said with a low growl.

Paul Kiel, once an executive of a Washington beltway alphabet soup agency and senior intelligence asset of the now defunct CMES-North American region, was totally clueless. Not being a sensitive within a paranormal community, Kiel had heavily relied on Lucia's nature and talents and now she was … gone.

"I don't have one, *Signore Presidente*. But what I do have are the charred remains of an envelope and letter that Lucia had opened. My surmise is that she had been attacked by something attached to those documents. Currently, the forensic lab is trying to make heads or tails of those destroyed remains. Frankly, sir, I think that exercise, while necessary, will come up empty. But, you never know. Perhaps some clue will be revealed."

"*Signore* Kiel, I don't like that answer."

"Respectfully, *Signore*, I cannot say anything else. You hired me to deal with facts. Currently, I don't have any, and currently we don't know who did this. But this is not my first crisis. Only four hours have passed.

Allow my people to dig into this. There is no such thing as a perfect crime. When under close scrutiny, clues appear. Connections are made. *Signore*, all I am asking for is forty-eight hours."

"*Signore* Kiel, you have twenty-four hours. But be advised, if you fail me *Signore* Kiel, I will not be firing you—I will be burying you—alive in the catacombs of the Fourth Level!"

*   *   *

Twenty-three hours into the investigation, one of Kiel's people found something while culling through the voluminous CMES database. It was the curious death of a member from Alexandria, Egypt, a physician named Dr. Hisham Ibrahim Matraway. The content of the coroner's report is what caught the attention of the security researcher.

> Subject died from asphyxiation due to the sudden loss of the diaphragm's structural integrity. Death was secondarily caused by multiple constrictions of the aortic network as the subject's skeletal structure had failed.

"*Mio Dio!* I must immediate contact *Signore* Kiel and *Doctore* Gomez-Ortiz!" In a virtual flash, both men retasked resources on this one, lone report of a man's death and the attendant circumstances. While not exactly the same, the conclusion reached by the

Alexandrian coven was the execution of an ancient, obscure, or totally *de novo* spell had claimed the physician. In any case, Kiel realized that he was up against something new which in the paranormal realm was *extremely* rare. Even with his limited experience, the security head knew that either case could potentially augur in a dangerous imbalance to a world based upon known rules and well-understood methodologies.

"Explain all of this to me *Signore* Kiel." DeSalvo ordered.

"What we have is a spell whisper's nightmare *Signore Presidente*. A spell, or better a series of interlaced spell's, which totally deny the adept's ability to identify the conjurer."

"That, *Signore* Kiel, is impossible." The Italian dismissed with a wave of a hand.

"Respectfully, *Signore Presidente*, you should not dismiss the 'impossible'. After all, that is our business, is it not?"

"Okay, Kiel, humor me." The man growled.

"Imagine the following, *Signore*. You wish to kill an individual with magic, anonymously. In essence, commit the perfect crime. How would you go about it? Up until now, we have relied upon the crafty abilities of spell whispers to uncover such things. But what if the magic targeted specifically those adepts? Blocked their senses? Clouded their finely honed abilities? That, *Signore*, is what we are up against.

"The process to achieve this miracle is surprisingly

straightforward and brilliant. It is nothing more than the layering of many simple spells, which like a length of linked chain, depend upon one another. We theorize that it begins in a near-sterile environment, like a laboratory. The adept is clothed like a researcher in garments and headgear that prevent any DNA contamination. This, in and of itself, is a tactic directed specifically against the forensic spell whisperer. In the mortal realm, such procedures have been employed and perfected over the past several decades.

"To continue, while so clothed and protected the adept builds, step-by-step, link-by-link, a series of spells that not only can kill an individual, but then destroy the mechanism of transmission itself, leaving behind absolutely no evidence that any spell whisper can analyze."

During this explanation, DeSalvo leaned into his desk, his head in his hands while he tried to concentrate. But two items competed for his attention. The loss of his wife practically immobilized him. But the other was the overall ramifications for the living.

After successfully swallowing back a sob, the chairman said, "What you are telling me is that the perfect crime can be committed."

"*Si, Signore Presidente.* But there are further considerations about the murder of the Alexandrian physician. In comparison to what we have just experience here, that murder was clumsily executed, whereas this one was a far more practiced and skillful act. *Signore*, I cannot stress this point enough. What we have just experienced is unique. Uniqueness in the paranormal realm is not a good thing, as there always has to be a balancing factor. Some sort of a corrective, a counter. But this method of conjuring represents a dangerous escalation, an open license to kill without recourse."

"*Signore* Kiel, is there any hint of who might have done this?"

"Not directly, *Signore Presidente*, but if I was a betting man, I would accuse TIIIS of this act."

"Why do you say that?"

Kiel steepled his fingers before his face in thought. "*Signore Presidente*, in my business, security and espionage, rarely does one have absolute proof of guilt. Instead, we work in a murky world of probabilities, tendencies, and yes, even outright hunches. Everything I know about TIIIS is that they do not overtly act, but when they do, it is with stealth and subtly. Their tendency is to reactively respond to injury or the threat of it." Now raising his finger for emphasis, "The only time that TIIIS became overtly proactive was during and immediately after The Contest in the Desert. That was the only time that they turned their Lictor of Magic loose."

"Can you give me an example of this proactive activity?"

"Most certainly, the sudden extermination of the Barcelona coven, and prior to that, the very public murders of several Eastern and Western European members of our coven. All of these took place immediately after the Contest.

"*Signore,* to continue, the conjurer of the Alexandrian physician's murder used ancient magic, ancient Egyptian magic, written in hieroglyphs, and even employed an *ushabti* magical figurine to ingeniously complete the casting. *Signore,* TIIIS is our most bitter enemy. I find it more than intriguing that among their brethren is an Alexandrian witch, who is a published scholar in Egyptian Demotic magic. Even more fascinating is her husband, a published scholar in ancient Sumerian demonology—their very own Lictor of Magic.

"*Signore,* if we follow this thread of speculation to its logical conclusion, that means TIIIS somehow, someway, became aware of Lucia's project and assassinated her before she could execute it. That means someone among us is a mole, a spy, *Signore.*"

DeSalvo sat back in his chair. *They* have a spy within *our* coven, here, in Rome. Frankly, upon reflection, it didn't surprise him in the least. *We* had spies at their campus in western Pennsylvania. Such a reality was the inevitable way of things.

But did that have to be? In that instant, he realized the real problem was him, fueled by his ego and emotional desire to irrationally injure and harm TIIIS, only exacerbated by his inability to counter their clever ploys and tactics. It always had been so, for whenever he tried, he had always failed—*The Gathering* recruitment project, the Contest in the Desert, the vampire Sigmund—clumsy failures all. His dear Lucia was just the latest. DeSalvo then realized his approach and policies were just as brutish and monolithic in their purpose as was his predecessor Giovanni Presto—a hateful man that he despised intensely. TIIIS, as much as it pained him to admit, had once again brilliantly defended itself. Then he had another thought. He had been forced into "retirement" once before, perhaps now it was time again, but he had to cut his losses. He made a decision.

"*Signore* Kiel, I want Lucia's special project shut down and disbanded, right now. Am I clear?"

"*Si, Signore Presidente.*"

When once alone in his cubical, DeSalvo, distraught, again made a decision, this time to do something that he had never before considered in his wildest of dreams. He dialed a number.

Meanwhile, of Lucia's seven assassination coordinators, only three obeyed their chairman's order to shut down the operation. The other four, relatively blessed by their highly predictable targets, stayed the course. They rightly believed that Rome's leadership had lost its nerve.

On the appointed day and time as established by Lucia, sub-governor Niall Ryan of Dublin was snuffed out by a car bomb. In the US, sub-governor John Strong of Maine was poisoned during a public luncheon. In

Canada, sub-governor Nathan Fournier of Halifax, while out walking his dog, was struck and killed by a hit-and-run vehicle. Demetrius Skuria of Nicosia was brutally slashed while strolling through the late-morning central marketplace of that city. He finally expired in the local emergency ward. The sub-governor of Amman, Yosef Hamdan, he and his body guards were blown to bits by a roadside bomb. And finally, in the US, the Midwestern regional governor, Klara Kotula, died horribly in a fiery car accident. In short, six individuals met their doom, proving once again that Rome's control over its membership was ephemeral at best.

* * *

In the wake of the world-wide assassinations, Silver Moon's security detail naturally was agitated about their president's latest plan for a European visit without them. Josh Remington, the head of IT and Security, didn't like it one bit, but the Navajo elder had firmly insisted. Silver Moon even made Remington promise that he would not alert or deploy any of TIIIS' old world resources. In return, she promised him, that the visit's duration would be a quick, in-and-out. Still, Remington made his president carry a satellite transponder, which she reluctantly agreed to do.

The TIIIS private jet landed at the Genève Aéroport on a Saturday around five o'clock local.

Silver Moon didn't take her luggage from the airframe. Instead, she went straight through Swiss control with only her purse and passport.

Once through customs, Silver Moon passed through the terminal and found at the curb an English-speaking taxi driver. Getting into the impeccably maintained Mercedes, she handed the driver a slip of paper with an address through the security divider. He read it, nodded once, entered the address into his trip computer, and began to drive.

Twenty minutes later, Silver Moon arrived at her destination a full hour and a half early. After paying her taxi fare, she decided that she would kill some time and walk about the quaint old world neighborhood with its cobblestone streets. It was a beautiful and clear early evening and she hoped that maybe a shop or two might still be open. At the very least, the Navajo was bound and determined to do some sight-seeing and window shopping. There were certainly enough churches about. This was, after all, Geneva, Switzerland, the city of Calvinism, banking, and diplomatic meetings.

*　　*　　*

Earlier that same Saturday morning DeSalvo sat at a window savoring a latte and sweet while the world rushed by. The lack of sensation was surreal from his first class seat as the Red Arrow bullet train raced for Milano three and a half hours away. He would arrive in time for lunch and then catch a train for Geneva. Four hours later he took a taxi from the Genève-Cornavin railway station and checked into the *Hôtel Les Armures*, tried to do some shopping, but his heart wasn't in it.

He then showered, changed, and at five minutes to eight, walked around the corner to *La Favola*—his favorite Italian restaurant in the city's old quarter. The warmth of its dining room's decor, rough-hewn wooden beams, and the aromas of its prepared cuisine, drew the man to this place like no other in Switzerland. That he knew the family who owned it, well, that story is for another time. As a personal favor, he requested that the two nearby tables remain unoccupied as he hoped to be joined by an important dinner guest. The owner just smiled and understood completely.

The chairman had arrived at eight sharp dressed casually in tan slacks, a tailored blue silk jacket, an open-collared white shirt with fine blue piping, and a red handkerchief peeking out of the jacket's breast pocket. It was his best attempt at the US tri-colors. Once seated, he ordered a bottle of a dry white that he favored. The waiter soon appeared with a bottle of sparkling water and a wicker basket of fresh warm bread. He poured out a slick of olive oil mixed with crushed olive and spices. Next, the sommelier arrived. The wine was deemed excellent and one glass was filled. The other remaining glass was left waiting, as was the chairman.

*   *   *

It had been a long time since Betsy Silver Moon had gone on a blind date and this pleasant evening sure felt like one. On her phone she had the benefit of several pictures of William DeSalvo, but when she saw him entering the restaurant precisely at eight, that told her more about the man than any photo ever could. Middle stature, lean, graying at the temples, a strong northern Italian face and nose, she saw in his gait a man who was comfortable with command, and perhaps the hint of a poor loser. Silver Moon took in a deep and calming breath, couldn't believe the glorious smells that teased her pallet, and entered the restaurant.

*   *   *

At precisely five minutes past eight, DeSalvo saw that a short woman with sun-beaten skin had made her entrance. She wore a modest bright teal and yellow patterned dress that draped nicely. A tastefully crafted Native American silver necklace with turquoise stones surrounded her neck. He stood and rounded the table in silent greeting as he recognized her face from the many photos that he had carefully studied. Her smile from across the dining room radiated like the noon-day sun.

"*Signore Presidente*, I am Betsy Silver Moon." She said as her hands met his. The intensity of his contact could only be described as psychically electric. "Thank you so very much for this kind invitation."

"*Presidente* Silver Moon," the Italian answered with a distinct British accent and a slight bow of the head, "I am William DeSalvo. And thank you so much for accepting my offer of dinner." It took all of DeSalvo's control not to jerk away at the woman's powerful psychic touch.

"Please, madam, allow me to seat you."

Once seated, DeSalvo offered Silver Moon some wine, which she accepted, swirled, and sipped. The woman thought its aroma reminded her of a breeze blowing over an iceberg.

"My, this wine is excellent. What is it?

"It is a French Sauvignon Blanc, a favorite of mine. I am pleased that you like it."

Silver Moon sighed and folded her hands in her lap. "*Signore Presidente*, I must say that my security detail did not like me coming here unattended. But for some reason I chose to do so anyway. There was something in your voice, I don't know, that I understood as a desire to speak with an outsider."

"Indeed, *Presidente* Silver Moon, you are correct, for I find myself at a crossroads. And, if you do not mind, please call me William."

"Then William it is, and, I'm Betsy."

With that pleasantry out of the way, both parties took a sip of wine.

"William. I don't have to be an adept to see that something is on your mind. What is it?"

"Betsy, you are direct and to the point. You are correct again, for I do have something on my mind.

Then the salad chef arrived, who made from scratch, at table-side, a divine Caesar, which paired brilliantly with the wine, so much so that both parties finished off the bottle with the salad. The conversation remained light, Silver Moon patient, but by the end of the salad DeSalvo finally spoke his mind.

"Now that was simply excellent."

"I agree." The Navajo said touching her napkin to her mouth with surprise as it smelled of fresh mint.

"Betsy, I wish to retire, but before I do, I wish to have in place an agreement between our … organizations … that will preserve the peace. As I do not know who my successor will be, and as succession in my organization can be sometimes chaotic, I wish to have something in place to ease the transition between us."

Silver Moon sat in shock at the statement, but fortunately the wine had helped ease it.

"First off, William, I do not know what the next course will be, but I am quite sure that you know what kind of wine will go with it. Especially as right now I need a glass."

DeSalvo chuckled at his colleague's observation.

"Agreed. The next will be a red," As he waved to get the sommelier's attention.

"So it's a peaceful retirement you want?"

"Yes, very much, both for me and my society."

"Well William, we're in the right city to craft such an agreement."

"Indeed. I suppose that my choice of Geneva was perhaps a bit too obvious."

"No, what I see is your commitment, your attention to detail. The real question is, will your colleagues follow your lead?"

"Yes, I know that will be initially problematic." He cryptically remarked as he fingered the narrow stem of his hand-blown wine glass.

"Peace, of any kind, must be embraced by both parties if it is to work. May I make a suggestion?"

"Certainly."

"When you tell your colleagues about this peace, do not use that term. Instead, use something French like *détente*, which will signal the idea of a cessation of hostilities. Further, I would tell them that *I* came to *you* with this overture."

The unfortunate use of the word "overture" caused the Italian to momentarily skip turn pale. *Focus William! Business first!*

"Betsy, are you sure that you are not a trained diplomat?"

"Trust me, William, practically every day I have to deal with a society of near-children."

The Italian smiled into his fist.

"But being serious once again, this *détente*, if successful, could eventually lead to something more substantive, such as a memorandum of noninterference. Allow me to be frank, William. There is bad blood between our societies that goes back millennia. We cannot banish that fact with a mere stroke of a pen. It will take time for that hatred to cool. Further, our societies serve different sectors of the paranormal world. We need each other to care for, manage, and if necessary, bring judgment upon those diverse elements. If we agree to not interfere with one another—that would be huge. By the way, this red wine is excellent."

"What then about the many issues surrounding treaty-bound allies?"

"Treaty-bound allies are not necessary if we are not at war." Silver Moon flatly said.

That elicited a grunt and a nod of agreement. "So true."

"William, I'm curious. What caused you to consider retirement in the first place, when right now you're seriously considering putting an end to our hostilities? You would be the perfect shepherd for your flock during such a transition."

"Frankly, Betsy, just between you and me, I am tired of being embarrassed by your society's cleverness and its damn Lictor of Magic. As for being 'the perfect shepherd' for my flock, that is doubtful. That role will have to be filled by someone younger and with more energy than I possess."

"Damn, and here I was just getting to like you William. And now here you go, running off and retiring. What your society needs right now is experienced leadership. That is what you possess above all others. On top of that, you think ahead. If I didn't know it, I'd swear that you were once a race car driver. They always are looking way, far ahead."

"My dear Betsy, as a young man, I *was* a professional F1 race car driver. Believe it or not, my predecessor was once my racing team's sponsor. And now that you mention it, we are here precisely because I do look far, far ahead. I am just glad that I found an outsider to listen to me.

"By the way, I am curious. Do you know a Dr. Erik Reissen?"

Silver Moon thought long and hard before answering. "Yes, he is an Egyptologist, and a quite famous one apparently. Austrian I believe. He now works for the Vatican as its director of Pro Deo's operations. My society has worked with him in the past. Why do you ask?"

"I would like to get to know him better."

"Well, that seems pretty easy to me, just invite him to dinner." The Navajo said as she raised her wine glass.

DeSalvo lightly chuckled.

"Oh, I almost forgot." Silver Moon said while leaning forward. "How is your security guard doing? The one that Stone returned to you?"

"Quite well, actually. And thank you for your assistance in that matter. Believe it or not, I offered him an early retirement, but he turned it down. What do you make of that?"

"A problematic marriage. The man is hiding from his wife."

"Yes, those are my thoughts as well." DeSalvo managed to smoothly say. But at that very moment, the international chairman of CMES came very close to breaking down and bearing his soul to this stranger. Came very close to blubbering out his immense grief over Lucia's loss. But DeSalvo didn't, for he had one last arrow in his quiver.

*   *   *

Upon DeSalvo's arrival back in Rome, he met first thing with his director of communications and security. During his train ride back, several things had crystallized in his mind. He ordered execution of one, last, swift blow of revenge for the loss of his wife, Lucia. The other was the drafting of a diplomatic memorandum that would handcuff all future opposition. This document would no doubt take some time, given that his inner cabinet would want to craft its outline and his lawyers to perfect its language.

As important that document was, as potentially complex it might be, it nonetheless remained far away and remote to DeSalvo.

"*Signore* Kiel, who is in charge of our remote assets?"

"*Signora* Isadora Ferroni, *Signore Presidente*."

"I see, please summon her."

"*Si, Signore Presidente*. May I ask why?"

"No, you may not." DeSalvo snapped with that face of stone that chilled the heart. Kiel got up to fetch the *signora*.

Moments later, *Signora* Ferroni appeared at his cubical. He stood, "Please, *Signora*, have a seat."

The nervous young woman did so, while wringing her hands.

"*Signora* Ferroni, please relax, I need a favor. That is all." DeSalvo soothed.

The woman nodded, but now sat on her hands.

"*Signora* Ferroni, is it not true that you manage all of our *outside* assets?"

"*Si, Signore Presidente.*"

"Do we have any who are currently at the Old Oaks Academy?"

The woman briefly searched her memory and confirmed, "*Si Signore Presidente*, currently we have only one."

"Who may I ask are they?"

"*Signore,* Andrew Alexander-Grissom."

"I see. Has he been sufficiently prepared for his mission?"

A single nod.

"Good. Then I want you to trigger his sub-conscious programming. His target is this individual." He passed her a piece of paper with a name.

"Today, *Signore Presidente*?"

"*Si, Signora* Ferroni. Today, as of five minutes ago. Have I made myself absolutely clear?"

"*Oh si, Signore Presidente! Subito!*" and the woman practically ran back to her station.

DeSalvo closed his eyes. *Oh how I miss you my Lucia ... have patience.*

CHAPTER 30

It was dinner time at the Stone's. Marvelous Mediterranean aromas wafted from the kitchen, which were the signature of Melaina's upbringing. Their home was one of the single-storey bungalows on Faculty Row that backed up against the surrounding oak forests of the Old Oaks Academy. Built in the late sixties, these clapboard one-storey structures had front and back porches with long flower boxes on their railings. Once a cookie-cutter architectural development project for temporary faculty housing, by the twenty-first century this neighborhood had matured into a tree-lined avenue of fine lawns and neatly trimmed hedges that delineated cozy homes.

From the street lined by a concrete sidewalk and grassy margin, J.J.'s and Melaina's house had a walk that led directly to the stairs of their front porch flanked by two flamboyant white cane chairs—both perfect places to sip a late afternoon tea or lemonade. Bordering the walk stood two majestic oak trees that provided cool afternoon shade in the summertime.

The rear porch was the Stone's favorite place to eat as the kitchen was right there with a screened backdoor. Sitting on the picnic table, the couple would sip their morning coffee, or afternoon drink. Halfway between the back porch's steps and the tree line, Stone placed in the backyard's lawn a large tree stump.

On this gifting platform, the Stone's would place treats for the *Argenti* who inhabited the forest beyond. They, in a complex treaty, agreed to establish a colony to guard the woods and the campus from all forms of demon-kind and intruders. Their favorite treat was dark chocolate wrapped in silvery tinfoil. Occasionally the pair would catch their furtive movements within the trees and hear their excited chittering. Only rarely did they actually see a bold one dash forward to fetch the prize. Roughly the size of a large chipmunk, the *Argenti* sought out all things silver to augment their diet. As a consequence, their teeth and claws were permeated with the metal making them natural enemies of demon-kind.

Stone's relationship with the *Argenti* went further, however, for they had taught him how to translocate, an ability that the Lictor of Magic had used to great advantage. Quite literally willing himself from place to place within a line-of-sight, Stone had multiplied his offensive and defensive capabilities.

While only fifteen hundred square feet, the Stone's modest bungalow had a central hallway that led directly to the kitchen in the back, while the rest of the home's rooms branched off of it—in all a two bedroom, one-and-a-half bath, with a small dining and front rooms.

*   *   *

Grissom knelt in his garden plot happily tending it, while ignoring his grumbling stomach. Glancing at his device, he saw that it was after six o'clock, but he had only a couple of more feet of bedding and he'd be finished. After a quick hand wash in the public bathroom, he would attend to his noisy digestive cavity.

Then his device went off. With a sour look on his face, he sighed, signed on, and opened up the message. He read the text, frowned, and then registered the attached graphic—Michelangelo's image from the Sistine Chapel of the Almighty reaching out to Adam. Much like the Red Queen of Diamonds in Richard Condon's novel *The Manchurian Candidate*, Grissom's conscious self was put on hold, while his preprogrammed deep sub-conscious completely took over. The incessant growling that had bedeviled his stomach was now long forgotten. Leaving his gardening tools and bucket behind, the young man with pants with dirty knees and hands with soil beneath his nails began walking in the general direction of Faculty Row.

*   *   *

Stone efficiently set the dinner table in the tiny breakfast nook of the kitchen, while his wife's fragrant efforts prompted his stomach to grumble noisily. Stone house rules were clear—the cook does not setup or clean up, and most of the time, the north Texan did the latter. But during the summer months, the roles reversed as Stone reigned supreme on the back porch with his Webber grill and Texas barbecue.

*   *   *

One of the many reasons that Old Oaks Academy was established where it was hinged upon the benign ley line that passed beneath its grounds. To best understand just what a ley line is, a phenomenon first coined by an amateur archaeologist named Alfred Watkins in 1921, consider the following. The human circulatory system, a complex collection of veins and arteries all powered by a central muscle, has a compliment to the earth's magnetic fields. This other network is made up of big and powerful channels of paranormal energies that course around the planet.

This circulating matrix of extraordinary paranormal energies, mimicked the biological system in another important respect. Just as veins and arteries are different in their purpose, the former oxygen-depleted and the latter oxygen-rich, so also were the *characteristics*, or as some conjecture *personalities*, of these semi-prescient conduits quite different. In the case of Old Oaks location, here the ley line was of a more benign nature, which, more often than not, allowed a respectful adept to tap in and use its power. Meanwhile, elsewhere this was not at all the case as a ley line could be far more aggressive, if not evil, in its intent. As proof of this dichotomy, it should be no surprise, nor coincidence, that New York, Baghdad, Rome, Cairo, Barcelona, Hong Kong, Minsk, and Berlin were well-known hot spots powered by such dark ley lines, which in turn fueled CMES' most active coven locations.

* * *

The northeasterner's programming was quite clear and specific. Locate a ley line. Next, through brute force link to it, and thereafter, much like a fire hose, direct its full power at the target. As the mortal's survival was not a concern, the sheer radiant power of just one bolt of the ley line's psycho-kinetic energy would consume the conduit—the conjurer, and the target. This admittedly blunt-force tactic was to be employed only in the most desperate of situations. Apparently for DeSalvo, this was such a time.

* * *

Grissom knew where the Lictor of Magic lived. He had walked by the location many times, while not knowing why he had done it. The young man also was well aware of the powerful ley line that coursed beneath the campus, for one of his classes had not only identified it and its characteristics, but had provided an introduction of sorts for each of the students. The ley line, referred to as Monongahela after the river, had become long accustomed to these amateurish pin-pricks by generations of student-adepts.

As he neared the modest bungalow, he took off his shoes and socks, ignoring the cold crispness of the early evening March air. Now standing before the structure in the brown grassy margin between the sidewalk and street, the northeasterner worked his bare feet back and forth into the turf to ensure the best possible connection, or grounding, with the ley line below.

With a deep sigh of commitment, and perhaps regret, he closed his eyes. The young man concentrated and reached down, down, down with his spirit until he found the nearest branch of the Monongahela. Upon contact, this semi-sentient entity recognized him from his other entreaties for connection, and allowed him to do so, like any mother Labrador would offer a free teat to her hungry puppy.

*   *   *

At that very moment, Melaina was in the kitchen fussing over a lamb dish. J.J. was sitting in their joint-office reading his e-mails.

SOUL CARRIER! MOVE YOUR WIFE TO THE BEDROOM NOW!

The extraordinary power and energy behind that command from Stone's First Soul propelled the former US Marine's legs into churning comic book wheels. Into the kitchen he went, where he picked up his wife with a dripping sauce spoon in hand. She never even had the opportunity to squeak out a protest.

*   *   *

Something attempted to pause, no, tried to stop Andrew

Alexander from opening his eyes. It was his alter ego, Andy Grissom who fought against what his other commanding self intended. He was not going to allow his good friend J.J. from being harmed. He'd promised.

But Andy lost his struggle, as his body's eyes opened to unleash a titanic maelstrom of psycho-kinetic energy directly into the center of the house before him, ripping a huge gash through its center and beyond.

*　　*　　*

Now in the bedroom, Stone fell onto the bed with his wife beneath him. It collapsed under the sudden shift in weight, while an awesome clap of thunder, and its following concussion, stunned the couple senseless. The center of their home had vaporized as if hit by a massive horizontal lightning bolt. The beam of unadulterated energy cleaved the house cleanly in two, beginning with an eight foot gash that widened to twelve, forming a pie-shaped gap. The extent of damage beyond the home ended at the half-charred gifting stump, because that was where the "conduit" failed. All that remained of Andy was a pile of dirty clothes, filled with a fluffy white ash.

The lone crack of thunder on that cloudless early evening reverberated throughout the campus and the trees of the oak forest. It was impossible to miss. The immediate neighbors lost windows. Cracks appeared in the newly installed stained glass windows of the campus chapel. Melaina and J.J., unconscious, were found bleeding from their noses and ears by the campus' firemen and paramedics.

*   *   *

Silver Moon, hearing the news, sat fit-to-be-tied and helpless in Santa Fe. Her rage was such that when she glanced at her favorite blue coffee cup, it shattered into a thousand pieces.

Get a grip on yourself girl. It was then that the guilt hit the Navajo right between the eyes. *You knew! You saw all the signs in Grissom's mind, and yet, you still failed to act! Thank God that they are still on this earth.*

Then Silver Moon entertained a bold move, wrinkled her upper lip, picked up her device, made a call, and then thought better of it. She was hot, irrational, and emotionally over-the-top.

Best not to blow up like a volcano, only to later regret every single word that had felt so right at the time. Remember that you're the president. Damn, I really need to meditate on this, she finally decided, as she snatched her truck keys.

J.J. was absolutely right. Go sit and cool off next to the rattlesnake mound.

Silver Moon again picked up her phone and attempted to call both Makris and Stone. Predictably, neither picked up. So she called the campus infirmary.

"Hello, this is President Silver Moon. I want to talk to someone right this minute who knows what's going on with the Stones."

"One moment, President Silver Moon."

After several moments of anxiety, a fresh voice broke into the line. "Hello, this is Dr. Porter."

"Doctor, this is President Betsy Silver Moon. How are the Stones' doing?"

"I am very sorry, President Silver Moon, I cannot release that information."

"HEPA be damned, doctor! Are they okay? And what about their baby?"

The chastened voice answered, "The family is stable. That's all I'll say."

"Fine, doctor, and thank you. But you damn better well polish up your resume, because when I arrive at campus, you're history!"

*   *   *

DeSalvo's day began poorly with the reading of his wife's autopsy report, which after an MRI scan, revealed that she had been pregnant. The technician's estimate was three weeks old. An impossible level of natal development for such a short time, DeSalvo knew, but vampire physiology at best remained a poorly understood subject. *My dearest Lucia ... please remain patient for me.*

The man's device briefly hummed. He saw the

telephone number and knew who it was from. They left no message, but then again, they didn't have to. Andrew Alexander must have completed his mission. At that news, a modicum of satisfaction passed through him.

CHAPTER 31

The fallout from the Ley Line Disaster, as it was now called within TIIIS circles, fostered sweeping policy changes regarding outside infiltrators, their detection, and detention. For the society, it was another sobering moment, much like the Christmas Eve Raid of several years back.

Stone now wore hearing aids as both his eardrums had been permanently damaged in the blast and concussion that followed. Makris was more fortunate, only one ear required an appliance. Miraculously, her baby seemed unaffected by the ordeal.

Their home was not redeemable, so before it was raised, the couple spent several days retrieving their possessions. With a considerable amount littering their front yard, one item had yet to be discovered— Melaina's family book of spells. That precious heirloom had been continuously handed down from mother to daughter since the fourth century. Over the intervening years, many spells had been added. Like all family heirlooms, it was irreplaceable.

"What am I looking for Mel?" Stone said as he stood amid the chaos that had once been their kitchen.

"Promise that you will not laugh?"

"Yeah."

"A rectangular cookie tin with a tight-fitting lid. It was black as I recall—a Jack Daniels' cookie box."

"You've got to be kidding!"

As the pair rummaged about Melaina spied the familiar shape, fully one half of its exterior burnt to a crisp, exposing its base metal. Dented, pitted, the witch held the seal container to her chest and went outside. When she opened it, miraculously, the flexible leather-bound book within was intact and in no respect harmed.

"How is that possible?" Stone asked. "I would have expected at least some charring at the edges."

"I don't know, Cowboy. Some things just happen for a reason, I suppose." She said with heartfelt relief.

"Has to be some sort of enchantment." Stone concluded.

"Must be, Cowboy. Must be."

Once the couple finished with their recovery efforts, the next day the contractors arrived with heavy machinery and the demolition began. The architect on site promised that once they were finished, the new home would not be any different from the other homes on Faculty Row. However, Stone insisted on one exception—the installation of a specially carved gifting station.

*   *   *

Throughout the diplomatic talks, Silver Moon never spoke of the ley line incident with DeSalvo. This she decided during the meditation session while at rattlesnake mound. While deep under her trance, the

Navajo realized DeSalvo's motivation in terms that he understood, specifically in terms of Biblical retribution, an-eye-for-an-eye, his actions made sense. But even in the ancient Germanic terms of *Wergeld*, or "man-money," his actions again, made sense. Sadly, those were the underlying cultural rules of both their societies—brutal and direct, which the woman acknowledged, but hardly agreed with. What Silver Moon realized above all, was that some sort of agreement had to be established between their societies in order to put a halt to such brutal acts in the future. And so, in the vernacular of the times, "Suck it up buttercup" fit her situation quite aptly. And, best of all, it worked.

*   *   *

Two months after the ley line accident, and after several rewrites, the historic announcement of the *détente* between CMES and TIIIS took effect. Both sides wished this project to go forward, as a monument to progress. This diplomatic understanding appeared nowhere in the mass media, but its effect on the world's stock markets was telling. Given the international nature and vast holdings of both societies, a subtle tension had suddenly been removed from the marketplace that both eased minds and loosened pocketbooks.

For some critics, the substance of the momentous

agreement left too many loose ends dangling, but for others of a more positive point-of-view it provided a basis for the lessening of tensions and offered the hope for a better future.

*   *   *

A Diplomatic Memorandum
Made This Day 1st of May 2019
Between:
The *Consilium Magorum et Sagarum*
Hereafter Referred To As CMES
And
The International Integrated Interface Society
Hereafter Referred To As TIIIS.
These Parties Hereto Agree As Follows:

Article 1: Ratification of a Diplomatic Memorandum

This diplomatic memorandum becomes valid thirty (30) days after its formal ratification, by both parties, CMES and TIIIS, and its publication and distribution among its members-in-good-standing.

1a. Cessation from this Diplomatic Memorandum

Either party, CMES or TIIIS, can withdraw at any time from this diplomatic memorandum. Any such a withdrawal must be presented to the Boards of Redress of both parties.

Article 2: Formal Recognition

TIIIS acknowledges CMES' existence, and grants CMES full rights of self-determination. Accordingly, CMES acknowledges TIIIS' existence, and grants TIIIS full rights of self-determination.

2a. Treaty Relationships

2a1: CMES
TIIIS acknowledges CMES' right to make and/or break treaty relationships with any organization, enclave, coven, or society as it sees fit. Similarly, CMES agrees that it will not coerce to its will, in any manner, any non-aligned organization, enclave, coven, or society.

2a2: TIIIS
CMES acknowledges TIIIS' right to make and/or break treaty relationships with any organization, enclave, coven, or society as it sees fit. Similarly, TIIIS agrees that it will not coerce to its will, in any manner, any non-aligned organization, enclave, coven, or society.

Article 3. Cultural Recognition

Each party, CMES and TIIIS, acknowledges the long history and traditions that make up and form the cultural identity of each party. It is acknowledged that each party, CMES and TIIIS, attract and gather members, which are not culturally compatible with the other. In order to prevent injury and misunderstanding, each party, CMES and TIIIS, acknowledge their opposite's right to cultural co-existence.

Article 4. Mechanism for Injury: The Boards of Redress

Each party, CMES and TIIIS, must, according to

their own established traditions and laws form a Board of Redress made up of three individuals, who are members-in-good-standing.

4a. The Boards of Redress of both parties must hold communications at least once every month during the calendar year. Such dialogue is encouraged and is considered mutually beneficial, which will foster better understanding between the parties, and the eventual formation of trust.

4b. Instances of injury must be petitioned to the Boards of Redress together, as one governing body.

4c. The Boards of Redress are granted the power to address and adjudicate any issues that arise between the parties. Their decisions are final.

* * *

Perhaps all too predictably, scarcely had one day passed since the establishment of the Boards of Redress, a flood of injured parties materialized. They clamored to be heard. Most of these early complaints came from the CMES membership, which were generally outraged that their society signed a document that granted parity with "that other coven, that late-comer." As proof that these protesting elements had not even read *The Memorandum* as it came to be called, not once did they note that their society, CMES, had always been mentioned first, out of deference to its ancient and hallowed tradition.

One "grievance," however, did gain traction. The

question posed to the Boards of Redress asked whether "any non-aligned organization, enclave, coven, or society" could simultaneously be a treaty member of both societies. After some thought, Article 2b was instituted to address this knotty and potentially inflammatory situation.

Article 2b. Multiple Treaty Memberships
> Any non-aligned organization, enclave, coven, or society may, at their discretion, enter into and ratify new or existing treaty-relationships with one or both parties, CMES and TIIIS, without fear of retaliation or abuse.

*   *   *

The day following the official ratification and establishment of Article 2b, tangible proof that *The Memorandum* had successfully functioned between the two parties, William DeSalvo was found in his black Ferrari. One of his estate's vineyard workers found him parked on a gravel overlook with a magnificent view. An opened bottle of red wine and two half-filled glasses had been carefully arranged on the consol as if the man was expecting a visitor. As for DeSalvo, he had several brake-dust-soiled silk scarves draped around his grotesquely slashed neck. He had completed his last hallowed promise to his impatient Lucia with a blood sacrifice—his own.

Appendix 1

Translation of *Vaticani Greci* 121.16.2.5

When Dr. Mahmud Iskiander first applied for the research grant, he was looking for a project that would launch his young academic career. After submitting his application, the young man waited two long years for the wheels of bureaucracy to turn. Even though a promising philologist and paleographer, fluent in the ancient Egyptian and Greek languages, Iskiander knew that the odds of him getting the fellowship were low. Still, the young scholar hoped to work within one of the richest library collections of the world—the Vatican's.

When an envelope stamped with the papal insignia of the crossed keys appeared in his university mail slot, his heart skipped a beat. As he held the thin missive between his fingers, Iskiander feared that it would be a rejection. He almost tore up the envelope, but then he opened it. The thin missive within stated that he had been granted unrestrained access to the Vatican library's collection by His Holiness, as part of a cultural exchange of scholars brokered by the Vatican with the government of Turkey. Additionally, the program would supply his flat, along with a generous monthly stipend for meals and incidentals. His dream had come true. Finally, a list of research contacts appeared along with their contact information. These scholars had approved his application. Further, Iskiander was encouraged to contact any of them while in Rome. One of those names was an Egyptologist by the name of Erik Reissen.

With his approved research pass in hand, Iskiander stood in the library's sunny courtyard. The long-haired scholar trembled under the intellectual weight of the task before him. He had only one year to find and complete his project. Then, if it was deemed acceptable by one of his research contacts, the work would be published under the Vatican's own imprint and distributed throughout the world.

*   *   *

A seemingly endless number of manuscripts are housed within the Vatican Library, shelved within the many arched corridors decorated with brilliantly painted Christian iconography and marble flooring, more utilitarian multi-leveled reading rooms, or intimately crafted, niche-like warrens. These artifacts of human endeavor, written in a variety of languages were carefully organized into separate collections. Fortunately, the entire inventory was meticulously catalogued online. But what Iskiander found shocked him. An army of scholars could easily be employed for centuries within this rich and overflowing research environment. The possibilities were practically endless.

It was then that the scholar understood the "why" behind the papal research fellowship.

After five solid days of intensive consideration, and more than a bit overwhelmed, Iskiander had his short list in hand. At the top of that list was one item in Collection Nr. 121 *Vaticani greci*. Iskiander scanned about and then actually found the item resting on the second shelf of the Fourteenth Carrel. It was a plain gray box. In faded black ink, its hand-written label, simply said,

Vaticani greci, 121.16.2.5
Anon. *il sacerdote di Set*
Greco 3 ° - 2 ° secolo aC
Provenienza sconosciuta. Memphis, Egitto (?)

Iskiander stood numbly, hyperventilating before the shelf. *It's actually here. Waiting for me. A text about a priest of Egyptian god Set!*

Carefully, he removed the gray box from the shelf. It weighed practically nothing. Prize in hand, he scurried off like a hungry mouse with cheese. Next stop, his assigned office to better examine this treasure.

As he walked, Iskiander's eyes glazed over as his imagination churned. *What might it contain? A biography? A hallowed promise of some kind? A history? Maybe some ancient ritual spells?* The library's catalogue had not listed its contents, just that it had not been studied. *Would it be a worthy project suitable for publication?*

By the time Iskiander had unlocked the door to his office, his head hurt.

Seated at his desk, he donned a pair of cotton gloves before he opened the box's metal clasp. Upon opening the lid, the scholar thought for an instant he smelled that special grass-like aroma that only could be pure antiquity. Smiling, and to a certain degree chiding himself as well for his sentimentality, he carefully lifted out the stacked sheaths of delicately yellowed papyri, each separated by a neutral medium layer of pressed, acid-free cotton. Originally united as a single roll, this document's carefully written columns of text had long ago been cut, divided, and then stacked—all in an effort to better preserve "that which was deemed so very old and fragile."

With tweezers, Iskiander arranged the first sheet of papyrus upon a prepared blotter-like surface of museum-grade, acid-free rag paper. Then, he gently covered the artifact with a clean sheet of glass sized for the purpose. Settling in, the paleographer began to read. His left hand unconsciously picked up a No.2 pencil. He started to take notes on a legal pad.

What Iskiander read brought forth a delightful mixture of wonder, amazement, and joy, which only escalated with the realization that the library catalogue had been right. To his best knowledge, the subject of this manuscript had never before seen the light of day, much less in translation. Two hours later, having finished a rough read of the entire papyrus, the young scholar knew that the text deserved a thorough philological and cultural analysis, translation, and commentary. And Iskiander began to do just that.

*   *   *

A paleographer's first task is to describe a manuscript's overall physical characteristics. Iskiander judged that this papyrus roll, when originally intact, had been between fifteen and sixteen feet long. As for the text itself, its Greek was crisply written in five-by-eight-inch columns with black ink. The scribe's hand was clear and precise. The subtle slant of the text, Iskiander noted with some pleasure, was left-handed—just like his.

The Greek itself was written in the *koiné* dialect that was in vogue from the fourth century BC through eleventh century AD. No additional adornments were noted—just straight monochrome text. This last detail caused Iskiander to make a note. *Is this document complete? There is no title or author mentioned.* With what was before him, there was no telling, as the rest of the papyrus had been trimmed away.

Next, the scholar devised a preliminary *schemata* or diagram of the manuscript's transmission history. Its *koiné* dialect suggested to Iskiander a broad period of some fifteen hundred years within which this particular manuscript could have been created. Consequently, this assessment caused him to assign the manuscript a designation of the letter "B." Preserved manuscripts were rarely originals. Be they made of papyrus, wood, ox hide, or parchment, such documents were susceptible over time to a destructive process called "burn," their slow deterioration. This is why modern library collections often smelled of ink and mustiness—their contents were in the process of "burning." This was also why, in antiquity, a working library was constantly copying deteriorating manuscripts to maintain their collection.

The other reason for Iskiander's "B" designation to was the nature of the content—the recounting of events that spanned from the thirteenth through eleventh centuries BC. Calculating that a working papyrus should last about two hundred years with careful handling, Iskiander estimated that stored ones could last much longer, maybe as long as five hundred years. Therefore, the document before him had to be a copy of a much older edition. Just how old, was the question. One did not often carbon-date papyrus without considerable reason, resources, and time. Furthermore, the dating process itself was a destructive one, meaning that a fragment would have to be sacrificed—and he did not have that authority. Iskiander had none of these resources. He needed another way.

Iskiander scratched his head in thought. Let us reasonably assume that the manuscript before me, B, was a late Byzantine, say eleventh-century, copy. That would mean, at least potentially, it could have made its way from Constantinople to Rome as plunder from the Fourth Crusade. If that was the case, then manuscript "a," the precursor document to B, could have dated back to sometime around the sixth century. If one again applied the five-hundred-year rule, then "a"'s precursor text, designated as "b," should be a first-century copy. If that was true, the ultimate original could have potentially been a work from the Alexandrian Library!

Even though Iskiander could not actually hold either the presumed precursor "a" or "b" manuscript versions to the B manuscript in his hands, he could postulate their existence based on "burn" alone. But given the age of the events described within, Iskiander further speculated that the original text was probably written in ancient Egyptian, which was later translated into Greek sometime between the fourth through first centuries BC. This intuitive leap he made because there were just too many instances in the text where the paleographer saw the Greek copyist struggling with the translation of difficult Egyptian words or concepts.

As to the fluorite of the Egyptian priest-magician Sethi, the central figure of this work, Iskiander read in Column 3.4 that Sethi's parents were none other than the famous Pharaoh Ramses II and his Chief Wife and Queen Nefertari. Fortunately for Iskiander, the chronology of that king's reign was well documented. After some calculation, the scholar reckoned that Sethi's birth probably fell somewhere between the years 1284 and 1255 BC.

Sethi, the son of Ramses II, and later priest-magician of Set, had lived a long life there could be no doubt, according to Column 16.4: "... **the priest and magician Sethi had already achieved over one hundred and eighty years.**" Furthermore, the text stated that Sethi, at the extraordinary age of two hundred twenty—approximately the year 1044 BC—was elevated to become the chairman or πρόεδρος of the συμβούλιο, *Consilium*, or council of all the *sem*-priests of magic in Egypt. This lofty post Sethi held until his death around 1000 BC, after reportedly living two hundred sixty-three years.

Iskiander wondered about the priest-magician's name itself. He doubted its authenticity. Seti was Ramses II's father, a good king, therefore making it a popular name for newborn baby boys. Secondly, Sethi was a priest-magician of the god Set. That, to Iskiander, seemed too facile. In the end, Iskiander had to consider whether the central figure of the text was real or imaginary, especially considering the man's extraordinarily long life span. Was he really Ramses II's son? It seemed so, as his name did appear amid the king's many family inscriptions. Or alternatively, was the papyrus meant as a fictitious propaganda piece—a hero's tale of the Set priesthood? In the end, the scholar had a sinking feeling that he would probably never know for sure.

Finally, the paleographer made an attempt to grapple with the slippery identity of the text's unknown author. After much consideration, Iskiander came to only one conclusion—whoever he was, his very literacy, references to monumental inscriptions, and the subject matter of the text made him a priest—most likely a well-traveled member of the Set priesthood.

* * *

The following is Iskiander's translation of the papyrus, which he entitled, *The Priest-Magician of Set*.

Column 1

For many years it has been debated who was the most formidable in Egypt. Who combined the mastery of the hidden arts with legendary military leadership? Who could wield the magical *was*-staff [1] of power as well as draw the bow, throw the spear, or drive the chariot? Who else led the council[2] as its first-voice for the span of a man's lifetime? Who else did so with a steady and just hand? Some have searched for the tombs of the most renowned magicians—Imhotep and his son Djedi.[3] Others have pointed to the great

---

[1] Greek transliteration of the ancient Egyptian *w3s*-staff. The *w3s*-staff had a stylistically curved head (of Set?) on its pummel and a forked end. On this powerful magical tool as a practical snake-stick, see W.J. Cherf, "The Function of the Egyptian Forked Staff and the Forked Bronze Butt: A Proposal," *ZÄS* 109(1982) 86-97 and *id.*, "Some Forked Staves in the Tut'ankhamūn Collection," *ZÄS* 115(1988) 107-110.

[2] Συμβούλιο. *Consilium* in Latin.

warrior pharaohs Mephramuthosis (sc. Thutmose III) and Rhaméssēs (sc. Ramses II).[4] Yet, none of these can match the priest-magician and council leader Sethi! While this view is a reasonable one, it is only partly correct, because the priest-magician and council leader[5] Sethi was a gatherer of knowledge and keen observer. It is also said that he eagerly listened to and sought out his predecessors, teachers, and brethren their guidance.

Column 2

Even in the days of King Ptolemy the Benefactor (sc. Ptolemy III Euergetes),[6] it is said that one of Sethi's faithful followers, he who buried his master, openly claimed that another, a certain *sem*-priest of Set,[7] was

[3] Greek transliteration of the ancient Egyptian names *Ii-m-ḥtp* and *Djdj*.

[4] Names as transmitted by the Egyptian priest and historian Manetho, *Aegyptiaca* frag. 50 (Waddell, p.101-103). Apparently, the author of the papyrus had access to this lost historical work.

[5] Πρόεδρος.

[6] Ptolemaic king and founder of the Alexandrian Library who reigned from 246-221 BC. His mention suggests that this tale was well-known at the time.

[7] A priestly level indicating a specialization (i.e., astronomy), cultic position (i.e., funerary, temple-oriented), or a special relationship with the royal court. See H. Kees, *Das Priestertum im Ägyptischen Staat vom Neuen Reich bis zur Spätzeit*, (Leiden, 1953) and his *Indices und Nachträge*, (Leiden, 1958).

Sethi's first master of magic, from whom he took counsel and example. To this opinion we give approval. And, as some are always wont to do, they passed on fantastic stories about this old magician of Set, saying, "He was a humble man, white of skin, with long flowing hair that reached his feet, who practically never left his temple's library." To this we do not give approval as it is nothing more than an ignorant invention designed to belittle a noble magician. Yet another example of so many incredible tales that are abroad, tales we will not stoop low to repeat. Thus, since the ancient scrolls have provided sufficient and noteworthy accounts of the priest-magician and council leader Sethi, we will do the same, gathering from them what we need, as we wish to make the ledger balance.

Column 3

Like the fury of a tempest, Egypt undertook many military campaigns that placed many cities and peoples under its yoke, or laid waste to them. In this regard, The Royal Annals record the many campaigns of Mephramuthosis (sc. Thutmose III).[8] It is recorded on monuments everywhere that these

---

[8] The Annals of Thutmose III, who reigned from 1479-1425 BC, adorn the outer walls of the Amun sanctuary at Karnak. See D.B. Redford, *The Wars in Syria and Palestine of Thutmose III*, (Leiden, 2003). The author of the papyrus speaks of them with remarkable familiarity.

same things occurred during the blessed reign of King Rhaméssēs.[9] In the face of such events, young Sethi, a son of the king by his own body and of his first chief wife,[10] made his presence known from the many others of the harem by offering himself willingly to the military cohorts. Sethi learned at a young age how to draw a heavy bow, throw a heavy lance, and hack with the war ax. Strong of body and will, Sethi excelled at the arts of war and soon came to the notice of the Commander of the King's Stables. It is said that when Sethi spoke to the horses of the royal stables, he used a calming voice, could tame the wildest of spirit, and bring them under his will as no other. He possessed the *way*.[11]

Column 4

An example of Sethi's gift of speaking to animals was his encounter with an angry mare, which was in her prime. With a coat black like

---

[9] Especially the Kadesh battle scenes of the Ramesseum. He reigned from 1279-1213 BC. See M. Lichtheim, *Ancient Egyptian Literature: the Late Period*, (1973) p. 57: "... the campaign was told at length in two separate accounts which scholars have called the Bulletin (or the Record) and the Poem....the two versions were not merely carved once on the walls of a temple but were repeated in multiple copies...They are inscribed on the walls of the temples of Abydos, Luxor, Karnak, Abu Simbel and the Ramesseum."

[10] This must be a reference to Queen Nefertari, the king's first wife.

[11] Odd use of the term τάση, "to have a proclivity for."

the night's sky, long of mane, and with eyes red with rage over the carelessness of her handler, she had crushed the wretch beneath her hooves. With the stable's straw still wet with the ignorant man's blood, Sethi entered, and confronted the horse as no one would approach the raging beast with foam dripping from its snout. Still filled with blood-lust and stamping the ground loudly as if to awaken the god Geb himself,[12] Sethi made an offering to it of a wide bowl of cool water. Desiring the water, the black mare approached, but Sethi retreated. Thrice the horse approached and thrice Sethi denied it. This teasing dance Sethi continued, until the horse allowed him to bring her to submission. The marvel was that the black mare was one of the king's favorites and therefore could not be destroyed. This Sethi did not know. After the passing of four days, Sethi hitched the mare to a chariot harness suitable for training.

Column 5

Shortly thereafter, the Commander of the King's Stable, a nobleman named Thutmose, took Sethi to his household. There, it is said, after much beer drinking, Sethi was assigned his own chariot and a team of horses. What the prince did not know was this team did not abide with each other, nor had they been trained to act as one. Thutmose had done this

---

[12] An example of the author transliterating the Egyptian earth god's name verbatim from Egyptian hieroglyphs into Greek.

as a test. He was curious, as were others, how Sethi would overcome this challenge. On the next day, however, the Commander of the King's Stables discovered Sethi leading the horses together, and then later in the day, they tolerated being tethered together. During the next days, the commander found out that Sethi had slept in the stables with his team, ate with them, and watered with them as well. Miraculously, Sethi was driving his team with a fully burdened chariot, to which he had added a considerable amount of weight. When asked about this, Sethi replied, "My team must pull me and one other into battle. Therefore, I train them as if going into battle the next day."

Column 6

The ability of Sethi to foresee the future was proven when an emissary arrived at the royal court from the lands near the city of Byblos. What had only been rumors were confirmed. The king of Hatti (sc. Hittites) had gathered an immense army of infantry and chariots without count in the plain near the city of Kadesh. King Rhaméssēs rebuked the emissary saying, "My vassal does not have such an army, nor so many chariots. What is your proof of such? Return to your homeland with three of my trusted scouts. Upon your and their return, only then I will make a judgment." Upon the return of the three scouts, who accompanied the emissary, they reported to the royal court, "What the emissary says is true, Great One. The plain before the city of Kadesh[13] is filled with the Hatti vassal's army. Our count of their chariots numbered over two thousand. The rumors say that Byblos, as well as the cities along the Great Green (sc. Mediterranean coastline),[14] are in danger. King Rhaméssēs then thundered to his generals, "Summon the chariot squadrons and infantry!"

Column 7

Since Sethi was the son of the god's own body, the Commander of the Royal Stables assigned him and his chariot to the Squadron of the Golden Horus, which accompanied the king. There are two versions of this account. The one goes as follows. Some say that Sethi performed well at the great slaughter that was the Battle of Kadesh,[15] that he reveled in the fray, lo' even bathed himself in the Hittite's blood, and then providentially came to his father's side when he was in dire need. As a well-muscled youth dressed in leather and bronze armor, Sethi stood next to his warrior father, whose armor gleamed like Re in his first appearance. "I am honored father that you have allowed me to accompany you to Kadesh to smite the treacherous Hittites! My chariot

---

[13] Greek transliteration for this Egyptian toponym.
[14] Greek translation of the Egyptian term, *Wdj-wr*. The scribe who copied this text reads Egyptian, but apparently does not know what the expression means.
[15] Said to have taken place in either 1275 or 1274 BC.

will be your shield-side. May we slaughter a multitude!" Sethi said with an upraised chin. "Father, may we drive through their ranks with blood up to our axles." "Sethi, you have more than earned this moment," his father replied. "I have observed you since your youth.

Column 8

"My son, you can draw the stoutest bow, hurl the heaviest spear, and swing a formidable axe. But your skill at driving a chariot is like no other. Tomorrow before that wretched city of Kadesh, we will be victorious as we drive their chariots into the river!" Then the war trumpets sounded the many chariot squadrons into formation. At the forefront, the Squadron of the Golden Horus, led by the king, jostled into position forming a broad front some fifty chariots wide. Lightly-built and pulled by matched teams of horses, driver and archer, as the horses, worked as one. Their astounding speed and maneuverability incited fear in the enemy. In comparison, the chariots of Hatti (sc. Hittites) were awkward—being massively built with four-wheels, and heavy—in that they carried three to four soldiers. They plodded forth like oxen. They waded into the fray of battle, attempting to crush under their wheels anything before them. At the second sounding of the war trumpets, **Rhaméssēs** goaded his horses and charged the Hatti (sc. Hittite) army. The remainder of the Squadron of the Golden Horus spread out behind him like a long, continuous thread from a weaver's loom.

Column 9

The chariots of the Egyptian king relied upon their speed and the penetration of their bronze-tipped arrows. Galloping toward the enemy like the wind, the Egyptian archers with their heavy bows could pierce a copper ox-hide ingot.[16] Upon nearing the enemy, the king furiously loosed his arrows. Their affect was immediate as the men of Hatti (sc. Hittites) dropped two ranks deep from a single cast. Before turning aside, the king had carved a piece out of the dreaded Hatti, much like a butcher with a bound calf. As the enemy advanced, the king's chariots, much like bees, continued to sting as their squadrons continuously coursed around in a great oval, stopping only at the main host to receive more arrows, before charging yet again. The enemy, however, fought stubbornly. While the speed of the king's chariots often caused their arrow casts to be errant, many did find their mark, which resulted in the upending of chariots.

Column 10

---

[16] "Heavy bows," a reference to the Egyptian compound bow. The piercing of a bronze ox-hide-shaped ingot is memorialized in a stone relief, where the Pharaoh Amenhotep II, while riding in a chariot, pierced a copper ingot five times with his arrows. Luxor Museum, red granite relief, Acquisition Number 6.

The king's driver had been twice wounded by the Hatti (sc. Hittites) during the first assault. Taking the reins from his wounded driver, the king returned to let him seek a physician and the king to replenish his arrows. At that time, Sethi too appeared to replenish as well, and seeing his father's driver being carried off, he left his chariot saying, "Father! Allow me to drive for you!" "You do not know the team nor they your voice!" The king answered. At that, Sethi patted the sweaty rump of the left-hand mare in a soothing manner. After one kick, she allowed him to do so. Now stroking her powerful neck, a large eye watched him as did one ear turn in his direction. "Easy, most powerful one. I am your master's son. Allow me to guide you." The mare snorted and bobbed her head. Now stroking her nose and facing both eyes with lashes that dripped with sweat, "I am your friend, most powerful one. After one more charge, I will water you and your partner well." The skittishness gone, Sethi repeated the process with the other horse. Finished, the son joined his father in the chariot and took the reins. "How did you know which was the master?" "I understand such matters. They are rested. Shall we go forth and destroy more of the enemy?" "Indeed my son. Let us teach them a lesson."

Column 11

The second version of this warrior's tale is

as follows. It is one that disparages Sethi's character and the worthiness of his exploits during the great battle by saying, "To return from any battle is a victory." With this opinion we do not abide, but it is true that both father and son did so and without serious injury. These others further say that if one requires proof of Sethi's unproven bravery in battle, upon their return to Egypt, then why did King Rhaméssēs announce before the court his son's priestly accession to the temple Set at Tanis? The king commanded further that Sethi learn of the god's secrets. While others' bravery in battle were recounted in song and rewarded with pectorals of gold, why did the king place his son's destiny within the sacred walls of a god instead of awarding him with honors of valor and victory? The answer to this doubters' question is that the king was satisfied, nay proud of his son's accomplishments in battle. Further, the king saw Sethi's destiny far beyond the present, as the high priest and first oracle of Set had the king's ear in this matter.

Column 12

The first oracle of Set, a gifted man named Herufankhhor, cared not one measure about Sethi's royal lineage or his proven prowess in battle. What the high priest prized most was the young prince's proven *way* with horses, which had even reached his ears. This divine gift, the priest had argued to his king, must be honed to a sharp edge along with a rigorous training in the secrets of his priesthood. So began Sethi's journey along a new and unfamiliar path. His first step began as the lowest of the low, a *wab*-priest,[17] fit only to sweep the floors and clean the animal stalls and pens of the temple. Next, Sethi applied himself to the scribal school within the temple, where he discovered both patience and discipline as the ears on his back felt the cane's wrath many times. After a year's time, the high priest Herufankhhor approved of Sethi's promotion to assist the temple's librarian and magician. Within the temple's library, the prince learned of the many religious and magical books by copying older versions and making new ones. In this industry, the much-revered librarian and magician by the name of Ptahsokar became Sethi's teacher in all things.

Column 13

In his tenth year of training within the temple of Set, Sethi was promoted from a *wab*-priest to a *sem*-priest dedicated to the temple library's care and elevated to an apprentice magician. Ptahsokar, his mentor in all things, during this time came to respect Sethi as if he were a son. During this time, the prince came to learn of many spells, both helpful and not, as the priesthood had many

---

[17] *Wab*-priest, literally, "cleaner-priest."

within its archive. "How does one choose, Great One?" "Only with a righteous heart may you decide," Ptahsokar answered. "To do otherwise would be an abomination." Then Sethi came upon a papyrus that described a potion, which could improve one's health and extend one's life. "Great One," Sethi inquired of his mentor, "should not this potion be proscribed for all of those of ill health?" To this Ptahsokar replied, "Should the granaries of the temple be emptied because there are those who hunger?" Sethi responded, "Only to those with promise should the temple's resources be so administered." The librarian and magician smiled, "A wise and just answer, Sethi. For you have realized only those of promise could repay their debt to the temple, while others could not." "By that logic Great One, then my father, the king, is surely one of promise. Should he not benefit from such an elixir?" "Indeed, Sethi, indeed," was Ptahsokar's rely.

Column 14

It is a matter of record that King Rhaméssēs lived long, and out-lived many of his one hundred and sixty-two children.[18] Therefore, it should be of no surprise that the king's health and well-being had been extended by the pious concern of his son Sethi.

---

[18] This is an interesting independent count of the Ramesside family. Modern Egyptologists range their number from between 88 and 103.

In the twenty-second year of Sethi's submission to the priesthood of Set, his mentor and master Ptahsokar undertook his journey West, and in his place, the *sem*-priest Sethi ascended to the position of the temple's librarian and magician. Having witnessed with his own eyes the effectiveness of the health and life-giving potion on his father, Sethi began administering himself with the same. While not the king, the new librarian and magician justified his decision since he considered himself as the pious son, the one-who-oversaw-the-bodily-affairs of his father the king. Others within the temple began to become suspicious of Sethi as they aged and he resisted this bodily weakness. During his forty-third jubilee in the service of Set, Sethi learned from his father of his desire to journey West. "I have become weary of this life, my son. It is not that I am resentful of your long care and ministrations on my behalf. It is time."[19]

Column 15

Sethi granted his father's wish in the form of a sweet potion.[20] Thereafter, his father, King Rhaméssēs, The Great Ancestor of the Egyptians, who had celebrated fourteen Heb-Sed festivals,[21] went West. Sethi witnessed the

---

[19] Modern sources place Ramses II's age at death between 90 and 96 years old.

[20] The "sweet potion" may have been one made with opium. The year was 1213 BC.

burial of his father that had been long-prepared. In that same year, the priest-magician, now in his majority, joined a συμβούλιο (sc. *Consilium* or council) of all the *sem*-priests of magic, who gathered at Memphis from throughout the Two Lands,[22] and included among their number those from the cities along the Great Green (sc. Mediterranean), the rivers who ran contrary (sc. Tigris and Euphrates), as far as the land of Hatti (sc. Asia Minor). Sethi, in his humility, considered himself an apprentice among so many accomplished magicians, and so applied himself once again, wishing to take on the role of a lowly *wab*-priest once again. However, the *sem*-priests of Ptah at Memphis knew of Sethi's many accomplishments and did not allow him to prostrate himself low. Instead, they raised him up and praised him openly before the council at his initiation. Many took notice their words, while others scoffed in derision saying, "Who is this royal child pretending to be a magician?"

Column 16

After seventeen years within the council, the praise of the *sem*-priests of Ptah came to fruition like a blossoming lotus flower. Those who had scoffed in derision had become few in number, some say due to witchcraft. Sethi's

---

[21] Heb-Sed festivals of magical renewal occurred after a king's thirtieth regnal year, and every fifth year thereafter.
[22] Upper and Lower Egypt.

agelessness caused many to wonder in awe, for it was said that he had already achieved over one hundred and eighty years. His counsel, whenever it was sought, was thoughtful, while his nature remained calm and just. By Sethi's thirtieth year, he celebrated a Heb-Sed celebration, much as would any pharaoh with his wives, children, and grandchildren in attendance. Again, some thought this act presumptuous—even if he was the son of his body, King Rhaméssēs. In the fiftieth year of his initiation Sethi was elevated by acclamation to the council's lofty position of first voice at the age if two hundred and twenty years. With great seriousness, Sethi declared that he would shoulder this burden like an ox. Several, however, were wary of his choice as first voice, and sought to test his resolve by nominating one from their temple. The next day, all had died horribly from the bite of a viper, proving that this priest-magician of Set was not to be trifled with.

Column 17

So began the ascension of the priesthood of Set within the council, and with it, the adoption of its oddly dark ways. For the next forty-three years, the first-voice Sethi led them with a just, firm, and oftentimes stern hand. Achieving the age of two hundred and twenty years, the priest-magician of Set had experienced first-hand far more than most magicians had read from their archives, excepting those long-lived kindred among the council, who out of necessity had to avoid the life-giving rays of Re.[23] Like his father before him, Sethi had long-prepared for his final journey to the West, having selected a most beautiful and select-of-places in the neighborhood of the Horizon of Tosorthros,[24] near the tombs of the magicians Imhotep[25] and Djedi. In this regard, his great-great-grandsons piously assisted him with every need, securing for him cedar wood from Lebanon, myrrh from the land of Punt, the architects, artisans, and stonecutters for his tomb, and the lands set aside for his funerary estate. Thus is the righteous record of Sethi, priest-magician of Set and first-voice of the council, who lived two hundred and sixty-three years.

---

[23] This is a curious statement. Were those "long-lived kindred" allergic to sunlight?

[24] Djoser (from Manetho, *Aegyptiaca* frag. 11 [Waddell, p.41), founder (?) of the Third Dynasty, and builder of the Step Pyramid atop the Sakkaran plateau.

[25] Manetho, *Aegyptiaca* frag. 11 (Waddell, p.41 n.4 and 42).

Appendix 2

Egyptian Priests & Priesthoods

The burden of performing the ritual functions for each god fell to the Egyptian priesthoods during the New Kingdom (1567-1085 BC). It was they who performed these myriad of acts on their king's behalf, which freed up his everyday existence.

Ritual acts required temples and resources that priestly bureaucracies managed for each god's estate. Just as naturally, priestly hierarchies developed in order to apportion the many tasks associated with the care and maintenance of a specific deity. At the top of this priestly ranking stood those who served the god directly in place of the king. These were the high priests, literally "the first servant of the god," who in some instances was supported by the "second," "third," and "fourth servant of the god." In contrast to these highly-placed priests, the vast majority of Egyptian priests, who shouldered the day-to-day temple duties, were the common priests, the *wab*-priests, literally "the cleaners."

This is not to say that specialty priesthoods did not exist, for they did, especially for those devoted to mummification and the necropolis. But one class of priests, the *sem*-priests, appears to connote a ranking of importance unto their own. While certainly not as powerful as high priests nor as lowly as *wab*-priests, the *sem*-priests were those associated with special cultic activities and even the royal palace itself. They are easily identified by the leopard skin that they wore over their shoulder.

While an old resource, the two volume work by Hermann Kees, *Das Priestertum im Ägyptischen Staat vom Neuen Reich bis zur Spätzeit*, (Leiden, 1953) and his *Indices und Nachträge*, (Leiden, 1958), remains the best place to begin the study of the high priesthoods of New Kingdom Egypt and later.

Sadly, English readers do not have such a resource. Instead, one must patch together disparate citations, which are often fragmentary and contradictory. A thorough-going overview of the history and development of the Egyptian priesthoods has yet to be written.

ABOUT THE AUTHOR

For W.J. Cherf, this is his fourth leap into the realm of paranormal archaeology. His first book of the Adventures of Paranormal Archaeology series, *The Magician's Tomb*, brought screams of delight from his passionate readership. *Netherworld's Gate* brought gasps for the who-done-it and why. *Dhampirica* appealed to a different, hemo-oriented audience.

Cherf is no novice to either archaeology or the ancient world, having excavated in Israel and Greece, along with extensive travel throughout the length of Egypt. Ask him sometime about what a sunrise looks like from atop the Great Pyramid. Or for that matter, walking ancient roads and surveying precarious mountain fortifications in Central Greece. Even better, inquire about a certain Fourth of July celebration atop Tel Beer Sheva in Israel.

As to why Cherf writes in his retirement years, he says, "I always wanted to write a book without footnotes." While this is surely true and is an oblique reference to his treadmill "publish or perish" days in academe, more than that drives the man. On more than one occasion, Cherf has said he has all of these stories in his head, which bedevil him until freed upon the world. In the end, you decide.

For free chapters of Cherf's works, not to mention a handy source for the latest and greatest in Egyptology, go to www.wjcherf.com. Cherf always says, "Sample before you buy." For reviews, go to www.amazon.com and search under "w.j. cherf." If you like this book, review it there. That's how authors find out if they still have the right stuff, straight from their readers.